W9-BOK-080

DARK HORSES

DARK
HORSES

Cecily von Ziegesar

Excerpt from "The Excrement Poem" from *The Retrieval System* by Maxine Kumin.
Copyright © 1978 by Maxine Kumin. Reprinted by permission of Penguin Books, a division
of W.W. Norton & Company, Inc. All rights reserved.

Excerpt from "Horse" from *45 Mercy Street* by Anne Sexton, edited by Linda Gray Sexton.
Copyright © 1976 by Linda Gray Sexton and Loring Conant, Jr., Executors of the Estate of
Anne Sexton. Reprinted by permission of Houghton Mifflin Harcourt Publishing Company
and by permission of SSL/Sterling Lord Literistic, Inc. All rights reserved.

Excerpt from "Us" from *Love Poems* by Anne Sexton. Copyright © 1967, 1968, 1969 by
Anne Sexton, renewed 1995, 1996, 1997 by Linda G. Sexton. Reprinted by permission of
Houghton Mifflin Harcourt Publishing Company and by permission of SSL/Sterling Lord
Literistic, Inc. All rights reserved.

Published in the United States by Soho Teen
an imprint of
Soho Press, Inc.
853 Broadway
New York, NY 10003

Library of Congress Cataloging-in-Publication Data

Von Ziegesar, Cecily, author.
Dark horses / Cecily von Ziegesar.

ISBN 978-1-61695-517-5
eISBN 978-1-61695-518-2

1. Horsemanship—Fiction. 2. Horse shows—Fiction. 3. Love—Fiction.
4. Jealousy—Fiction. 5. Self-actualization (Psychology)—Fiction. I. Title
PZ7.V94 Dar 2016 DDC—dc23 2016003782

Horse illustration © VectorPic/Shutterstock
Interior design by Janine Agro, Soho Press, Inc.

Printed in the United States of America

10 9 8 7 6 5 4 3 2 1

For Agnes, never dark.

PROLOGUE | RED

'm dying. Whatever I drank from those boxes has made me very, very sick. I can't find my stall. The ground lists and sways beneath my hooves as I stagger around in the dark, looking for it. I stop to get my bearings. My sides heave and my head hangs heavy, almost to my knees. Every loud moaning breath startles me, but there's nothing I can do to fix me. This is the end.

I'm outside the barn now. The storm is over and the skies have cleared. The earth is a just-baked pie left out to cool. I splay my long legs like a newborn foal and pump giant breaths of sweet steam through my distended nostrils. In, out. In, out.

Over in the main ring the jumps loom, huge and beautiful in the moonlight. In just a few hours she and I are supposed to jump that course. We're supposed to ace it. We're supposed to win. That's highly unlikely now. More like, Bye-bye my American pie. You made living fun. But this must be the day that I die.

I find a patch of muddy grass and lie down to sleep and replay my favorite dream. In the dream we're together again, just the two of us, with no interruptions. I have her all to myself and she's not distracted by anyone, girl or boy. We're not competing either. We just hang out, like old friends.

It was an accident how we came to be in the same field at the same time, looking into each other's eyes, forgetting everything and everyone else. I wasn't looking for her, and I'm pretty sure she wasn't looking for me, but I could sense then—exactly then— that everything was about to change; it had already changed. Standing in front of me was my whole reason for existing. Actually, I hated her at first. I hated everybody, and she hated me. But then I liked her. I didn't care, and then I did care—a lot, too much maybe. It's almost impossible to explain, especially in my current state. But I will try.

PART 1
The previous October

1 | MERRITT

There's this thing I do when I know something's expected of me. I a) run away, b) make a big mess of it, c) all of the above. It's like instead of anticipating failure and disaster and doing my best to avoid it, I go right ahead and make the disaster happen, so I can be right about it being a disaster and a failure, and the resulting disappointment is like a perverse triumph. Like, see what you made me do? I told you I was going to mess up.

Today's disaster began last night when I decided to go to a party instead of eating a nice healthy dinner and going to bed early. My parents were at a screening for a film about Pythagoras made by one of their former students. They ordered sushi for me and made me promise to get in bed at ten.

As soon as they left, I went out.

I didn't even really know Sonia Kuhnhardt, the Chace senior hosting the party, but she lived near Lincoln Center, which was semi-convenient. Besides, all the Upper East Side private girls' schools like Chace and Dowd are so small everyone recognizes everyone else. It feels like we know each other, even when we don't.

Sonia lived in a brownstone, not an apartment. Girls sat on the stoop smoking cigarettes. Music drifted out of the open windows. Upstairs, the kitchen was huge and messy. Boxes of wine were lined up on the counter with real wine glasses. It was so private-school superior to serve wine at a party instead of beer, but I didn't mind. Wine is stronger.

I picked up a glass and an entire box and carried them over to the large sectional sofa, claiming a lonely spot on one end. I didn't come there to socialize. I'd come to obliterate the SAT, which I was due to take the next morning. Setting the box on the coffee table, I dispensed the red wine into my glass and began to gulp it, gagging on its sickly sweetness. My hangover was going to be so huge I'd have to name it. Gunther. Voldemort. Lucifer. The Beast. Sorry I messed up the SAT. Blame it on The Beast.

"Hi." Some blond boy who was trying to grow a mustache sat down beside me. "Do you go to Chace with Sonia?"

I nodded, figuring that was good enough. I didn't really know how to talk to boys. No brothers, and no boys at school since I'd transferred to Dowd toward the end of last school year.

The boy was drinking water, or something that looked like water. "I'm Sonia's brother, Sam. We're twins. And you are?"

I took another vomity gulp of wine before answering. "Merritt. Like the Merritt Parkway?"

The boy twin, Sam, chuckled. "Your parents named you after a parkway?"

I nodded again. "Yup."

And that was the last thing I said all night, until several glasses of wine later, when Sam hailed me a taxi, before I "messed up the white carpet," and I had to give the driver my address. My parents were still out when I got upstairs, so I raided the medicine cupboard and took two of the Percocet pills Dad had been prescribed for his hamstring tear. Then I passed out. Mission accomplished.

"You might want a little sea salt." Mom placed the salt grinder at my elbow and touched her toes. Her purple Lycra leggings stretched tautly over her muscular legs. Her hips popped.

It was morning, the morning of the SAT.

"Somebody needs to limber up," Dad observed cheerfully from the living room, where he was doing crunches on the floor.

My parents were both fanatically healthy. They were professors at Columbia and they ran to work and back every day. They had me when they were well into their forties, and it was like they were trying to beat the clock somehow by getting healthier and fitter every year. A couple of years ago they had run half marathons; now they were running full ones. I preferred to walk. I was also pretty sure that all the exercise they did together was a form of premeditated alone time, a way of accomplishing two goals at once. My parents were very practical. Why not get fit and spend time together instead of going to a gym and seeing a couples counselor? I wasn't sure if it was working. There was a lot of forced cheeriness at home that felt insincere to the point of creepy. But what did I know? Misery was my middle name.

Eggs and kale squirmed on my plate. The Beast was in full force. I pushed back my chair. "I have to get going," I said, desperate for some fresh air.

"Go get 'em!" Dad called from the floor as I tromped toward the elevator.

"You won't make it through the test without brain food." Mom tucked a Ziploc bag full of raw almonds into the pocket of my faux leather jacket. I turned my head so she wouldn't smell my sour wine breath. "Don't stress this, it's really not a big deal."

I hated when she did that, just pretending to have no expectations when she was really worried I might crack and go all Unabomber again.

It had been like this since my grandmother, Gran-Jo, died last spring. I refused to go to school or even leave my room for weeks. My parents tried to get me to see a psychologist, but I refused to go to the appointments. Finally I transferred from my huge public school to Dowd Prep and started going to school again even though the school year was almost over. But even at tiny Dowd, I went from being a good student with friends to a student who barely scrapes by, has no friends, and prefers to stay in her room watching reruns of creepy reality TV shows like Extreme Cheapskates and 19 Kids and Counting with the door closed. Gran-Jo was the most important person in my life and suddenly she was gone. Sorry for feeling sad.

"I'll text you when I'm done," I promised Mom, and turned to go.

Dowd Prep is a crosstown bus ride away from my building on Riverside Drive, through Central Park and over to Lexington Avenue. I bought a can of Red Bull at a deli and drank it on the way, but The Beast was still winning. My hands shook. My eyelids were coated with a film of cold sweat. I was freezing and suffocating. My knees wouldn't stop bouncing.

"Phones and other electronic devices should be in your lockers with your coats," Mrs. T, our proctor, declared as I arrived. I sat down at the only empty desk in the Dowd gym, two number-two pencils clutched in my fist. Mrs. T's last name was Greek and sounded exactly like "testicles," so she stuck to "Mrs. T" for obvious reasons. "If you need to use the ladies' room you must do so now, or wait for the first break in approximately one hour and fifteen minutes."

I stood up. My pencils rolled off the desk and onto the floor.

"Miss Wenner, do you need to use the ladies' room? Are you all right, dear?" Mrs. T asked kindly. "You look a bit pale."

I nodded, ignoring the accusing stares of my classmates, particularly Amora Wells and Nadia Grabcheski, the two most annoying girls in the class. They were always posting selfies on Instagram, flaunting the blue ribbons they'd won at winter horse shows in Florida or the new monogrammed blankets that fit their sleek ponies just so. Right after Gran-Jo died I'd actually gone up to them at a party to talk about riding, but they'd just stared at me with their heads cocked to the side, as if I were speaking gibberish. Maybe I was. That was at the beginning of the sadness, and the sadder I got the more wasted I wanted to be. The morning after that party Amora had posted an out of focus picture of me on Instagram. I was slumped on the floor outside the bathroom, waiting to go. Beside the picture she'd written the snarky caption, *Dowd Welcomes Promising New Student*. Nadia was the first follower to "like" Amora's post. Needless to say I wasn't going to spend the weekend at either one of their country houses any time soon.

"I think I need a drink of water," I told Mrs. T.

Ann Ware, my best friend, or rather *former* best friend, frowned at me as I waited for permission to leave the room. Ann and I had gone to public elementary and middle school together. She'd gone to Dowd in ninth grade, which was why my parents thought I might like it.

"Very well then, run along," said Mrs. T. "But hurry back."

And so I ran. I ran out of the gym to my locker, got my coat, and ran straight out the main door.

It was October, the weekend after Columbus Day, but still warm. Some of the leaves were tinged with gold or bronze, but they clung to their branches, refusing to fall. I felt the weight of my phone in my pocket and thought of calling home. I could say I wasn't feeling well, go home, and crawl back into bed. But I didn't want to go home.

Eighty-sixth Street and the 4 train were only a short walk

away. The subway was nearly empty, too early on a Sunday even for tourists. In my badly hungover state the darkness and gentle rocking of the car might have lulled me to sleep, but two sharply dressed old ladies caught my attention. They were huddled together, talking intimately and laughing, like schoolgirls who had grown up together. The taller one was wearing Gucci loafers with gold horse bits across the foot. She handed her friend a tube of lipstick and then held open a compact mirror to help her put it on. The train lurched to a stop at 59th Street and the taller one stood up abruptly, forgetting that her purse was open in her lap. The contents spilled everywhere.

"Hurry," her friend snapped, crouching down to pick up the scattered items. "This is our stop!"

I staggered after a runaway glasses case and handed it over.

"My varifocals!" The taller woman gasped. "Thank you, angel."

"They're Chanel," her friend said in an exaggerated, mocking whisper.

The women smiled gratefully and scurried off the car just as the doors closed. I watched them on the platform as the train pulled away, fanning themselves and laughing before they headed up the escalator to Bloomingdales.

Something rolled back and forth beneath the seats across the car. It was a green plastic bottle of prescription pills from the woman's purse. I knelt down and picked it up.

The pills were white and harmless looking. "Every four hours for hip pain," the label read. The subway car was empty. I removed the childproof cap, took two pills, and tucked the bottle into my pocket.

If someone asked me at that moment where I was going and what I was doing, I would not have been able to answer. I was on autopilot. At 42nd Street I got off and went upstairs to Grand

Central Station. I used to spend a lot of time there, going to or returning from Gran-Jo's house in Connecticut. I hadn't been there since she died.

I stared at the green ceiling painted with glimmering gold stars until my neck cramped up. Then I headed downstairs to the Oyster Bar, one of Gran-Jo's old haunts. It feels more like a secret vault under a bank, or a catacomb beneath a cathedral than a restaurant. It was only ten-thirty in the morning, so it was empty. Gran-Jo liked to sit at the bar. I zipped up my jacket to hide my Dowd Prep T-shirt and took a seat.

"What can I do for you, Miss?" the young guy behind the counter said brusquely. He was busy rolling white cloth napkins around clean sets of silverware and didn't even bother to look up.

"An Old-Fashioned and two Wellfleets," I said equally brusquely, ordering Gran-Jo's usual pre-train cocktail and snack. Oysters were not my thing, but it felt wrong not to get any. Besides, I do like the way they come, all self-contained in their shells, pearly and blue-gray on the inside and rough and dirty looking on the outside.

The guy placed my oysters and drink on the bar and went back to rolling napkins. I held my nose, slid the oysters down my throat in quick succession, and washed them down with the drink, which tasted like sweet gasoline. I squeezed my eyes shut and swallowed a few extra times to make sure nothing was about to come back up. Gran-Jo must have had a stomach made of lead.

There were two twenties in my jacket pocket with my Metrocard. I laid one on the bar just like Gran-Jo had always done and slipped out of the restaurant before anyone else who worked there noticed that they'd just served a minor a very large quantity of bourbon.

The train schedule hadn't changed by more than a minute or so since Gran-Jo died. The Sunday morning 11:07 Stamford train with a connection to New Canaan was still on Track 107, just off the station's main hall. I walked upstairs and crossed the echoing expanse of marble automatically, allowing my legs to take me where they knew to go, because my brain wasn't working very well at all.

An ancient man with a little cart was selling plastic pint glasses of beer beside the first car on the train.

"Do you have any Coke?" I asked.

"Only beer," the man said in a thick accent.

"Fine." I handed him my last twenty.

He took it and squinted at me over his eyeglasses. "You twenty-one?"

"Almost," I lied.

He shook his head and handed me a dripping pint of beer. "Only one."

I reached for it, a crooked, freaky half-smile that I didn't even know my face could make reflected in the lenses of his glasses. "Keep the change."

"This is the 11:07 to Stamford stopping at Greenwich, Cos Cob, Riverside, Old Greenwich and Stamford. Change at Stamford for the New Canaan line. All aboard," the conductor announced as I settled into a vinyl seat by the window.

A curt whistle sounded and without further ceremony the doors closed and the train departed, moving slowly toward the long, dark tunnel leading out of Manhattan and into the Bronx. Only three other seats in my car were occupied, all of them by exhausted-looking middle-aged men. I stared woozily at my distorted reflection in the smudged glass. When the train emerged from the tunnel, my phone vibrated and bleeped four times.

I took the phone out of my pocket. The first text was from Ann Ware.

hey, where'd u go?? hope ur ok. lmk.

The second text was from Mom.

Are you walking home? Warm bagels here!

Then there was a voicemail message.

"Hello? Merritt? I don't know why you're not picking up. Ann Ware just called and said you left the SAT and you looked like you weren't feeling well. It would be nice if you could let us know where you are—Quiet, Michael, I'm leaving her a voicemail. Merritt, please do call us back."

And another.

"Hi, it's Ann. I hope you're not mad, but I just called your home number because it's the only number I had. Your mom gave me this one. I just wanted to make sure you're okay. The SAT wasn't as hard as I thought. I know we haven't really talked in a while, but call me back when you get a chance."

And then one more from Dad.

"Merritt, it's a gorgeous day. Your mother and I want to get out there for a bike ride, but not until we know you're safe. We're waiting for you at home."

That was it.

Out of habit, I trolled my Instagram feed. I never posted anything myself, but I was guilty of following a few of my classmates. It was my way of being there without being there. I never felt like I was missing out on anything anyway since most of their pictures featured cupcakes or selfies in dressing rooms at Forever 21, and as a rule I never liked or commented on any of their posts. What would I say? *OMG, I so wish I was there!!!!?*

Nadia Grabcheski had posted something an hour and a half ago. She must have snuck her phone into the gym because it was a picture of me walking out of the SAT while all the other girls sat in their neat rows, about to take the test. Beneath the picture was the caption *Just gotta grab my flask*. I powered off my phone and rested my head against the window.

"Miss? This is Stamford. Your ticket please?" I jolted awake at the sound of the conductor's voice and squinted up at him.

"I don't have a ticket." I felt in my jacket pocket for my money, realizing with a sinking heart that I'd already spent both my twenties. I hadn't thought about a train ticket. I hadn't really thought at all. "I'm sorry." My tongue was sluggish, my mind scarily blank and unhelpful. A red heat crept up my neck and spread across my face to my hairline. I kicked my empty beer cup under my seat. "I don't have any money."

"Well, is Stamford your final destination?" the conductor asked. His face was severe and weather-beaten, neatly trimmed white hair peeking out from his navy blue conductor's cap. But his voice was kind.

I shook my head. "New Canaan." I would have to change trains across the platform.

"If you give me your name and home address I can send the bill there. No extra fee," the conductor said patiently.

"Merritt—with two *t*s and two *r*s—Wenner—with two *n*s," I responded automatically. "Three hundred Riverside Drive, New York, New York, 10024."

He punched a few holes in a paper ticket with his hole punch and handed it to me. "That'll get you to New Canaan. You'll need another ticket to return. Hurry now. That train's just about to depart."

"Thanks." I took the ticket and dashed out of the car. The New Canaan line train was waiting across the platform. I leapt on, my whole body trembling with the effort, just as the bell sounded and the doors slid closed.

2 | RED

A horse's life is all about the people we belong to, but I never belonged to anyone. I never even met my owner until my first race.

The race was at Keeneland, my home track, where I had been practicing. I shouldn't have been nervous, but the stands were full of people and the new noises, sights, and smells made me anxious, despite my blinders and earplugs. The jockey assigned to me was a girl. I had never been ridden by a girl before. She patted my neck before she mounted up and I swung my head and nipped her in the arm. She elbowed me in the nose and I pinned my ears and shook my head so hard I almost fell over on top of her. I was already covered in lather and I could feel through the reins as soon as she was up on my back that she was nervous too.

Then it was time for the post-parade. The sky was black and lightning flashed way off in the distance. There were only five three-year-olds in the race, all new to the track, and we whinnied to each other and jogged in place while our riders tried to calm us down. My jockey might have said something soothing to quiet me, but I had wool in my ears, so I couldn't hear a thing. She was like a flea up there on my back, a silent flea, while a sturdy palomino lead pony and his cowboy rider wrangled me to the starting gate.

I was number five on the outside and last in. As soon as the metal gate closed behind me, the gates in front of my chest flew open.

"And they're off!"

All but one.

I stood frozen in place, mesmerized by the zigzags of lightning on the horizon that looked even more captivating in my blinder-induced tunnel vision. My whole body trembled. Rivulets of sweat ran down my forelegs. Then my jockey flashed a whip in front of my eyes and I leapt forward into a manic gallop, swerving toward the inside rail as I'd been taught. Faster, faster.

When I reached the rail I didn't straighten out. Instead I jumped right over the rail, across the grassy median in the middle of the track, straight through the shallow duck pond, through a flower bed and toward the rail on the far side. Lightning flashed even closer this time and the vibrations rumbled the turf beneath my hooves. There was another vibration too—my jockey's frantic pleading as I soared over the rail once more, cutting off the racing pack in the far turn.

My jockey sawed at the reins, causing the metal bit to cut into the soft corners of my young mouth. *What's she doing?* I wondered. I was out in front. The other horses were literally eating the dirt ricocheting off my flying hooves. I thought I'd done a very good job in a very bad situation. Didn't she want to win?

She kept on pulling and pleading, but I was stubborn. I sped up instead of slowing down. Then a familiar scent filled the air. It was a filly from the herd of broodmares with whom my mother and I had grazed and frolicked when I was a foal. She was gaining on me. I nickered and turned my head to greet her.

Things happened very quickly after that.

The filly slammed straight into me and we both went down. Our jockeys flew through the air in opposite directions and landed clear. The crowd of people watching was both loud and hushed at the same time.

"Number One and Number Five are both down. The jockeys have given the signal that they are safe. Can we get a vet truck please? A vet truck to the three-quarter post now, please."

The other three horses thundered past. One of my earplugs had been dislodged and I could hear someone shouting. "Her leg! Her leg!"

I was already standing. My legs all felt fine. It was my shoulder that hurt, and something was funny with my jaw. I let my tongue loll out of my mouth and shook my head. The blinders must have slipped over my eyes because I was almost completely blind.

"This race has been forfeited. Wagers will be refunded at the nearest booth. Thank you for understanding, folks." The announcer sounded louder than before, and not because my earplugs had fallen out. He seemed to be the only person speaking above a whisper in all of Kentucky.

Beside me the filly thrashed and moaned in the dirt. A young groom from our stable ran out of the clubhouse and across the track to crouch at her head. Tears streaked his cheeks as he sang to her in Spanish. She didn't belong to him, but she was his all the same. They gazed at each other adoringly until a rumble of thunder sounded from above and the filly became frantic.

"No, no, no!" The groom's cry echoed around the hushed track as she gave a mighty thrust and stood up almost all the way.

Both our jockeys tried to help the groom prop her up, but it was no use. The filly let out a shrill shriek and fell back down again. She didn't move anymore, but I could still hear her pained breaths.

I stood alone in the spot where the filly and I had collided. My shoulder throbbed and the bridle's leather straps felt like a vice around my swollen jaw. The vet truck rumbled its approach behind me. Several other vehicles arrived with it. A groom came to my head and held my bridle while a small crowd gathered around the filly.

"She'll have to be destroyed," a man said. "Quickly now. She's in a lot of pain."

"Her first race," said a man in an overcoat as the vet injected the filly with something to put her out of her misery. "What a waste."

He was our owner, I realized. I'd never seen him up close before.

There was another man with him, a big man in a shiny gray suit. He gave off a strong odor of oranges and wood. A small woman wearing a pair of enormous sunglasses clung to his arm as she minced carefully over the turf in spiky-heeled shoes. Her lips were painted bright red and her black bobbed hair gleamed in the sun.

Within seconds, the filly's breathing stopped and she was gone. The vet's assistant unfolded a tarp and put it over her. Soon she'd be taken away and sold for parts, like a totaled car.

"That chestnut horse should be destroyed too, while you're at it," my jockey said of me. "This is all his fault. He's a nutcase."

"Completely loco," the groom holding me agreed.

"Go ahead and put him down too," my owner told the vet without even a glance at me.

"Wait a minute," the man who smelled like wood and oranges spoke up. He turned to the vet. "I'll take him. Unless you think he's a lost cause."

"I was a lost cause," the woman at his side interjected. She spoke quietly, in a strange accent. "You haven't destroyed me yet."

The man in the suit laughed without smiling. "I suppose I specialize in lost causes."

The vet came over to examine me. "Broken jaw. Contused eye socket. Shoulder seems to be bothering him but I won't know the extent of the damage till we've done x-rays. Legs seem to be perfectly fine. Obviously he likes to jump, and he's pretty enough to make a nice hunter prospect. If he's not lame."

"Lame or not, he's not safe," my jockey insisted. "I'm lucky he didn't kill me."

I snorted, spraying her with dirty horse snot.

"And he's an escape artist," my groom added. "Gets out of his stall. Knocks down rails. Lets the other horses out, too." This was true. I wore a muzzle in the barn except for when I ate.

"Maybe racing just isn't his thing," the vet continued. "I've seen horses with more lives than cats. A nice big three-year-old Thoroughbred like this one? Mr. de Rothschild, if you give him a chance and work with him, he could do anything."

My owner just stared at me, frowning. I stared back with my one good eye.

Mr. de Rothschild came over and ran his large gloved hand over my sweaty neck. I could really smell his perfume then. It smelled like gold.

"Maybe Beatrice would like him," he mused to his female companion.

"Maybe," the woman said and shrugged her shoulders. She began to mince away toward the ringside VIP bar, already bored with our little exchange. It was clear to me that horses weren't her thing.

I never raced again. I was gelded and shipped East to my new home to recover from my injuries and to wait for my someone to belong to, my own girl—Beatrice.

3 | MERRITT

"Last stop!" the conductor shouted. I jerked awake. He was standing very close to me, his wide body blocking the aisle of the empty train car.

I glanced out the window, but my vision was all blurred.

"Is this New Canaan?"

"That's right." The conductor pulled a little notebook out of the pocket of his navy blue uniform, glanced at something written there and then put the notebook back in his pocket. "I'm quite sure you have someone meeting you here. Hurry up now, this is the last stop before we head back to Stamford."

I clutched the back of the seat in front of me and pulled myself upright. The conductor stood aside to let me pass, and I staggered toward the open doors. He must be confusing me with someone else, I thought. No one was supposed to meet me. No one even knows I'm here. The platform seemed incredibly bright and hot and I was so tired. But Gran-Jo's house wasn't far, and I knew the way so well I could walk there with my eyes closed.

New Canaan is this totally old-fashioned, frozen-in-time town, with no chain stores or fast food restaurants or even a movie theater. It hadn't changed at all since I'd been there last. I turned left at the gas station. A few cars slowed down as they passed, checking me out. It was unusual to see someone walking along the road in New Canaan. Most of the residents had a BMW or three.

Gran-Jo wasn't that rich, but well-off enough to keep a horse in her backyard and have a gardener tend to all the flowers she was addicted to looking at but didn't have a clue about taking care of. She'd lived in New Canaan for almost fifty years, in the house her husband—my grandfather—had grown up in. They raised my dad there, and she stayed even after my grandfather died, despite the influx of Mercedes SUVs and giant McMansions. Gran-Jo in New Canaan was like me at Dowd Prep—she didn't really belong there, but you can get used to anything.

I came to the spot where the road split. Gran-Jo's driveway was coming up on the right. The gravel sparkled beneath the rubber soles of my gray Converse sneakers. Gran-Jo's house was red, but the sun was so bright it seemed more like a pinkish coral color than red. Yellow chrysanthemums grew in white flower boxes outside every window. Gran-Jo hated chrysanthemums, so that was weird. She liked roses because they came back every spring, bloomed all summer, and were hard to kill.

My eyelids were leaden and I kept stumbling. If the conductor had let me, I would've stayed on the train and slept until the next morning. This drinking alcohol and taking pills thing—I couldn't handle it. Maybe it was the healthy diet I'd been raised on. I just wanted to get to Gran-Jo's house and lie down. I leaned against the white clapboard fence that ran along the driveway. The fence was part of the large rectangular paddock where Gran-Jo kept Noble, her horse.

Noble was huge and beautiful and amazing, dark bay with a thick black mane and tail. He and Gran-Jo had been together for twenty years and competed all over. I read something for Social Studies once about certain Native American religions that believed in familiars—animal spirits that are part of you, that guard over you and complete you. Noble was sort of like that for Gran-Jo. They were connected somehow. And even though I loved them both, I was always a little jealous of their bond.

I heard a whinny and looked up. A dappled gray horse with an arched neck and a very full white tail trotted over to the fence where I swayed tiredly. The horse sniffed my hand. I hung my arms over the top rail to prop myself up. The horse blew deep, warm breaths into my light brown tangle of hair. I closed my eyes and inhaled deeply. The smell of horse is my favorite scent in the entire world.

"I'm sorry I'm such a mess," I told the horse. "You're probably like, 'What's your problem?'" I lifted my head to look into his golden brown eyes. He stared back at me expectantly, as if he were waiting for something. I missed riding so much.

"Anybody ever ride you, huh?"

The horse just stood there. I glanced at the house. It looked quiet and empty. I climbed shakily up onto the top rail of the fence and sat down. It took some effort to stay there without falling over backwards. I felt like I'd been clobbered in the head and stomach with a club. But I didn't regret what I'd done. I was glad not to have taken the SAT. I was glad to be there at Gran-Jo's with this beautiful, friendly horse. This was what Gran-Jo's house had always been for me—an escape, a relief. I just wished I didn't feel so awful.

The horse and I were eye-to-eye now. He turned his head away and then back to me again, interested and not interested at the same time. Horses are sort of like cats that way. Noble used to prick his ears and nicker at us when we when we brought grain or hay to his run-in shed, or when we came into his paddock to groom him or ride. But after we'd untacked him and rubbed him down and picked out his hooves, he'd stalk away to roll and graze, ignoring us completely.

"I think I need him more than he needs me," Gran-Jo would sigh.

But I needed her, and Noble, too. They were the thing I ran to every weekend and all summer—any chance I got.

The gray horse ducked his head and nudged my thigh with his muzzle. It had been forever since I'd ridden, and he seemed so gentle. It was too tempting to resist. And what was the harm? I'd stay inside the paddock. Nothing bad would happen, and no one would ever know.

I stood on the middle rail of the fence and reached out to grab a handful of the horse's gray mane. He snorted but stood his ground, as if he knew what I wanted. I used his neck to steady myself and swung my right leg up and over his withers, heaving onto his broad back just as he stepped away.

"Good boy." I patted his neck, unable to keep the stupid smile from spreading across my face. Something fell onto my jeans, staining them darker, and I realized I was crying. Smiling and crying at the same time. I really was a mess.

"Hello?" I heard someone call from off in the distance.

I looked up. A man stood in front of the house with a bucket in one hand and a phone pressed to his ear. The horse nickered and trotted over to the fence. His body trembled beneath my legs.

"Hello?" the man called out again as he walked toward us.

The horse was going crazy, nickering and prancing as the man approached. I slid around on his bare back, trying to keep my seat without squeezing him with my legs too much.

"Whoa," I murmured and grabbed another handful of mane.

The man was over the fence now and walking across the paddock. He was older, with a neatly trimmed white mustache, wearing pressed khakis and a light blue button-down shirt.

"Someone just telephoned," he told me cryptically. "They're on their way." He held out the bucket and the horse shoved his nose into it greedily.

I slid off his back, landing heavily on my unreliable, staggering feet. Someone was coming. It sounded like they were coming for me.

"I'm sorry," I tried to say, but my voice was completely wrong, like my tongue was made out of socks. "Who's coming?"

"Your parents," the man said, still holding the bucket for his horse. "The conductor at Stamford found your cell phone on the train. I understand you're Joanne Wenner's granddaughter. I bought her house." He frowned. "Are you all right?"

I pressed my forehead into the gray horse's shoulder. I didn't mean to be rude, but I felt truly awful. The horse lifted his head from the bucket and snorted. A beige Prius wobbled down the gravel driveway—my parents.

4 | RED

Still no sign of "Beatrice," but how could I complain? Life in my new South Hampton home was five-star, first-class, premium deluxe. My leather halter was lined with genuine sheepskin. A brass plate emblazoned with my full name, Big Red, hung from my stall door, and the stall itself was even more spacious than the large birthing stall I'd been born in. It had a heated floor. Its walls were padded with foam encased in leather. My hayrack was made of brass and filled with the freshest, tastiest hay I'd ever eaten. The bran and oats and molasses and corn in my sweet feed were organic. My water was filtered and chilled and came through an on-demand automatic watering system. I just stuck my nose near the stainless steel basin and the cold, fresh water kept coming until I could drink no more.

Most of my aimless days were spent outdoors, munching on acres and acres of fresh grass turned salty from the ocean air. After breakfast I was turned out in a small field with a black dressage horse named Mozart who did nothing but weave neurotically back and forth in front of the gate, waiting for his owner. She came to ride him in the afternoons and spent hours talking to him, petting him, and feeding him carrots. All the other horses in the stable seemed to have owners like her, who petted and doted on them, all except me.

Where was Beatrice?

Late in the afternoons I was brought inside to be vacuumed, brushed, combed and polished until I gleamed and you could eat off my glistening red coat and my bleached white face. Then I was put away in my stall to watch the parade of chauffeured black SUVs creep up the driveway. The barn would fill up with adolescent girls hugging their horses and ponies and gossiping with each other as they got ready for their riding lessons. My neighbors on either side of my enormous, leather-padded box stall were chisel-headed warmbloods, imported from Europe and bred for their perfect conformation and athletic ability. The warmbloods were owned by two tall teenaged girls who doted on them and fed them sweet mints.

"Poor boy," they'd say, removing my muzzle and offering me a mint out of sympathy before slipping it back on again.

But I was fine, really. As the track vet had predicted, there was nothing seriously wrong with me after the crash at Keeneland except a fractured jaw, a badly bruised shoulder, and a messed-up eye. Those would all get better, except for maybe my eye. I'd already adjusted to having limited vision on that side.

I was fine, but so lonely.

For months I did nothing but eat and sleep and pine for a girl I hadn't met yet while my body healed. Beatrice had become mythical in my mind. I couldn't wait to meet her. She would feed me treats and talk to me and pet me, just like all the other girls, except she would be special because she would be mine.

Five months after my accident at the track a girl with angry brown eyes got out of her small black car and stomped down the aisle to my stall.

"Perfect," she said, inspecting my leather muzzle. "Dad got me Hannibal Lecter from *The Silence of the Lambs*."

It was Beatrice—finally. But her voice and her laugh weren't friendly. And she didn't give me carrots, or rub my forehead, or pat my neck. She just glared at me with her hard brown eyes and puffed on some sort of odorless cigarette with a glowing end. She didn't look like the other girls either. They wore their long hair braided down their backs or pinned up and secured with a hairnet beneath their black riding helmets. Beatrice's hair was clipped very short. The other girls wore colorful T-shirts, stretchy beige riding breeches, and tall leather boots for their lessons. Beatrice wore only black—black shirt, black jeans, and a pair of chunky black steel-toed boots.

"Want me to tack him up for you, Miss Beatrice?" one of the grooms offered. "He can be kind of wacko." He peered at me over my stall door. "Red? You going to be nice?"

Beatrice just laughed. "No thanks. The longer it takes to get him ready, the less time I have to ride."

"Whatever you want, Miss," the groom said. "But shout if he tries anything."

"Oh, I'll shout all right," Beatrice said in her laughing-but-not-laughing way.

So this was Beatrice. The girl I was supposed to belong to after months of jealous yearning and endless waiting. My disappointment was so acute I could taste it.

I hated her.

I was surprised to discover that she really didn't need the groom's help. She was very good with all the brushes and tools in the grooming box. She put the tack on correctly, and even loosened the right cheek strap on the bridle a hole where it had been buckled unevenly. Obviously she'd been around horses a lot and knew a great deal, but that didn't mean she liked it, or me.

"Watch it!" she warned harshly when I put my hoof down too close to her boot after she'd picked it out.

"Over, fatso," she ordered, shoving my rear end out of the way so she could straighten out the saddle pad.

I snorted and pawed the floor in annoyance while she brushed me, tried to bite her shoulder when she tightened the girth, and half-reared when she tried to lead me forward into the indoor ring. That only made her laugh. "Gee, Dad," she said. "You sure picked a winner."

The indoor ring was empty. It was morning still and a weekday. This Beatrice girl didn't go to school like the others.

"He's a beautiful horse, isn't he, Bea?" Mr. de Rothschild called from the viewing area beside the ring. Golden cufflinks flashed on his wrists. I could smell the same citrus-and-wood cologne he'd worn at the track in the spring. He winced as Beatrice jabbed her heels into my sides and I bolted forward.

"Careful now, Beatrice. He hasn't been ridden in a long time and he's very young. I wanted to have Todd come down and train him for a few months before you came home from school, but then you came home unexpectedly."

"I know how to ride, Dad," Beatrice insisted.

She was a terrible rider. I could feel that she knew what to do, but she did the opposite. She stuck out her stomach and slumped her shoulders and flapped her elbows and knees, posting heavily on the wrong diagonal. Then she'd pull on the reins and lean over my neck, shouting "Whoa! Whoa!"

Soon I was galloping on the wrong lead around the ring, occasionally kicking my hind legs out with an irritated buck. Beatrice flapped up and down, but she stayed on. Then, without warning, she steered me toward a three-foot jump.

It was just a plain white rail with three feet of air beneath it, lower than the fences I'd jumped that fateful day at the track. But I'd never been asked to jump. Just before takeoff I skidded to a halt. Beatrice flew over my head and crashed into the rail.

"Ow! Shit. Stupid horse."

Mr. de Rothschild stood up. "You're not hurt, are you? I don't know why you insist on no one helping you. If you're going to ride, you need a trainer. You should be having a lesson."

Beatrice dusted the peaty footing from her black jeans. "I know how to ride," she growled.

I stood by the jump, the reins dangling from my bridle. She went around to my left side and undid the girth. Then she pulled off the saddle and tossed it on the ground. It was a Hermés saddle, very expensive.

"What are you doing?" her father protested.

Beatrice ignored him. She removed my bridle and tossed it on top of the saddle. Then she whacked me on the hindquarters.

"Go! Shoo! Run away!" she shouted at me. She picked up a handful of dirt and threw it at my hocks.

I took off and tore around the indoor ring a few times, thoroughly enjoying the riderless run. Then Beatrice stepped in my path and held out her arms. I ducked away from her and galloped across the diagonal, straight over a big oxer. Another jump shaped like a chicken coop stood beyond it only two strides away, so I jumped that, too.

"Marvelous!" Mr. de Rothschild cried.

I eased down to a trot, swinging my head toward Beatrice to see what was next. She turned her back, and without another word to me or her father, left the ring.

I walked over to the viewing area. Mr. de Rothschild held out his manicured hand for me to sniff. I pinned my ears and gnashed my teeth. He withdrew his hand.

"What am I going to do with you? Both of you?"

We stared at each other for a few minutes. Despair hung over him in a cloud of cologne. Finally he got up and left me penned in the indoor ring, forgetting how good I was at opening gates.

Within seconds I unlatched the gate and sauntered outside. Beatrice was in her small black car with the windows rolled down and the radio blaring. She honked the horn when she saw me. I reared and galloped off toward the ocean.

A groom found me grazing in the tall grass on a sandy hill near the beach. He led me to a small paddock with a run-in shed and put my muzzle back on. And that is where I stayed, day and night, instead of in the barn. Every couple of days a new person would try to ride me—one of the more advanced teenaged girls, an older man—but I always got them off my back within minutes. I was furious—with myself and all humankind. Beatrice didn't love me and I certainly didn't love her. I wasn't even sure I was capable of love.

A few weeks later, Beatrice and I were sent away together.

5 | MERRITT

"It's perfectly normal for her to be upset right now. It's a lot to take in. Plus there's all the overstimulation. Her urine sample shows high levels of caffeine, alcohol, and muscle relaxers, a homemade cocktail of whatever's easily available at the drugstore or in your cabinets at home, anything she can get her hands on. It's very common."

I stared out the window of my new bedroom, ignoring the know-it-all woman. Her name was Dr. Kami, I'd gleaned that much. And she'd been talking about me as if I wasn't lying right there ever since I'd woken up. I felt awful, as if my body had been detached from my head and rigor mortis had set in.

"It's just such a relief," my mother said. "Good Fences was mentioned in an article about equine-assisted therapy in *The Wall Street Journal* last spring, and I had an 'Aha' moment. I just wished I'd acted on it sooner. Michael was against it. His mother was a horse person, you see. Their relationship was . . . troubled. He thinks horses are just pretty pets for spoiled girls. And especially with the de Rothschild association, but I—"

"I wasn't against it," my father interrupted her. "I just thought it sounded a little half-baked."

My parents were masters at talking about me as if I wasn't there. They particularly enjoyed quarreling about me in public, as if it were perfectly acceptable to demonstrate how dysfunctional our family was in front of complete strangers. And I had fallen into the habit of tuning out or walking out, whichever was more convenient. Except I couldn't walk out now. I didn't even know where I was.

"There's never a right time," Dr. Kami reassured them. "And it's never too late. Anyway we're very new. We only opened in May."

Mom beamed at Dr. Kami. "Well anyway, when I called this morning I was just so relieved that you had an opening. It's just exactly what we've been looking for." She shot Dad a meaningful glance. "Today it became very clear that things are not going to improve with Merritt at home."

I understood then that Good Fences was some sort of equestrian-themed loony bin for teenaged girls. It was just off the Merritt Parkway, ironically, about an hour north of New Canaan. My parents had picked me up in Gran-Jo's driveway and we'd driven straight here. I'd fallen asleep briefly, and the next thing I knew, there was Dr. Kami.

"I'm hoping the horse element here will provide meaning for her," Mom added. "It's exactly the sort of place her grandmother should have gone to as a girl."

Mom and Gran-Jo had never gotten along. Mom was too modern, urban, and efficient. She wore stretchy new-age fabrics that were easy to clean. She didn't like old things or clutter. She ate a lot of salmon, kale, and raw nuts. She didn't drink cocktails, only wine in moderation. She once said that Gran-Jo had been "raised by wolves," because Gran-Jo had gone to a horsy boarding school in Virginia at the age of twelve and had proceeded to run away with her best friend's older brother (my grandfather) at the age of eighteen. Mom hated how much time I spent with Gran-Jo and Noble out in New Canaan. She didn't understand that it was out of necessity. There was only so much

TV I could watch while my parents trained for marathons and graded papers and shopped for sustainably harvested fish.

Gran-Jo and Noble were the best part of my life. But they'd both been dead for over a year, and today I'd tried to go see them.

"What's your success rate?" my father was asking Kami now.

"Well, as I said, we only opened in May, but our girls seem very happy for the most part," Kami explained. She had frizzy brown hair and wore her reading glasses propped on top of her head. Her stocky legs were shoved into ugly denim Bermuda shorts and a pair of worn work boots.

"We move in baby steps here at Good Fences," she continued. "We call them 'cross-rails.' When you jump a course of fences on a horse, the only way to do it is one fence at a time. I think Merritt will get a huge boost straight away from linking up with one of our equines. Our girls' self-esteem is at an all-time low when they arrive, and then this gorgeous animal, this gentle giant, picks them for a friend and confidante. It has an immediate impact. And then there are the routine chores of the barn. All the responsibilities that go with taking care of a horse. It's a lot of work, but it does a world of good."

I turned back to the window. Outside, horses grazed in a green field surrounded by a pretty white clapboard fence. Bright orange and round, the sun sank behind a stand of conifers, setting their branches on fire. The quaint horse barn was painted red with white trim. It looked exactly like the toy barn Gran-Jo kept my plastic Breyer horses in when I was little. If she fell asleep on the sofa after dinner I'd play with them until I got tired and put myself to bed.

"Merritt, I think it might be best if you say goodbye to your parents as quickly as possible so you can get ready for dinner,"

Dr. Kami said, addressing the back of my head. "We operate on a tight schedule here. The sooner I get you acquainted the better."

I whipped around and glared at my parents. "Wait, you're just leaving? But how long am I staying? What about school?"

Mom crossed the room to join my father by the door. She took his hand as if to demonstrate their solidarity. Both my parents were still dressed in their Saturday workout clothes, Fitbits strapped to their wrists.

Dad coughed and averted his gaze from mine. "Dr. Kami?"

"Just Kami is fine," Dr. Kami assured him. "Don't worry, Merritt. We have a nice balance here of therapy, school work, barn work, and fun."

I'd helped Gran-Jo take care of Noble every day all summer and every weekend. We didn't call it work. Everything else was work.

Dad squeezed my mother's hand. "Sounds great to me," he said, forcing a smile.

Mom let go of his hand, pulled down the ankle zippers on her track pants, and kicked her legs out in front of her one at a time, the way she did before a run. Then she walked over to the bed, bent down, and kissed me lightly on the cheek. She smelled like sweat. I felt bad that she hadn't had a chance to shower.

"Get better," she said brusquely.

I stared up at her, too angry to cry. "I can't believe you're just leaving me here."

"There are horses," Mom said, a pleading note in her voice.

"It'll be easier if we just go, Susan." Dad strode over and kissed my other cheek. He smelled even sweatier than Mom. "Good luck. Try to . . ." He faltered and sighed, as if whatever he wanted to say was really too much to ask. Then he took my mother's hand again and led her toward the door. "Try to lighten up a little," he called out finally, over his shoulder.

"I'll be in touch," Dr. Kami promised as they made their way out.

I glanced up at her, feeling very exposed on my new plain white bed in my new plain white room. I hugged my knees to my chest and shivered even though I was still wearing my jacket. Dr. Kami had a lot of smile wrinkles around her eyes and mouth, but I bet she just pretended to be all fuzzy and approachable. Pretty soon I'd be doing jumping jacks on the manure pile at three o'clock in the morning in the rain for acting so spoiled and ungrateful to my parents.

"Your mom unpacked your things for you. They're in the top two drawers of the bureau and the left-hand rail of the closet. Your schedule is right here on your desk. Why don't you have a look at it? I'll meet you downstairs in the dining hall in fifteen minutes. We can talk then."

I stayed on the bed, still hugging my knees. I wanted to get under the covers and not move until morning, or maybe for a whole year. I definitely didn't want to eat dinner with a bunch of strangers. "I'm not hungry," I mumbled.

Dr. Kami smiled patiently. "Dinner is part of the program. No exceptions. You'll see why when you get there." She turned to leave. "Fifteen minutes."

I slid my feet to the floor and stood up, noticing for the first time that there was another bed in the room, wedged diagonally across the far corner, behind another desk. The bed was unmade. A pair of cream-colored satin pajamas lay in a rumpled pile on the pillow.

I bristled. "Wait, I have a roommate?"

Kami stopped in the doorway. "Oh yes. That's Beatrice. She sort of rearranged the furniture. She's been to all sorts of boarding schools, so she's used to getting creative with her room." She smiled her friendly, can't-hide-from-me smile.

I glared back. I didn't want a roommate, especially not one who wore satin pajamas.

"See you at dinner." Kami backed out of the room, pulling the door closed behind her.

6 | RED

My new home was shabby compared to the de Rothschild's fancy Hamptons stable, but I had a grass paddock and run-in shed all to myself, while the other horses shared the little red barn and the larger fenced-in pasture down the hill from me. Here the horses—some of them ancient—were never ridden. They stood dozing stupidly in the sun, or were led around in circles and talked to by girls in sweatpants and rubber boots. I kept watch from my lonely hill.

Beatrice was the only one responsible for my care. She kept me beautiful, I'll give her that. My coat gleamed, my hooves were conditioned and free from stones, the shavings on the floor of my run-in shed were spotless, my water buckets scrubbed. But she never talked to me or scratched me behind the ears the way the other girls talked to and patted their horses. Her voice was always sharp and angry. When she wasn't feeding or grooming me or cleaning out my shed, she ignored me, sitting with her back against the fence, reading a book.

Sometimes she played with the electric fence.

The parkway ran behind my paddock, beyond a thickly wooded forest. In order to keep me or anyone else from escaping and getting run over, someone had installed a very high-voltage electric wire all along the back side of the paddock.

Beatrice was fascinated by it. We'd been there for two weeks, and she would not stop hovering over that fence.

"How bad could it be?" she said aloud one evening, just after sunset. She held her finger over the wire.

Was she talking to me or to herself?

The fence thrummed threateningly. I could tell the current was strong, I just didn't know how strong. I sniffed it and tossed my head as my nostrils picked up the scent of singed hair.

"Chicken!" she guffawed loudly.

She held her hand even closer to the fence. Her fingernails were painted black and her black hair was even shorter now than it was when we'd first met. She'd cut it herself. I'd watched her through the tack room window of the little red barn a few nights before, using the clippers meant for buzzing the horses' whiskers and ears.

"If I get seriously shocked what will you do?" She glared at me for a moment and then snorted to herself. "Probably nothing."

A bell sounded from the big log house where all the girls lived.

"Dinnertime." Beatrice pulled her hand away from the electric fence and walked across the grass to the gate.

I pawed the ground and snorted. She lifted the waiting feed bucket from outside the gate and poured my grain into the feed pail inside my run-in shed. Then she unstrapped my muzzle from my halter.

"Don't look too happy," she warned as I attacked the grain. "I'll be back."

7 | MERRITT

At Good Fences dinner was served family style. Three "servers" were assigned the task of carrying platters of food from the kitchen to both of the big round tables in the dining room. The others remained seated. Since I was new, I wasn't expected to serve. I sat down next to Kami at an otherwise empty table set with six places. My stomach still felt strange, both bloated and empty at the same time. All I'd eaten that day was a bite of eggs and two oysters. Some solid food might be good.

A very short guy in his twenties who looked like he might be Mexican or South American placed a platter of gooey lasagna on the table. He pulled out the chair on Kami's other side and sat down. I was surprised to see a guy at all, since Good Fences was only for girls.

"Merritt, this is the amazing Luis. He takes care of the equine side of things—the barn and grounds and the horses. Luis knows everything about everything. He used to be a jockey, but I think he's happier on his lawnmower. Safer anyway."

Luis grinned, his tan skin creasing around his mouth and eyes. "I have broken, like, fifteen bones," he told me. "Nice to meet you, Merritt."

Kami picked up a serving spoon and dug into the lasagna.

"Our best dinner on your first night here." She grabbed my plate and served me a huge portion.

I stared down at it. At least there was no kale.

A morose-looking chubby girl with rings all over her fingers placed a bowl of salad on the table and sat down next to Luis. A tall, extremely thin blonde girl sat down next to the chubby girl and pushed a plate of garlic bread and a bowl of meatballs into the center of the table.

Kami cut another enormous slab of lasagna and sloshed it onto her own plate. "The lasagna is veggie. We try to be healthy here at Fences, although the red velvet cupcakes are so disgustingly good they should be illegal."

"Totally!" The skinny blonde squealed. "I live for those cupcakes!"

I rolled my eyes. All the girls at Dowd were so into cupcakes. It was like their passion to make and decorate cupcakes, or to buy fancy cupcakes at one of those special cupcake boutiques like Baked by Belinda. As if cupcakes somehow represented something more than just small cakes with way too much frosting on them. As if cupcakes were magical and gave you special powers. I hated cupcakes.

The blonde girl scowled at her lasagna. She was dressed like Valentine's Day Barbie, in pink short-shorts and a pink crop-top. Her fingernails, eye shadow, blush, and lipstick were all the same shade of baby pink. She was older, too, eighteen maybe— too old to wear that much pink. Clearly the girls here were pretty messed up.

Luis served her a small piece, gave the chubby, many-ringed girl a normal-sized piece, and then dunked three huge pieces onto his own plate. "I love being the only guy here. Nobody eats, so more for me."

Kami snorted. "Hello Mr. Eighty-five Pounds?"

Luis laughed and reached for Kami's hand. "One hundred and seventeen. I weighed myself this morning."

I noticed with alarm that everyone at the table was holding hands.

Kami grabbed my left hand. Oh no. Were they going to pray? I didn't do God stuff. I hadn't even been baptized. Typical of my parents to not ask whether Good Fences had any religious affiliation. They just wanted to get rid of me. They didn't care if I had to pray and go to confession and hold hands and hug everyone all the time.

"Thanks for another great day," Luis said, his head bowed. "The food looks freaking good too. Let's eat."

"Let's eat," the rest of the table chorused.

They released each other's hands and picked up their forks.

Kami cleared her throat. "Since Merritt's new, let's introduce ourselves while we eat. Tell us your name and what your goals are. Tell us about the horse you've been working with. Then we'll do the Word of the Day." She frowned at the empty chair next to me. "And maybe Beatrice will decide to join us at some point."

I looked around the room. There was only one other table. Two male staff members I hadn't met yet were sitting with some younger girls. And that was it. Good Fences was tiny, which meant it would be impossible for me to escape. Although my roommate seemed to be doing a pretty good job of it.

"I'll start," said the chubby girl, who'd been quiet until now. Her face was pale, her green eyes marble hard. She pushed away her lasagna, her fingers heavy with silver rings. "My name is Tabitha. I have anger issues. The food here is too healthy. I can't sleep. I miss my bed at home, and my Komodo dragon, Heyoncé. He's very clean. My horse sleeps in his own poop." She spoke in a monotone, looking down at the table. "I used to post a lot of pictures of myself in like, rage poses, or pretending to do weird shit like stick razor blades between my teeth, on Instagram. That was fun." She sighed. "I miss my phone."

I snuck a glance around the room. It was true: not a cell phone in sight. My parents still had mine.

Luis was next. "I'm Luis. I was working at Saratoga, you know, the racetrack? I exercised the horses, but I wanted to be a jockey and I used to starve myself and party a lot to keep from gaining weight." He rubbed his concave belly. "I started getting more and more rides and I even won a stakes race. That felt good. Then one time I was still sort of high, and I forgot to put up the girth and I fell off and broke my back. That was it, no more racing for me. I did a lot of work on myself and then I started the job here. I like how they use the horses to help the girls. And like Kami says, I like my mower and I like to eat." He shrugged and dove at his lasagna again.

Sharing was not my thing. I nibbled a piece of garlic bread, already anxious about what I was going to say. This was my worst nightmare, why I'd refused to see a shrink.

The tall blonde was next. "I'm Celine. I'm eighteen, so the oldest one here. My goal is to feel ready to leave here and go to college, but I love my horse, Lacey. She's so sweet, she just gets me." She sighed deeply, her big blue eyes misty with emotion. "I think I like it here a little too much. Everyone is so nice. I'd stay here all the time if I could." She glanced at me and smiled. "I was the first girl here when they opened. It was supposed to be like summer camp, but now it's October and I'm still here . . ."

Her voice trailed off. A shadow loomed behind me. I turned around. A tough-looking girl with short black hair, dressed head-to-toe in black, yanked back the empty chair to my right. She sat down two feet away from the table with her knees splayed wide.

"Hello, Beatrice," Kami greeted her. "You're not going to be able to eat much sitting like that."

Beatrice dragged her chair forward. She leaned in to see what was left of the food. "Hey, what the hell, guys? What happened to the garlic bread?"

I blinked at the center of the table. Someone had dropped the remaining pieces of garlic bread into the bowl of meatballs.

Tabitha bit her lip. "My bad."

"You're disgusting," Beatrice growled.

"What did we talk about earlier today?" Kami asked, her voice even and cheerful. "Treat others the way you would like to be treated. If you want to eat dinner here with us I will ignore your lateness, but only if you can be respectful and nice."

Beatrice rolled her eyes. She lunged forward and grabbed the entire bowl of meatballs and bread, picked up her fork, then began to eat right out of the bowl. "Is it sharing time? Is it my turn to share?"

Kami glanced at me, her cheeks flushed an irritated red. It was the first time she'd registered any emotion other than patient understanding. Obviously Beatrice knew how to push Kami's buttons.

She turned back to Beatrice. "Go ahead."

Beatrice took a slow, dramatic sip of water and then put down her glass. She wiped her mouth on the back of her hand and cleared her throat. "I would just like to say again what I say at every sharing time: This place is so lame. They don't even let you ride the horses. Not that I actually like riding." She turned to me, her dark brown eyes in a permanent glare. "It's basically a petting zoo. I'm only here because I got kicked out of all the other zoos, so my father created this one. Just wait till it snows, then it'll really suck."

Kami pushed back her chair and stood up. "Thank you, Beatrice. Once again, I think you'd be better off eating in the One-Room Schoolhouse. I'll take you there myself."

Beatrice grabbed a cherry tomato out of the salad and popped it into her mouth. "Fine. Absolutely. Love it there."

I watched Kami lead her away, anxious about meeting Beatrice one-on-one, whenever she came back to our room. Anxious, but a little intrigued.

"That girl is so scary. Everyone calls her 'The Bear,'" Celine explained to me as she reapplied her pink lipstick. "Her dad basically funds this whole place. He's like this amazing philanthropist, but his daughter's a nightmare. She's his adopted daughter though. They're not actually related."

"I saw her spit in Kami's face," Tabitha added. "It was kind of funny. That was the first time they put her in the Schoolhouse."

"What is that, anyway?" I asked, poking at my lasagna. I could eat some plain toast maybe, or some saltines, but not lasagna.

"Solitary," Celine explained. "It's where they put you when you're really bad, so you can relax and regroup. It's just like this modern shed with no windows. I've never gone. I hate being alone."

"I like it," Tabitha said. "I purposely blow off my barn chores so I can go there. There are all these beanbag chairs and a whole library of CDs to listen to. The Schoolhouse rocks."

"You know that Beatrice is good with the horses though," Luis put in. "I watched her. She knows what she's doing."

"She never talks to anybody," Tabitha said. "And she's totally obsessed with this poet who committed suicide in like the 1970s or something."

I was still mulling over what Beatrice had said about not being allowed to ride the horses. What did they do with them then?

Before I could ask, Kami returned with a plate of chocolate

chip cookies. "I brought dessert. Now, where were we?" she said, as if nothing had happened. "Ah yes. Merritt. Your turn."

I put down my fork. My palms were clammy. I wished I could speak my mind like Beatrice, tell them to leave me alone, but I couldn't imagine drawing that much attention to myself.

"I'm Merritt," I began, my eyes on my plate. "Um, I used to ride my grandmother's horse. She and her horse both died a little over a year ago. I really miss them so . . . my parents thought I'd like it here? That's it, I guess."

I kept staring at my plate.

"Thank you, Merritt," Kami said after an awkward pause. "Now my turn."

I picked up my fork and looked up.

"I'm Kami. I'm a recovered bulimic. I used to be a social worker who liked horses. But then I got certified in equine-assisted therapy and helped get Good Fences started. Every time I match up a horse with someone I get seriously jazzed." She shot an enthusiastic eyebeam at me. "You'll see tomorrow. It's magical."

There was an index card lying in the middle of the table with the word "Intentions" printed on it in careful black capital letters. Kami stuffed a forkful of lasagna into her mouth and picked up the card.

"I *intended* for us to do the Word of the Day now, just like I *intend* to eat only one cookie for dessert," she said, still chewing. "But why don't you two girls take Merritt down to the barn to meet the horses instead?"

I followed Celine and Tabitha across the lawn and down the hill to the red-shingled barn. It was nearly dark and the air was chilly, but the barn aisle was brightly lit. Inside it was small and orderly, but not fancy, with ten large box stalls—five on either side of the cement-floored aisle. Above the stalls was a hay-loft full of neatly stacked bales of hay. I breathed in the sweet, musty scent of hay and horses—the scent I loved and missed so much. It was like food for me, like some essential nutrient that my system required but that I had been deprived of for far too long. I inhaled deeply, filling my lungs with it. One of the horses swung his enormous brown and white head in my direction.

"Who's this?" I reached out to stroke the massive velvety nose.

"That's Arnold. He's a draft horse rescue. They're all rescue horses here," Celine explained. "Kami told me Arnie was on the Budweiser wagon team when he was young, and then he was used to drag logs around at county fairs. When she got him at auction he had sores all over and he was foundering. He's only sixteen, but he acts like he's thirty."

I nodded as if I understood, but I realized then how limited my exposure to horses actually was. Noble, Gran-Jo's bay Irish Sport Horse—schooled in dressage and show-jumping and probably with far fancier bloodlines than any of the horses at Good Fences—was the only horse I'd ever known. I smoothed Arnie's dark brown forelock against his broad, white forehead. He bowed his head, his eyes half-closed.

Next to Arnie was a squat Shetland pony who craned her neck to sniff my hand. Her fuzzy, peach-colored nose barely reached the top of the stall door.

"That's Chamomile," Celine said. "She's a thousand years old and will probably outlive us all. Apparently she used to work on an Amish apple farm, although I'm not exactly sure what she did there. And I think she's had a few babies, too. You should see her when they turn them all out in the field. She bosses everyone around."

I hung over Chamomile's door and scratched her between the

ears. She shook her head and tottered away to root for strands of hay that might have dropped into her bedding.

"And this is Lacey, my girl." Celine's voice brightened as she opened the door to the next stall and went inside to hug the flea-bitten gray mare inside. "Lacey was a jumper. Like, a really fancy one. She did all the big shows. Then she fractured both knees in a jump-off. Her knees are still kind of arthritic, but she's okay."

Celine pressed her face into the horse's neck. Lacey stood very still, her brown eyes soft and unblinking. She didn't seem particularly fond of Celine, but she didn't seem to mind her either.

"Lacey knows everything about me. Oh no!" Celine dashed out of the stall and grabbed a pitchfork. "Poor baby. You can't sleep with all this mess in here." She began to pick out clumps of manure and dump them into a bin in the aisle. "Go ahead and meet the others," she said. "The Appaloosa is Cinnamon. She belongs to Luis. Then there's Rex, the little black one. He's Tabitha's. And the two gray ponies in the field are Greta and Ghost. They live outside at night. These guys go out during the day."

I went down the line, greeting the horses and patting them. They looked at me with mild interest, but I could tell they were used to girls coming and going. I was nothing special to them.

Tabitha was in the tack room listening to music on an old radio, humming to herself while she cleaned a pile of leather halters with glycerin soap. She'd used so much soap and water that the halters looked like they were covered in shaving cream. "Less is more," Gran-Jo always told me when it came to cleaning leather. Too much water dried it out. She used to take apart all of Noble's tack and lay it out on her living room floor. She'd sit in her armchair, drinking bourbon out of a crystal tumbler, watching me like a hawk while I cleaned it and put it all back together again.

The sky was dark now, with no moon. A few of the outside lights began to turn on. Celine continued to sift through the bedding in Lacey's stall. Two younger girls stood by the pasture fence, giggling hysterically while the two gray ponies grazed. Luis hosed down the flowerbeds outside the main house—or "the Lodge" as Kami called it.

A flash of white caught my eye up on the hill across the driveway from the main pasture. It was another horse, a big one, with four white stockings and a long white blaze down its face. Some type of muzzle contraption was strapped over its nose. The horse looked sort of scary, like something out of a horror movie.

A girl sat on the ground nearby, her back against the fence, a book propped against her knees. I recognized the dark head and black clothes. It was Beatrice.

Something glowed red in her hand, giving off its own tiny halo of red light. Celine came up behind me and grimaced.

"See? She goes up there and reads. She never talks to any of us. She just reads and smokes her stupid e-cigarette. We're not even allowed to smoke them, but they made an exception for her because her dad owns the place."

"What about the horse? Why isn't it down here with the others?"

"Oh, that's another one of Mr. de Rothschild's charity cases. He was rescued from the track. I think he was supposed to be Beatrice's show horse."

"Really?" It was difficult for me to imagine Beatrice at a horse show, unless she was there to terrorize everyone.

"Oh yeah. Beatrice was a big time pony rider. She won everything. Spent the winters in Florida and the summers at Saratoga and the Hamptons. She used to be all tiny and cute with these long black braids and dimples. But when she was around fifteen she got too big to ride ponies anymore. She started acting like she didn't know how to ride at all and refused to compete. She's just spoiled," Celine concluded. "Kami says that horse has some major issues anyway. He's scary, just like her."

I nodded, nervous again about meeting Beatrice in our room. Curfew was at nine o'clock and it was already after eight.

I helped Tabitha wipe the soap scum off the halters, then we hayed the horses while Luis watered. I actually enjoyed the barn chores, but I was so exhausted I was truly grateful when Luis finally turned off the barn light and we headed back to the Lodge.

My room was dark. I switched on Beatrice's desk light. Her bed was still messy, her satin pajamas untouched. It didn't look like she'd been back to the room at all.

I changed into my old cutoff sweatpants and my favorite green Ox Ridge Hunt Club T-shirt and got into bed. The plain white sheets felt new and scratchy.

Beatrice's desk light was still on. Maybe we could get to know each other a little bit before we went to sleep, I thought. That way it wouldn't feel so bizarre, sharing a room with a complete stranger. My head felt like lead on the flat foamy pillow. This morning I'd gone to school to take the SAT. The night before I'd barely slept. I felt like I'd been awake for a whole year.

In just a few seconds I was completely gone.

8 | RED

Beatrice returned after dinner to strap the muzzle back onto my halter. Three times a day the muzzle came off for an hour or so, allowing me to eat my grain and hay and to graze. Then it went back on.

The days were getting shorter. There was hardly any light left. As usual Beatrice sat down by my fence to suck on that glowing pipe of hers and read the same book she always read. From my quiet, grassy hilltop I watched the other girls hay and water their horses in the little red barn, laughing and chattering the whole time.

Beatrice stayed with me under the pretense of keeping me company, but she was just using me to avoid the others. The fact that I was her horse, that I belonged to her, was a complete joke.

The lights went out in the barn below and the girls traipsed back up to the main house. Beatrice threw down her book. She swatted at her arm. "It's too dark to read. But of course there are still mosquitoes." She sucked on her pipe and fingered the dry leaves on the ground.

Now that my muzzle was on I couldn't eat anymore. I began to doze off. Sleep was my only escape. Lucky for me, horses can sleep on their feet.

• • •

The smell of smoke startled me awake.

Beatrice had taken apart her pipe and was crouched over the ground. "I've always wanted to try this. I saw it on the Discovery Channel." She was holding a foil gum wrapper around the tiny battery from inside her pipe. The wrapper was smoldering. "Hey, it works!"

Suddenly it caught fire and she tossed it on top of a small pile of dry leaves. Then she picked up a stick and held it over the flame. The stick caught fire and Beatrice stood up with it in her hand. I backed away.

She stamped on the leaves, putting out the fire, still holding the burning stick in her hand like a torch. I backed away even more, as far as I could. Horses have the good sense to be afraid of fire. She ducked under my fence and began to walk with the burning stick toward the little shed where she'd been spending a lot of her time. The shed door was padlocked shut, but she pulled it open a crack and shoved the burning stick inside.

"Bonfire tonight!"

I snorted and pawed the ground as smoke seeped out the shed door. I wasn't too panicked though. The caretaker, Luis, had watered the flowers around the shed so the ground there was damp. Plus, I'd caught the scent of rain in the gathering dark. The clouds were already low and heavy. There were no stars.

Beatrice ducked under the fence again and kept walking through my enclosure toward the electric fence and the parkway beyond.

I followed her, unworried. Now I was just curious. As she might say, I was watching "solely for entertainment purposes."

Beatrice stopped by the electric fence. "Okay. This is either going to blast me straight to hell, or it's going to do nothing. Either way, I'm out of here, so who cares?" I stopped about a yard away. She turned to look at me. Then she came over and took off my muzzle. "Let's give them something else to deal with while we're at it, huh?"

For the first time since I'd met her, I felt happy. Without a muzzle there were so many things I could do. I wandered away to nibble at the patchy grass. Flames licked the door of the little shed. Beatrice went back to the electric fence and took off her heavy black boots. Her arms were pearly white in the darkness as she stretched out the fingers of both hands. Then she grabbed onto the thrumming wire.

The air around us became charged with electricity. I could smell the current. It seemed to hold her, rather than her holding it.

A long minute passed, then she fell down.

"Ow," she moaned softly. "That was awesome." She rolled onto her back and took out her pipe. The end glowed red.

I drifted away toward the gate, still grazing. One of the grays in the pasture across the driveway whinnied at me and I nickered in return. My hooves felt light on the cool ground. It began to rain. It was going to be a great night.

9 | MERRITT

A commotion woke me up. Sirens outside and shouting inside. Beatrice's desk light was still on, just as I had left it, and the bed was untouched, satin pajamas in their rumpled spot. I knelt on my bed and pulled the white roller blind away from the window. It was very early, not even fully light. A murky blue fog clung to the ground. Kami and Luis were leading horses into the barn. A red fire truck sat in the driveway, lights flashing but silent now. Firemen tramped around a small shed, which I assumed must be the "One-Room Schoolhouse."

I squinted. The shed door looked like a half-eaten piece of burnt toast.

"Not my problem!" a girl's angry voice echoed throughout the Lodge.

It was Beatrice. Had to be

Outside, a car engine revved. A black Escalade, shiny in the dim morning light, appeared from behind the fire truck. It sped away down the driveway.

Good Fences was suddenly quiet.

I got out of bed, padded across the cream-colored carpet to the door, and peeked out. The narrow hallway was empty. Rubber boots stood in neat pairs outside the three doors facing mine. I recognized Tabitha's shiny red ones. They seemed way too cheerful for a girl like Tabitha.

Celine's sleek, platinum blonde head popped out of the doorway next to mine. She was wearing some sort of pink terry-cloth romper with matching slippers. The only trace of morning on her face was the slightly smudged eyeliner beneath her big blue eyes.

"What happened?" I demanded.

Celine furrowed her perfectly plucked eyebrows. "I thought you'd know. She's your roommate. Didn't you see anything?"

"Just Beatrice's car leaving. I mean, I think it was her car. She didn't come back to the room," I explained. "Not even to sleep. I just woke up when I heard her yelling."

Celine stretched her long, skinny arms out in front of her and rolled her wrists until they cracked. "Well it's only an hour till breakfast. I'm sure Kami will tell us everything."

Breakfast was a serve-yourself situation, with bins of cereal lined up on the kitchen counter, pitchers of orange juice and milk, sliced bread and a toaster to toast it in, a bowl of bananas, and a platter of melon slices and green grapes. Yawning, I filled up a bowl with raisin bran and drizzled some milk over it. My parents would be so proud. They had all these theories about behavior and diet. As long as I ate well, they said, I would feel well.

I joined Kami and Tabitha at the same table where I'd eaten last night. Amanda and Sloan, the two inseparable fourteen year olds paired up with the two gray ponies, were whispering quietly at the table by the window.

Celine was right behind me, balancing a few grapes and a slice of melon on her otherwise empty plate.

"Beatrice got kicked out," Tabitha announced immediately. "She tried to burn down the Schoolhouse, and then she let out all the horses."

"She did not," Kami snapped grumpily. She looked awful, huddled over a mug of black coffee, her frizzy hair sticking out in fuzzy brown clumps around her tired face. "Well, yes, she started a fire. But the rain pretty much stopped it. Her horse caused the most trouble. He has to wear a muzzle or he gets loose and lets out all the other horses." She heaved an enormous sigh. "Mr. de Rothschild sent them here to bond with each other and now look what's happened."

The cereal in my bowl went soggy as I waited for her to finish. "Beatrice is gone and they've left us with her awful horse."

"Do we still have double Study Hall?" Tabitha demanded. Two slices of cinnamon raisin toast smeared with marshmallow fluff were stacked on her plate. I would have to try that tomorrow.

"No Study Hall," Kami said with her eyes closed. Her fingers gripped her coffee mug as if it were supporting her whole body. I don't think I've ever seen anyone look that tired, except for maybe me in the mirror last night when I was brushing my teeth. I wondered if there wasn't more going on than a small fire and some loose horses. She opened her eyes again. "Would you mind just doing barn chores and free time until lunch today?"

"Woo-hoo!" Tabitha cheered.

Last night before dinner, I'd learned a little about the routine from skimming the brochures and pamphlets my parents had left on my desk. Days at Good Fences were broken down into one-and-a-half-hour blocks. We were supposed to do two blocks of Study Hall a day, working on schoolwork that came in packets from our regular schools. The supervisors—Kami and two other tutors—were supposed to be on hand to help us. I didn't even have my first packet from Dowd, so I was happy to skip it.

"What about Merritt?" Celine said. She cut a piece of

cantaloupe into bite-sized cubes without actually eating it. "She hasn't been paired up with a horse yet."

"She can do my barn chores," Tabitha offered.

I pushed away my half-eaten bowl of cereal and was about to go back to my room and crawl back into bed when I realized Kami was frowning at me.

"Will I be getting a different roommate?" I asked her.

"How good are you around horses?" she responded, ignoring my question. "You said your grandmother had a horse."

I was instantly suspicious. "She kept her horse behind her house. I used to stay there all summer and on weekends. She pretty much taught me everything."

Kami nodded. "And was her horse green at all? Did he behave himself?"

Noble was pretty well-behaved, except around umbrellas and bicycles. And when it snowed we'd have to lunge him for an hour before either of us could ride him. "He was kind of old when he died, but he definitely had his moments. I fell off him a few times. I never got hurt or anything though."

"Maybe we should try," Kami said, more to herself than to me.

"Try what?" Try was not one of my favorite words. Try this delicious salmon and kale burger. Try to do better on your next Math test. Try to smile more. Try to make more friends. Try not to think about the past so much and focus on the future. Try not to yawn so much. Try to get involved in some new activities.

"Well, now that she's gone, someone will have to take care of her horse," Kami said slowly.

"Whose horse?"

"Beatrice's. His name is Red."

"He's in his own field, right? I saw him last night, up on the hill."

"Don't do anything with him before I get there," Kami

warned me, as if I'd already agreed to the assignment. "That horse is a handful. I can introduce you to him this afternoon." She pushed her glasses up on her head and zoomed in on me with her tired, froggy eyes. "Promise?"

"Sure. Yeah, I promise."

"Good." Kami pushed her chair back. "I'm going to go lie down for a bit and maybe take a shower. I'll see you all at lunch."

I'd never been good at keeping promises.

"I'll catch up with you guys in a sec," I called as the others headed down to the barn. Ignoring the demarcated path, I stepped off the Lodge porch and tromped across the dew-dampened lawn and across the dirt driveway. It was a beautiful morning. The sun was bright and there were no clouds. Tall trees bordered the driveway, their yellow-leafed branches full of singing birds.

I walked up the hill past the One-Room Schoolhouse. The little shed was soggy and charred, but it was still standing. I imagined Beatrice would have been disappointed that it hadn't burned to the ground.

Red ambled out of his run-in shed as I approached his paddock. The same leather muzzle was strapped to his halter, preventing him from grazing. He stood by the fence, head up, ears pricked, as if he'd been waiting for me.

"Hello," I greeted him. "You look kind of like a serial killer in that thing."

The tall chestnut stared at me, his ears flicking back and forth. His eyes were a beautiful amber color, orangey-brown with flecks of gold. He was even bigger than I'd first thought. And he was gorgeous.

He sniffed my hand as best he could with his muzzle on, then snorted and stalked away, as if I bored him. Bobbing his head up and down to ward off the flies, he walked back to his run-in shed and stood half in and half out of it, his hindquarters to me.

"Nice to meet you, too."

I don't know what I expected. Noble had always been so friendly. I glanced around his paddock. The grass inside his enclosure was cropped close to the ground. He must have been allowed to graze at certain supervised times. I was tempted to take his muzzle off, just to see what he would do. There was no one in sight. I climbed over the fence and walked toward the run-in shed.

Gran-Jo had taught me never to approach a horse from behind without talking to him.

"I'm just going to take that thing off so you can eat," I said, standing to one side. I touched his hindquarters to let him know exactly where I was and that I wasn't a threat.

Red's head went up. His ears went back. He swished his full, rust-colored tail and cocked his left hind leg. It was a warning. If I got any closer he would kick me.

10 | RED

could have really kicked her hard—it wasn't like anyone was paying attention, the nitwits.

"Fine," the girl said quietly and stepped out of the way. "Suit yourself."

I heard her walk away, but she wasn't walking toward the barn or the house. She was going the wrong way, toward the parkway and the electric fence. What was it about that fence? Curiosity got the better of me. I backed out of my shed and took a peek.

She was just a regular-looking girl. Brownish-blonde, not big or small, blue jeans, gray T-shirt, sneakers. I'd seen a million of her at the fancy Hamptons stable. Sometimes they gave me carrots. A couple of them even tried to ride me when Beatrice refused to, but I was always impossible. I lay down on one of them. I broke the reins for another. I scared them all away.

She held her hands over the electric fence, daring herself to touch it.

"They must really not trust you," she said. "Hey, look at all this clover." She ducked under the wire and pulled up a fistful of flowering clover. She held it out to me. "Let me take that muzzle off so you can have some."

I snorted at her and swished my tail. I knew the drill. She

might seem nice—nicer than Beatrice anyway—but soon enough she'd be shouting at me and running away.

"Fine." She dropped the clump of clover and turned back to the fence. "I don't even think this is on." She held her hands over the charged wire.

I trotted over to the little pile of clover and nudged it with my muzzled nose. It smelled delicious. I nickered. If she wanted to take my muzzle off now, that would be great.

She laughed. "Oh, now you want to say hi."

Her back was turned, hands still hovering over the fence. I nickered again. Now that I'd smelled the clover, I really wanted it. I strode up behind her and butted her hard in the back.

"Hey!" The girl spun around to face me.

Here we go with the shouting. Girls, they were all the same.

I did a fancy dressage horse move, half-rearing and dancing sideways. Then I planted my hooves, pressed my ears flat to my head, rolled my eyes, flared my nostrils, and thrust my head at her.

"What's wrong with you?" she demanded.

We stared at each other for a moment. Her eyes were dull gray with dark rings around them and her skin gave off a sickly sweet, fermented odor that I couldn't quite place. I waited for her to back away in fear, but she wasn't afraid. She took a step toward me. I didn't move. She took another step and reached for my head. I could have stood quietly and let her do whatever she wanted to do, but I'd had enough of these girls. Why couldn't she just leave me alone? I squealed at her in warning and reared up, dancing backwards on my hind legs and ramming my tail and hindquarters into the electric fence.

"Hey, watch it!" the girl cried.

The jolt was intense and agonizing and impossible to get away from. The fence bowed with my weight and made a crackling sound. I lost my balance and crumpled to the ground in a deflated heap.

11 | MERRITT

Beatrice's horse wasn't just green, he was completely insane. I waited for him to get up, but he just lay there, staring at me creepily and sort of wheezing through his muzzled nostrils. I wasn't even supposed to be in there with him. I wanted to run down to the barn and join the others, pretend like nothing had happened, but maybe he was hurt.

"Stay there," I said and turned to run back down the hill to the Lodge.

Kami was in the Common Room. Thank goodness—I wouldn't have had the guts to wake her up from her nap.

She glanced up at me when I pushed open the front door and then went back to labeling a stack of index cards. I waited as she wrote the words Small Moments on one and put it on the stack. "Done with barn chores already?" she asked without looking up. "I couldn't sleep. And there's no point in taking a shower when I'm going to be around horses and horse manure all day. Soon as I'm done here I can take you out to meet the de Rothschild horse."

"Um. See, that's the thing, I—" I stopped. I'd been at Good Fences less than twenty-four hours and I was already in trouble.

Kami put down the index cards and peered at me over her reading glasses. "What happened?"

"I went up to see him," I admitted. "I was just walking

around in his paddock and he ran at me and got into the electric fence. He fell down. I think he's hurt."

Kami stood up and pulled her cell phone out of her back pocket. She sent a text and then reached for my arm, pulling me toward the door. "Show me."

From afar Red looked like he was just dozing in the sun. As we drew closer, I could see his amber-colored stare. We stood over him, watching the flies land and get twitched away, only to land again. His big ribcage rose and fell with every long, slow breath. He didn't seem to want to get up.

"I was just talking to him," I explained. "I just wanted to see what he was like. And then he sort of charged me and did this rearing thing and backed right into the fence."

Kami frowned down at Red and pushed her reading glasses up on top of her head. "Well, at least he saved you from getting blasted. That fence is wicked strong. The county made us put it in, some sort of code about livestock being so close to the parkway. It's the same sort of fence they use in prisons and big cattle ranches. I wasn't ever even going to use this pasture for the horses, but Red is sort of an escape artist." She shook her head. "I thought the fence would help."

I squatted down and poked Red's coppery neck. Maybe all he needed was a little prodding. He'd get up and be just fine. He pinned his ears back and snorted warily. I pulled my hand away.

"Watch it," Kami warned. "He's pretty unpredictable."

Red's ears flicked back and forth. His amber eyes blinked sleepily in the sunlight.

"You know Mr. de Rothschild, Beatrice's father, basically funds this entire operation?" Kami said. "Good Fences only got started because of him. I suspect it was all with Beatrice in mind." She sighed. "My phone call to him this morning could not have been more difficult. Beatrice and Good Fences were just not a good fit."

I didn't respond. I was worried that Kami was working herself up to ask me some big favor. People always confide in you before they ask you do something. Like, here, I gave you this present that you didn't even want, and now, in exchange, you'd better give me something. But I didn't owe her anything.

"Eventually we plan to build new buildings and hire a big staff of teachers and therapists and really grow," she continued. "My vision is for Good Fences to become a real equine-assisted therapy boarding school with a riding program, not just a small place for a few girls. But I can't do it without Mr. de Rothschild."

A white pick-up truck bombed down the driveway and pulled up at the bottom of the hill. A small woman with a bleached blond ponytail hopped out. She waved at Kami and began to walk up the hill toward us.

"That's Dr. Mitchell, the vet," Kami said. "She's terrific."

I wondered if I could leave now. I'd done what I needed to do. I'd gone to get help and now help was here. I could go on one of the computers in the Common Room, maybe find a book or a People magazine. I shoved my hands in my jeans pockets and took off toward Red's paddock gate.

"Merritt?" Kami called out sharply. "Where are you going?"

"Back to my room?"

"No way," Kami insisted. "You're going to stay here and answer all of Dr. Mitchell's questions, and listen to what she has to say, and do everything you can to help Red."

"What? Me?"

Kami smiled. "He's your horse now. I just assigned him to you. Mr. de Rothschild will be so pleased." She said it forcefully, as though trying to convince herself and me that it was true.

"Good Fences didn't work for his daughter, but I promised him I'd find a use for this horse."

"But he's crazy," I protested. "You said so yourself. You called him an 'awful horse' at breakfast. What about the draft horse, or Chamomile?"

"Who's crazy?" Dr. Mitchell asked as she joined us. She was tanned and smiling and healthy looking, the type of person my parents gravitated toward.

"He is," I mumbled and jutted my chin at Red.

All three of us looked at the big chestnut horse, still dozing in the grass.

Kami shook her head. "Wouldn't you just love to know what he's thinking?"

12 | RED

Some sympathy would have been nice. A carrot, a scratch behind the ears, a few kind words. I thought this girl wanted to make friends, but she'd already changed her mind and started talking trash about me. She was no different from Beatrice. At least I knew her name now: Merritt, like the parkway.

The vet opened her bag, fastened with Velcro. You wouldn't think a horse would encounter that much Velcro, but we do. It's on everything: the muzzle on my face, the protective wraps and boots they put on our legs, the blankets we wear in the winter, the jackets and gloves our riders wear. Not a day goes by that I don't hear that sound—*rrriiiip*. Maybe I'm a little sensitive, but it's one of a bunch of sounds I could do without. Also paper bags, squealing tires, thunder and lightning.

I was still lying down. Dr. Mitchell stood by my head, assessing me.

"Why's he wearing a muzzle?"

"He gets out. Let's out all the other horses. It's a pain in the ass," Kami explained.

"Does he bite?"

"Yes, that too."

"Well I'm going to take it off for now. You know they make grazing muzzles with slats at the bottom so the horse can still eat? I'd try one of those and see how he does. This thing may keep him out of trouble, but he'll be less restless if he can graze."

Rrrriiiip. She unstrapped the thing and pulled it off. Instant relief. Still lying down, I bobbed my head up and down and nibbled at a few tiny shoots of grass. Dr. Mitchell prodded my knees and ankles. I stayed put. I felt dazed and shaky. Beatrice had said the electric fence was "awesome." What a freak.

"He didn't fall funny? You didn't hear any cracks or crunches, right?" she asked Merritt this time.

Merritt shook her head. She was scowling at me. I glared back.

Dr. Mitchell took hold of my halter and tugged it upwards. "Come on, stand up. You got a lead rope handy? I'll need you to jog him to see if he's sound."

"His lead rope is on the fence post by the gate," Kami told Merritt.

Merritt just stood there.

"Go and get it," Kami ordered.

Merritt returned with the lead rope and the vet clipped it on. "Come on, time to get up. Let's go!" the vet shouted and yanked so hard on my halter I wanted to bite her. Finally I stretched out my front legs and rose to a stand. I shook myself, trying to appear dignified and bored by my little audience.

"He's not favoring any of his feet. Standing square. Go ahead and give him a jog."

Kami turned to Merritt. "Go on. You know how to jog a horse, right?"

"I guess." Merritt took the lead rope and pulled on it. "Come on. Let's go."

I decided to be a good boy. I stepped smartly out at a brisk jog.

They'd forgotten that I was a Thoroughbred, a big one.

"Hey!" Merritt gasped as I dragged her along. She broke into a run to keep up. "Slow down."

"Whoa!" Kami shouted after us. "Get in front of him! Lean your shoulder into his chest if you have to! Make him walk!"

But Merritt didn't need Kami's instructions. She knew what she was doing. She was already doing it.

"Nothing wrong with that horse," Dr. Mitchell remarked as we walked back. "Maybe he was just stunned or something."

"Or maybe he's just nuts," Merritt murmured under her breath.

The vet shone a little light into my eyes and ears and nose. She ripped the plastic off a disposable thermometer with her teeth, lifted up my tail, and thrust the thermometer into my anus. No comment.

"Don't you dare kick me," the vet warned.

We waited for the thermometer to read my temperature. Merritt stared at the ground. She was different, this girl. Strange. Sort of damaged by life, but not rotten or depraved, like Beatrice. Or me.

At last Dr. Mitchell removed the thermometer. "One hundred point four. Perfectly normal. But I'd like you to watch him carefully for the next hour or so. Make sure he eats and drinks. Can we leave the muzzle off if someone's watching him?"

Kami nodded. "Sure. I hate muzzles. He came with it though, so we were just following instructions. Last night he let out our whole barn. The ponies were up in the woods."

"He's probably bored," Dr. Mitchell said.

You think?

"I'd put a few big balls in here, and a radio. Music, even talk radio, can be soothing. He needs daily exercise, too. Doesn't anyone ride him?"

Merritt lifted her head and looked at me for the first time

since I'd run into the fence. Her eyebrows were all knitted together and she still radiated unhappiness, but at least she was looking.

"Nobody's been able to," Kami said. "His owner didn't know what to do with him. That's why he's here."

Dr. Mitchell opened her bag again—*rrrriiiip*—and stashed her vet things inside. "Someone should at least lunge him or chase him around. He's a young Thoroughbred. If he doesn't get worked, his behavior is going to get even worse."

Kami nodded, but she didn't look happy about the idea. "I'll see what we can do."

The vet gathered her things and left. Merritt was still holding my lead rope.

"I have a bunch of phone calls to make before lunch," Kami told her. "The insurance inspector. Our contractor. Why don't you stay here and keep an eye on him and get acquainted? Make sure he's eating and drinking like the vet said. You okay with that?"

Merritt nodded sullenly.

Kami followed the vet down the hill. I went back to eating grass. The shakiness was fading. Merritt shuffled along at my head, holding the lead rope and sighing these long, exhausted-sounding sighs.

I stopped eating for a moment and stretched out my nose to snuffle her armpit. She didn't jump away or shout or even move. She just scratched my forehead sort of absentmindedly.

"So you want to be friends now?" she asked.

And that was the thing. This had never happened to me before. I did want to be friends. I really did.

13 | MERRITT

When I got back to my room after lunch, Beatrice's things had been removed, the bed stripped, and the furniture pushed back to its correct position against the wall.

There was an email from Mom on my pillow. This was how the outside world would communicate with us, via email printouts. We couldn't email back. We could only write actual letters and mail them with stamps or wait for our Sunday phone call.

Dear Merritt,

I can't say it's been quiet around here since you've been gone because you've always been very quiet, but it is different and we miss you. Your father and I have both been busy with our advisees and endless department meetings. Yada yada yada. Sorry to bore you.

Dr. Kami tells us you've been matched up with quite a horse. How exciting for you. She also told us your roommate has left Good Fences, but you'll soon be getting another one. I requested that you not have a single, since you've spent so much time alone in your room at home. We want you to make friends, and Dr. Kami agreed.

Please try to write us a "snail mail" letter—I think Dr. Kami told us there are stationery and stamps in the

Common Room. And did you know that every two weeks there's a trip to the mall? Fun!

Your dad and I are going to compete in our first 50-mile ultra marathon next month. He thinks it will be good for us to do together, and with you gone we have lots of time to train. Tomorrow morning we're running to Coney Island and back.

Hope you're settling in well. Give your horse a hug for me.

Love,

Mom & Dad

I crumpled the letter into a little ball and tossed it in the trash. Dr. Kami? I'm sorry, but last time I checked a two-year master's degree in social work does not make you a doctor. I turned and stared grimly out the window. Red was standing by the fence, his nose strapped into his leather muzzle, looking like a prisoner on death row waiting for his last meal.

My very first Group Therapy session was in a small, unfurnished sunroom off the Common Room. A huge picture window faced the lawn. The other girls were all there when I arrived—Tabitha and Celine and Amanda and Sloan—seated cross-legged in a circle on a red and blue Persian rug.

Kami entered the room right behind me. "Take a seat."

As usual there was an empty spot next to Tabitha—the other girls seemed to be afraid of her—so I sat there. Kami wedged herself between Amanda and Sloan, much to their dismay.

"I can't have you two whispering to each other in Pig Latin the whole time, can I?" she joked.

Amanda and Sloan shot each other looks and giggled. They seemed perfectly normal and happy. I couldn't help wondering why they were even at Good Fences.

"Big circle, girls," Kami instructed. "Spread yourselves out to the edge of the carpet." She pulled a pink balloon out of the back pocket of her pants and began to blow it up, her face red and her eyes bulging with the effort. "There." She tied the end of the inflated balloon and cupped it in her palms. "Now, I want you to start passing this balloon back and forth to each other. It's light, so you need to sort of spike it with your fingers like a volleyball. Just keep it moving, keep passing, any which way. Keep passing it until you feel the urge to say something, then grab it and we'll listen. If it's a question directed at me, I won't answer till later. I want this to feel more like a call and response or a conversation, not you hammering me with questions. Just keep passing and catching and talking. If the balloon's in your hands, you get to speak. And try to stay seated, please. I don't want anyone getting hurt."

She spiked the balloon into the air and it soared in my direction. I spiked it away. I didn't feel like talking, although I did have about a thousand questions to ask the good "doctor," mostly about Red and the possibility of maybe not getting a new roommate to replace Beatrice.

Celine reached out and caught the balloon. "When we go to the mall next Saturday, I'm going to use my Bath & Body Works points to buy everyone a mini hand sanitizer. They have the most amazing scents like S'mores and Key Lime Pie and these little holders so you can put them on your belt loop or your purse strap." She smiled, her teeth pearly and perfectly straight. "Everyone can choose their own scent." She spiked the balloon into the air again.

Tabitha batted it in my direction and I swatted it away. Amanda poked it and Sloan caught it. "Where are we going t[o] go to like, relax and toast bagels and listen to music if there[] no Schoolhouse?" she asked and spiked the balloon toward t[he] ceiling.

Amanda grabbed the balloon out of the air. "Yeah. And is Merritt going to get a different roommate or is Beatrice coming back?" She tapped the balloon into the center of the circle.

I lunged for it. "Um, I don't mean to sound ungrateful or whatever, but didn't you say I would have a choice of horses to link up with or whatever? What about Chamomile, isn't she free?" I hugged the balloon to my chest. "Also, I'm really fine with having my own room. I won't spend all my time alone in there, I promise. I only do that at home because I have a TV. I'll just go there to sleep."

I spiked the balloon away and Tabitha caught it this time.

"Can I room with Merritt?" She smiled creepily at me, like she wanted to cut me up into little pieces and store me under her mattress to snack on whenever she was consumed with rage, or whatever her problem was. I had a feeling her creepiness was all an act, but that was creepy in its own way.

"You guys." Celine crossed her bony arms prissily. "We weren't supposed to ask Kami questions, remember?"

Tabitha spiked the balloon and Kami caught it this time.

"I'll handle this, thank you Celine. There are only five of you here at the moment. I don't need an assistant." She took a deep breath and pushed her glasses up on her nose. All of a sudden I felt a pang of pity for her. She was annoying, but we were worse. "This is what happens when I skip lunch with you guys," she apologized. "Sorry I wasn't there to answer all of your questions."

Through the picture window I could see Red up in his sunny paddock, pacing the length of his fence. Now and then he would stop and stare off into the distance.

Kami followed my gaze. "I've ordered the grazing muzzle the vet recommended from SmartPak Equine. It should come tomorrow. And I told Luis to pick up some balls at the sports

store for Red to play with. He's buying a cheap radio for Red's shed, too. Let's hope it helps."

"How come her horse gets all that fun stuff?" Sloan whined. "It's not fair."

"The vet said Red needs to keep busy so he won't get bored," Kami explained. "And to answer your other questions: I haven't made up my mind about Merritt's roommate situation. Beatrice is not coming back, not if I can help it. And sorry Merritt, this time I chose the horse for you. Fingers crossed it works out." She tapped her chin. "What else? Oh, the Schoolhouse. I'm still talking to the insurance guys, but we're going to fix it up as soon as we get a check from them. I think we can do without it until then, don't you?"

Nobody answered.

She scanned our glum faces and then smiled. "You know what? I have an idea. Let's go outside. It's so warm and sunny, and it won't stay this way for long. We can combine Group with afternoon barn chores."

Celine, Amanda, and Sloan cheered and rushed for the door. Beside me, Tabitha moaned with dramatic weariness as she rose to a stand.

I followed along behind the group as Kami led us through the Common Room and outside to the barn. "It's been so hot, and the horses are all so dirty. I'm going to supervise while you each give your horse a bath," she announced.

More cheering. Tabitha moaned even louder this time.

I glared skeptically at "Dr." Kami's back. Did she seriously believe Red would allow me to bathe him?

She stopped and turned just outside the barn door. "Merritt, you head up and take Red's muzzle off and get his lead rope on while I get them started. I'll meet you up there in a moment and we can decide how to proceed."

I nodded curtly and headed up the hill to Red's pasture. He stood half in, half out of his run-in shed, his head low, ears facing sideways, which meant that he was relaxed, probably dozing. But when I picked up his lead rope and unlatched his gate, his head shot up and he spun around to face me, his ears pricked.

"I'm supposed to give you a bath now," I told him.

He stared right at me, looking just as wary and skeptical as I felt.

I walked to his head, unstrapped his muzzle, and clipped the lead rope on his halter. He snorted and butted his big head against my shoulder, not violently, but hard enough to knock me off balance.

"That's enough," I said firmly. I gave the lead rope a quick yank and began to lead him toward the gate.

"Gran-Jo and I used to give Noble a bath and trim his whiskers every Sunday," I told him as we walked. Gran-Jo had taught me that talking quietly was the best way to calm a nervous horse. It didn't really matter what you said. "The whole day would go by with us doing stuff like that and we wouldn't even notice."

It was true. All the time I spent with Gran-Jo, learning how to groom and take care of Noble, learning how to walk, trot, canter, and jump, was the only time that seemed to go by quickly, the time I missed so much. The rest of my life—school, home-work, meals with my parents talking at me or over me—was just a slow, monotonous blur.

"At least there's only three hours of school here," I went on, absentmindedly picking bits of hay out of Red's thick auburn mane. "It's still pretty boring though—"

"Well, you haven't even been here twenty-four hours," Kami interrupted. "I'm sorry we're boring you."

I looked up. She was standing at Red's pasture gate, cell phone in hand. How long had she been there?

"It's nice to see you so comfortable talking to him," she said. "And he seems to want to listen."

Kami was so irritating with all her little observations. "I wasn't really talking to him. I was just talking."

"No explanation necessary. It's all good. I was just speaking with Mr. de Rothschild—Red's owner—and he said you should be safe with the horse if all we're doing is giving him a bath or grooming him or leading him around. Which is all you will be doing. He also said he is absolutely overjoyed. He hates the idea of that valuable horse doing nothing, going to waste. And he said you have good taste."

"But I didn't get to choose—" Red tossed his head violently to ward off a fly, almost knocking me over me in the process. I gave the lead rope a sharp yank. "Stop that. Behave yourself."

Kami smiled approvingly. "There. Just like that. You're the boss. Bring him down to the barn and we'll see if he'll let you give him a bath."

I led Red down from his paddock. Kami followed close behind. We crossed the dirt driveway, Red's unshod hooves scuffing the loose gravel and sending pebbles flying. All of a sudden his head shot up and he swung abruptly around, nearly yanking my arm out of the socket. Luis and Cinnamon, the small Appaloosa mare with two different colored eyes, were trotting up the driveway toward us.

Cinnamon was all tacked up in an English saddle and bridle. Luis halted her and grinned. He was so tiny, his legs barely covered the little mare's barrel. "How do you like your new horse?" he asked me.

A lot of girls would kill to get this close to a horse, any horse. I didn't want to sound like a spoiled brat, so I just patted Red's neck and shrugged.

"We're doing baths," Kami told him, striding ahead of me into the barn. "Hurry up and get her untacked so you can join us."

Luis dismounted and ran up his stirrups. I couldn't help but envy him for getting to ride. "Cinnamon is really old, like twenty-nine or so," he explained. "I walk her out to keep her from getting too stiff. She used to be a lead pony for the post parades."

Red pinned his ears and tossed his head at the old mare.

"Hey," I told him. "That's not nice."

Luis laughed. "He's just jealous. He wants all the attention. He's got you now though. That's good."

I wanted to protest—Red didn't have me, I was just stuck with him. But Luis walked on, leading Cinnamon down the aisle. I followed with Red at a safe distance. The other horses were already tied up along the fence behind the barn. The area had been designated for horse baths, on a slight slope for good drainage, with rubber mats on the ground and a hose neatly coiled beneath the spigot. Each girl stood at her horse's head with a black bucket filled with soapy water and a big sea sponge. An extra bucket and sponge stood at an empty space on one of the rubber mats by the fence.

"I filled that one up for you already," Tabitha told me, pointing to it. She was really milking this roommate idea.

"Thanks," I mumbled and led Red over to the bucket.

"I want you to talk to your horses," Kami told us as she watched me tie up Red with a loopy slipknot that I could undo quickly if he did anything dumb. "Tell them what you're going to do before you do it. Like this." She picked up the sponge in my bucket, squeezed out the excess water, and held it over Red's withers. "I'm going to give you a nice warm bubble bath now, mister."

Red sidestepped away from her and rolled his eyes so the whites showed. Kami shook her head and dropped the sponge back in the bucket.

"Just hold on a moment before you do anything with him," she muttered.

I stood close to Red's head while Kami went to help Amanda with her gray pony.

"Don't be silly," I murmured to Red. "You're dirty. And this water is nice and cool."

"I wish someone would sponge-bathe *me*," Tabitha complained as she gingerly rubbed soapy water on her horse's urine-stained knees. "Ever since I got here all I can smell is piss and manure."

"That's you, not your horse," Celine commented. Her permasmile returned as she squeezed her sponge all over Lacey's forehead. The gray mare closed her eyes and relaxed her long neck, clearly enjoying it. "You love this, don't you girl?" Celine crooned. Lacey flapped her gray muzzle comically, revealing a row of huge yellow teeth.

"See, that doesn't look so awful, does it?" I asked Red. I reached into the bucket and grabbed the wet sponge. "I'm just going to drip some water on your neck," I told him as I held the dripping sponge over his mane and squeezed it. Water splashed down and seeped into his coat, staining it darker. Red stood his ground.

"I wouldn't do that if I were you!" Kami yelped at me. "I thought I told you not to do anything!"

I ignored her, letting go of Red's halter so I could stand at his side. I held the sponge high over his withers. Noble used to love it when I did this. Water ran down Red's massive shoulders. He put his nose into the air and flapped his lips, grinning like a cartoon donkey.

"See? I told you you'd like it," I murmured and dipped the sponge in the bucket to wet it again.

"Well, well, well," Kami breathed, marching over to us with

her hands on her wide hips. "Have you noticed anything that might be slightly amiss about this picture?"

I frowned and took a step back, sponge dripping from my hand. Red swung his head in my direction as if to say, "Hey, why'd you stop?" His head was bare. His halter was on the ground, his lead rope still tied to the fence.

"Shit!" I dropped the sponge and reached for the halter.

"Well I'll be darned." Kami just stood there, staring.

I fussed with the halter, trying to untangle it so I could put it back on Red's head before he got away. God, was he a pain. How could he have escaped from his halter so easily and quickly when I was standing right there?

Kami was still staring at us.

"What?" I demanded, growing more and more annoyed.

"That horse wouldn't let me get him wet. And now he's just standing there without a halter or anything while you splash water all over him."

I slipped the halter over Red's head once more, buckling it a little more tightly this time. I wasn't sure what kind of response Kami was fishing for, and I didn't really care. "I guess he likes it."

She raised her eyebrows. "I don't know about that. But I do know one thing: he likes you." She shook her head, pulled her phone out of her pocket and snapped a picture. "The way his owner described him, he's like a known terrorist. But with you he's like a big puppy dog."

"Not exactly." I retied the lead rope around the fence, pulling the slipknot tight.

"He's a completely different horse," Kami went on.

I shrugged and ran my palm over Red's damp chestnut neck. "Good boy."

14 | RED

"Good boy."

It wasn't just the words. It was the feel of her hand on my coat and the almost absentminded way she praised me when I didn't even deserve it. I took my halter off for the hell of it, but I didn't run away. I didn't break anything. I didn't bolt off in a farting gallop and take the fence with me. Because I didn't want to leave her.

"Good boy."

A horse's life is all about the people we belong to. Until now I was certain I'd missed out—that I'd never belong to anyone. But at exactly that moment I became hers. Sure, technically I was still owned by Beatrice, or Beatrice's father, but I didn't care who paid the bills. I was Merritt's, all Merritt's. Finally.

After my bath, Merritt and Luis took me back to my run-in shed for my afternoon hay. She spread the flakes out in the grass outside the shed so I could eat and dry off in the dwindling sun. Still holding my lead rope, she rubbed my coat down with a soft towel and combed out my mane and tail, completely absorbed with what she was doing. And I was completely absorbed with letting her. Luis tossed four soccer balls into my paddock while I ate. Then he hung a radio with baling twine to a beam up high in my shed.

"Only station that comes in clear is the classic rock station,"

he called as a song with an insistent beat and a shrill male voice
singing in quick staccato reverberated inside my shed.

"Another man bites the dust-ah . . ."

It was an odd song, but I liked it. I liked the beat echoing
inside my head and in the air around my shed. Listening to music
was like doing something without actually doing anything. Merritt kept combing my tail. I kept eating and listening, totally
blissed out. A soccer ball flew past my nose. I pawed the ground
and snorted loudly through my nostrils.

"Hey!" Merritt cried. "You scared him."

"He's not scared. He's curious," Luis said. "Let him go and
see what he does."

I stood with my head up, quivering with anticipation. Merritt
unclipped the lead rope from my halter.

"All right," she said quietly. "Go play."

I ducked my head and trotted away, tail up. Then I planted
my feet for a moment, snorted snot everwhere, and galloped off
toward the soccer ball, stopping abruptly in front of it. It rolled
away from me and I pushed it with my nose along the ground,
nudging and nudging until it got completely away. Luis ran up
and kicked the ball into the far corner of my pasture. I whinnied
shrilly and galloped after it, my tail flying out behind me.

"Look at him go!" Luis cried, laughing.

"Maladopted!" the strange song continued. I'm sure I had
the lyrics completely wrong, but so what? It suited my mood
perfectly.

Hello ball. I zoomed it away with my nose and trotted after
it. Goodbye ball.

"He likes soccer," Luis observed.

"He's a lunatic," Merritt said.

Excuse me?

"But he's a good mover. Beautiful trot," she added.

Beautiful everything.

The song ended and a new one began. This one was about magic carpet rides. I chased after the ball at a trot and swatted it across the grass with my nose.

"Well, you don't know . . . where . . . we will climb . . ." the throaty voice warbled.

Again, I probably had the lyrics wrong because I wasn't listening very carefully, but it was the beat that mattered. I could feel myself getting sillier and sillier. I lay down to roll—a must after a good bath—then sprang to my feet again and bolted away, farting and bucking and waving my head back and forth. I hadn't frolicked like this in weeks, months! And why not? I was a four-year-old Thoroughbred. I needed to move.

I don't know if it was the music that worked me up into a frenzy, or the sound of Merritt's and Luis's laughter, or the hope that Merritt was beginning to like me just a tiny bit, but I could not stop running. My fenced in paddock was only about five hundred feet on each side. As I galloped I became a running blur. Around and around the perimeter I went, my sides grazing the fence. Then I bucked and spun halfway around, cutting across the paddock at a diagonal and lengthening my stride toward the gate. Five, four, three, two, one! I soared over the white clapboard fence rails and clattered onto the driveway.

"Red!"

I skidded to a stop and spun around. Merritt was at the gate.

"Come back here, Red."

My whole body trembled as I hesitated. Then I burst into a gallop again, back toward her. It was uphill this time. Four, three, two, one and up and over the fence once more. I was winded now. I jogged over to her and snorted. Halting, I shook myself hard, like a wet dog, as if to shake out all the crazy energy that had consumed me. She snapped the lead rope back onto my halter and bent down to examine my legs. They were fine. I was fine.

"I'm not going to tell anybody about that," Luis said, coming up behind us with the soccer ball tucked under his arm. "He's okay, right?"

"Yes, I think so." Merritt prodded my knees with her bony fingers. She stood up and smoothed out my forelock, staring at me with her pale blue eyes. They were brighter now. She didn't look as tired as she had before. "He can really jump though."

I stared back at her. Of course I can jump, I wanted to tell her. I can do anything you ask me to do. All you have to do is ask.

15 | MERRITT

I t was Saturday, mall day. I wasn't as excited about the trip as the other girls. I didn't need any clothes or cosmetics, we weren't allowed electronics, and I was already eating more at Good Fences that I ever did at home because the food was actually edible. What was I going to do in a strange mall in a random town in Connecticut?

"Please don't do anything stupid while I'm gone," I begged Red as I finished cleaning out his shed.

He was so much happier in his grazing muzzle. He'd already pummeled all his soccer balls into misshapen blobs. And the radio seemed to keep him entertained when he was alone.

"Be good."

The mall's Apple store was all shiny, bright, and clean, with wafer-thin electronics displayed on sleek, white display tables. I was still wearing the same jeans I'd worn to muck out Red's stall that morning. I felt dirty and out of place and I found myself missing him. Had I remembered to fill his water bucket? Had he escaped somehow despite his muzzle and let out all the other horses? Anton and Matthias, Good Fences' two cooks and academic tutors, would be on the premises the whole time we were gone, but they weren't horse people. And it was so easy to forget about Red, all alone up on his hill, like a prisoner in solitary confinement.

"Finally," Tabitha sighed and made a beeline for the iPhones.

Celine snatched up a laptop and began tapping away. "I wonder if I can access my Forever 21 account. I could order stuff through PayPal and have it shipped to Good Fences."

I went over to an iPad and automatically logged onto my Instagram account. Right at the top was a picture of Ann Ware wearing a ton of makeup. Beneath the picture were a series of smiley face and musical note emoticons followed by the caption, "listen to my song #f-edupwiththesat—500,000 YouTube hits and counting!!"

I hit the home button on the iPad, clicked the YouTube app and searched for the song "F-ed up with the SAT."

There was Ann again, dressed in our Dowd Prep uniform and school tie, wearing red lipstick and black eyeliner, sitting on a stool with a banjo in her arms. I pressed PLAY.

"*I don't need to prove that I'm smart. I know I'm smart,*" Ann sang, strumming her banjo and looking directly into the camera.

I turned up the volume and bent over the display table so I could hear better.

> *Ace this test for a college that's pop-u-lar*
> *But I know who my friends are*
> *And we're gonna go far . . .*
>
> *I don't need to prep for your stupid test*
> *a, b, c, d, e—none of the above*
> *What does it say about me?*
> *Why don't you ask me and see?*
> *I'm so F-ed up with the S-A-T*
> *I just wanna be free to be me, me, me*
> *Let's walk out of the S-A-T*

All those losers can fill in their a, b, c, d, e
None of the above, thanks, it's not for me . . .

Hey!
If you have any guts you'll walk out with me
Hey!
Here's your chance, baby, follow me . . .
Hey!
Or not . . . Or not . . . Or not . . .

I was dumfounded. It wasn't a terrible song. Ann had always liked to sing and play weird instruments and make videos for fun. I'd even held the camera for some of them when we were younger. But Ann wasn't the one who'd walked out of the SAT. She'd even taken a prep course. She was bound for Oberlin or Julliard. I was the one who'd walked out. The song was about me. And I was going nowhere.

I didn't know what to feel. Angry that she'd used me as inspiration for a song? Flattered? Was she trying to tell me something? Did she think I was brave for ruining my college chances, or seriously stupid?

Tabitha leaned in to see what I was doing. "Oh, so funny! I just listened to that like, two seconds ago. It's trending on Twitter and Instagram right now."

"It's a stupid song." I powered off the iPad and pushed it aside, not even sure why I was so angry. So what if my former best friend had written a song about me that had gone viral?

Tabitha reapplied the dark red lip gloss she'd bought at Sephora and rubbed her lips together. She seemed so much more content at the mall than she did at the barn. "I don't know. I like it. I mean, I really hated having to take the SAT."

I stomped over to Celine at the laptop table. There were ear buds in her ears and she was bobbing her blonde head up and down. I looked at the screen and there was Ann Ware in her school uniform again, mouthing the words to her SAT song. Unbelievable. For the first time in my life, I understood what "going viral" actually meant. The song was a virus and everyone had been infected.

"I thought you were online shopping," I growled. I turned away to glare at the shiny white walls and the nerdy Apple helpers in their ugly blue polo shirts.

"Oh my God, have you heard this?" Celine trilled annoyingly. She offered me one of her ear buds. "Come listen with me."

I shook my head and went to wait for Kami by the entrance. I'd begun to think that the girls at Good Fences weren't as bad as the girls at Dowd. But they were just as bad, maybe even worse. Or maybe, like my father said when he'd left me at Good Fences, I just needed to try and lighten up.

I was quiet on the ride back, still stewing while the other girls compared purchases. I hadn't bought anything and I couldn't stop worrying that Red had somehow broken loose and gone on a rampage. The sun had set by the time we turned down the long dirt driveway and the outside lights were on. I could just make out Red's stark white face in the half-dark, still waiting by the fence. He wasn't maimed or dead, and the other horses were still safely in the barn.

I stepped out of the car and breathed out a long sigh of relief. It was as if I'd been holding my breath, just the tiniest bit, ever since we'd left. The others went inside to change, but I headed directly up the hill to Red, eager to get started on my evening barn chores. My feet crunched the gravel in the driveway. Red nickered softly and pricked his ears as I approached. His eyes glistened in the darkness. He looked happy to see me.

"You miss me?" I called out.

He nickered eagerly in reply. He was probably just hungry, but it was still nice to hear.

16 | RED

The day after Merritt spent the whole day away in a van somewhere with the other girls, we tried something new.

Kami and Merritt led me down to the small round pen behind the barn, the most boring place I'd ever been. No grass. No hay. No balls. Not even any music. Nothing to do but stand there and whisk away flies with my tail. The horses in the end stalls of the barn watched us as Merritt unclipped the lead rope and let me loose. I hung my head and sort of rooted around in the dirt for a little while. Finally I dropped down and rolled.

"Do you know why this horse never raced but the one time?" Kami asked while I got good and dirty.

Merritt just watched me roll, her lips pursed and her eyes steely. She was the one who would have to clean me up. I didn't feel bad, though. There's nothing like a good long roll in the dirt.

"He has great bloodlines," Kami went on. "There's some Seattle Slew in there somewhere. And there's no denying he's built to run. But right out of the starting gate, first thing he did was go sideways and jump over the inside rail. Then he ran through the grassy area in the middle of the track and jumped over the fence in the far turn, back onto the track. The other horses crashed right into him. One of them—his half-sister actually—had to be put down on the spot. His owner was going to put him down, too. Racing people are very superstitious, like baseball players. Thank goodness for Mr. and Mrs. de Rothschild."

I clambered to my feet and shook myself. A cloud of dust rose up around me. I snorted and groaned, then folded my knees and dropped down to roll again. It felt heavenly.

"Idiot," Merritt murmured, but she didn't sound mad. She was smiling at me, like she was calling me by a pet name. "Was he hurt?" she asked Kami. "In the race?"

"Oh, his right eye got pretty banged up. You know how he holds his head sometimes, kind of down and cocked to one side? He can't really see out of his right eye too well. And I think he broke his jaw and bruised his shoulder pretty badly. But that was it. He's okay, physically."

They remained in the center of the pen, eyeing me as I stood up and shook myself off again. I swung my head around to look at Merritt. Was there something I was supposed to be doing?

"Idiot," she said again and held out her hand.

I sniffed the air. There was nothing in her hand, but I didn't mind. I walked toward her anyway and pushed my nose into her palm. She stroked the wide white blaze down my face and straightened out my forelock. Then she reached up and scratched me behind the ears. I snorted and looked at her with my one good eye.

"You're filthy," she said, but it didn't sound like she minded.

"You know Merritt, the reason I'm telling you about him," Kami said gently, "is that I'd like you to try and tell him about you."

Merritt stopped scratching and stuffed her hands into the back pockets of her jeans. "What do you mean?"

"I mean, I want you to tell Red, not me, all about why you're here. What happened to you. You heard his story. Now it's your turn. It was over a year ago, wasn't it? When your grandmother died? Can you tell Red what happened?"

Merritt kicked at the dirt with her sneakers. "I'd really rather not," she muttered.

But Kami wouldn't let it go. "Red can't help you if you won't let him."

Merritt rolled her eyes and raked her fingers through my tangled mane. Then she gave in. "Fine. Red isn't even listening. But I'll tell him anyway."

She took a deep breath.

"I spent February break at Gran-Jo's house in New Canaan. Just me and her, like always. It snowed almost the whole time and it was a lot of work, shoveling everything and making sure Noble was warm."

She continued to untangle my mane with her fingers while she talked. And she was wrong: I was listening.

"Noble was Gran-Jo's horse," Merritt went on. "He was pretty old, but she'd done everything with him. Show jumping, dressage, hunter paces. He was huge, seventeen hands. Dark bay, with a black mane and tail."

She ran her hand down the length of my neck. I didn't move, except for maybe my ears.

"One day it was sunny and I rode, but the rest of the time it was just too cold and snowy. Anyway, Noble was sort of off when I rode him. We decided to just keep his legs wrapped, and we put him in his stall with all his blankets on, and hand-walked him twice a day, up and down the driveway. We watched *Gone with the Wind*, which is like ten hours long, and then I made Gran-Jo re-watch *The Black Stallion* because it's my favorite movie of all time. We made popcorn and she drank her cocktails and I drank hot chocolate. Everything was fine and normal and then I went home."

Merritt took another deep breath.

"The next month or so I had stuff to do with my friend Ann on the weekends and my mom took me shopping and I didn't go out to see Gran-Jo. I talked to her on the phone though, and when I asked her about Noble, she just said he was fine, everything was fine."

She twined her fingers in my mane, pressed her forehead into my neck, and sort of hung there. I didn't want to hurt her or scare her, so I just stood still, watching Kami watching us out of my one good eye.

"Then it was spring break. I took the train out to see Gran-Jo, just like I always did. She met me at the station and we drove back to her house. When we pulled in the driveway I didn't see Noble in his paddock. He wasn't in his shed. And Gran-Jo didn't get out of the car right away."

Merritt trembled, still clinging to my mane, her forehead pressed hard into my neck.

"Go on," Kami urged. "You're doing great."

Merritt took another deep breath. "Gran-Jo didn't get out of the car and she was acting sort of strange. I kept asking, 'Where's Noble?' Finally she told me she had to put Noble down. She didn't want to tell me on the phone."

Merritt was shuddering now, her breathing more like gasping. My neck was damp with her tears.

"I was so mad. I'd never been mad at Gran-Jo, but I just couldn't believe she didn't tell me. She could have told me she was going to do it and then I could have come out and said goodbye to him. He was my horse too, and she never let me say goodbye."

She could barely talk now. My neck was soaking wet.

Kami reached up and put her hand on Merritt's back.

Merritt waved her away. "I'm not finished."

She took another long, shuddering breath and then went on.

"We never even got out of the car. Gran-Jo was acting so strange. She wouldn't look at me and she was wearing too much perfume and sucking on these mints. I didn't want to be there anymore, not without Noble, so I told her to drive me back to the station. Her driving was really bad though. She kept slamming on the brakes. I was worried she was drunk. I asked her to pull over so I could walk and Gran-Jo just snapped. She said I sounded just like my mom. We got to the station and I got out of the car and slammed the door. I went right to the platform. I never even turned around. And when she was pulling out of the station—"

Merritt stopped talking and made this wheezing sound.

Kami patted her back. "That's all right, sweetie. You don't have to—"

"She pulled out of the exit the wrong way and a truck slammed into her. She was killed instantly. Right behind me. I didn't even turn around!" Merritt shrieked.

I flinched, but I managed to keep my hooves firmly on the ground while she fought to catch her breath.

"It was my fault because I yelled at her and she was so upset she didn't even know what she was doing." Her voice fell to a whisper. "I never saw her again. I never saw either of them."

She let go of my mane and sort of slumped into me with all her weight. I had to push back to keep from falling over. Kami came around to my head and rubbed my forehead. I didn't pay any attention to her. I was concentrating on keeping my balance.

"Merritt?"

Merritt didn't respond. She just kept on sobbing into my shoulder. I think there was more snot on me than tears.

"Red is hungry now," Kami said. "He needs his dinner. Grab his lead rope and take him up to his shed."

Merritt pulled away from me and wiped her nose on the back of her hand. Her face was all red and splotchy. She blinked at me. "Okay," she said robotically.

The sun sat on top of the trees like a giant egg yolk. Merritt walked over to the gate and picked up my lead rope. I followed her so she wouldn't have to walk back and get me.

"I think we've all underestimated that horse," Kami observed as Merritt led me away.

17 | MERRITT

The other girls were right. Sundays sucked. My session with Red was the last of the five "equine-assisted therapy" sessions that day and it was already dusk.

I stumbled up the hill with Red, led him into his run-in shed, and poured his grain. Leaning against the shed wall for support, I waited for him to finish so I could put his grazing muzzle back on. The radio blasted some bizarre rock song with flute music about a guy named Aqualung. I felt like there was something wrong with *my* lungs. Like someone had punctured them with a pitchfork and I wasn't getting enough air. I just wanted to curl up on my bed and go to sleep, or watch back-to-back episodes of *Survivor*. But there was still more sharing to do.

Sunday dinner was an hour earlier than usual. It was followed by Double Group, where we were meant to respond to what we'd shared during our equine therapy session. After Group we were supposed to feel all warm and fuzzy from sharing so much and desperately in need of some comfort food, because Sundays always ended with warm brownies and ice cream in front of a movie in the Common Room.

And of course, Sundays were also the day we got to call home. After breakfast and morning barn chores, while the other girls were either having their equine therapy sessions or cleaning their rooms and doing laundry, we'd each taken turns with the house phone in the Group room. The tradeoff went on throughout the day. I got my turn after lunch. No one answered when I called the home phone, so I dialed my mother's cell.

"Merritt?" she shouted. "I'm so sorry, I can't hear you very well. We're in Dick's Sporting Goods in this god-awful mall off the New York State Thruway. It was your dad's idea. I hate malls."

"I'm just calling to say hello," I said, not raising my voice. I wanted to tell her about Red, about how he was this disaster of a horse and everyone was afraid of him, but how Kami thought I could handle him, or fix him, or something. But I didn't want to shout it. I hated shouting. Besides, it wasn't the sort of thing you could shout.

"Ugh, Michael, you look like a toreador," I heard my mom say. "Merritt, your dad just came out of the dressing room wearing this wind-resistant running suit he thinks is spectacular. He wants me to get one too. But I don't care if it's the best performance fabric in the world. I won't be seen in that." There was a fumbling sound. "Sorry. Merritt?"

"Should I call back?" I stared out the big picture window. Red was in his pasture, his muzzled nose halfway under the bottom rail of the fence, trying to get at the last long shoots of grass that bordered the driveway. "Actually I don't know if I'm allowed to call back. I'll just talk to you next Sunday if that's better."

"I'm sorry, honey. We're just trying to get ready for that ultra marathon we entered. I think I mentioned it in one of my emails? You dad is bored of regular road marathons, so he wants to try ultra marathons and longer trail races. We've entered a fifty-mile race in Massachusetts next weekend. With all this freedom I figure we might as well."

I wasn't sure if I'd heard her correctly. "Freedom?" I repeated.

"You know, now that you're not home? Your dad thinks it'll be good for us as a couple to spend more time together, training and traveling. I'm sorry, I think I have to go try this horrible thing on. You're doing great though, yes? Dr. Kami and I have spoken at length on the telephone and she sends me daily updates. She told me there wasn't a suitable roommate match at the moment, which I'm not so happy about, but your dad says I should just let her do her job—"

"She's not really a doctor," I said, cutting her off. I wondered what exactly she and Kami had spoken "at length" about. Knowing that my parents and Kami were talking about me behind my back really pissed me off.

"Oh, and I spoke to Mr. de Rothschild, too," Mom went on, not picking up on my tone or mood or anything I'd said. "Such a nice man. He seemed to know everything about you. He's just so thrilled you can handle that horse. He's been at his wits' end about him apparently."

So Mr. de Rothschild—a man I'd never met—knew everything about me. My hand shook, banging the phone against my ear.

"Say hi to Dad for me," I said brusquely. Then I hung up.

I picked at my dinner—lasagna and meatballs again; I was beginning to see a pattern—dreading Group, wondering just how Kami had weaseled the whole miserable story of Gran-Jo and Noble dying out of me. Maybe after talking to my parents "at length," she'd picked up on the fact that they never listened. It was if she knew after my call with them that I'd be ready to talk. I had to hand it to her, she was pretty good, even if she wasn't a doctor. But I was done talking for the day. Seriously done.

"Something wrong with the lasagna tonight?" Matthias demanded. He and Anton stood over our table. Their hair was combed and they'd changed out of their stained white chef's jackets. Both of Good Fences' chef-tutors were from Switzerland.

Both were tall, with strawberry blond hair and bright blue eyes. But Matthias was very heavy and never exercised, while Anton was into CrossFit and lifting weights.

"Merritt, you are a gifted mathematician, but not such a gifted eater," Anton said, indicating my barely-touched lasagna.

"I'm just not that hungry," I mumbled feebly.

The other girls had been fighting over which movie they wanted to watch. Kami had given us a choice of *Frozen* or *Despicable Me*. I guess she thought we were too emotionally unstable for more challenging films.

Kami pulled my plate toward the center of the table. "What about your garlic bread? I'm not letting that go to waste."

I nodded. "Go ahead."

Matthias picked up a spare fork and skewered a meatball with it. He was about to pop it into his mouth when Anton slapped it away.

"We're about to go out for a nice meal and you eat meatballs? I don't think so."

"I'll take it." Luis reached across the table to grab the fork.

"Every Sunday we go out for sushi and sake," Matthias told me. "We get to sleep in on Monday." He lowered his voice. "Which is necessary for Anton especially, because of the sake." He put his arm around Anton's shoulders and pulled him away. "Have fun, girls. Don't stay up too late."

There was no Word of the Day on Sunday, thankfully. I helped Celine and Tabitha clear the table and scrape the plates into the huge waste bin in the kitchen. Then I opened the dishwasher and began to load it, not really caring how neatly the plates went in.

"Someone's in a bad mood," Celine observed as I crashed plates and bowls together and stabbed the forks into the utensil carrier all covered in tomato sauce and cheese.

I wanted to stab her porcelain Barbie cheek with one.

"I told you Sundays were shitty," Tabitha said. "The first Sunday I was here I dumped an entire wheelbarrow full of manure in front of Kami's bedroom door. She keeps it locked, otherwise I would have put it on her bed."

"That's why Beatrice was in such a bad mood the night you arrived, remember?" Celine said. "We didn't do movies or Double Group that night. We took you down to meet the horses instead."

I turned on the dishwasher and followed them into the Group room. I could listen, I just wouldn't speak. And maybe I could skip the movie and go up to bed instead. I had nothing more to say. I just wanted the day to be over.

Sloan and Amanda came in, giggling and whispering and bumping into each other as usual, followed by Kami. We sat in a circle on the floor.

"So what's the verdict? *Frozen* or *Despicable Me*?" Kami asked, smiling her friendly smile, like she hadn't just spent the entire day torturing us and emailing our parents sneaky updates.

"*Despicable Me*," Tabitha and I said.

"*Frozen!*" Sloan, Amanda, and Celine chimed in.

Kami laughed. "Interesting. I was going to vote for *Despicable Me*, myself. We'll let Luis be the tiebreaker after Group. Now, back to business. Who wants to respond to their session with their horse or their call home today? Does one of you have something on your mind that you can't wait to say? Go ahead. Be brave, girls."

"You know how we were talking about Sundays being hard?" Celine asked, looking at me.

I nodded.

"Well the first Sunday I was here I scraped my knuckles with a grapefruit spoon—on purpose."

"What's a grapefruit spoon?" Tabitha asked.

"They're sharp and pointy, with little ridges on the edge of the spoon," Celine clarified. "I brought one with me. I love grapefruits, they're the perfect food."

"But you really don't need a special spoon to eat them with," Tabitha scoffed, rolling her eyes.

"Girls," Kami warned.

"It took me a while to locate my parents," Sloan said. "They're getting our beach house ready. The one outside of Sydney, in Australia. Where we dock our yacht."

"Actually I talked to your mom this afternoon," Kami said in the same friendly tone. "She's at home in Montclair, New Jersey, right where she always is."

Sloan blinked at Kami. Maybe that was her problem. I hadn't been able to pinpoint it before. She had some sort of pathological lying disorder.

"I hate my parents," Amanda volunteered.

"You're angry with your parents," Kami suggested.

"No," Amanda insisted. "I hate them."

"I also am angry with my parents," Tabitha said, mocking Kami's turn of phrase. She picked at her molars with a very long pinky nail that she'd recently painted black.

"I'm just angry," I heard myself say and instantly regretted it.

Tabitha laughed. "If I'm ever allowed back into the world again and I get my driver's license, I want a bumper sticker that says that. 'I'm just angry.'"

Kami's smile faltered, clearly not too happy to be facing a semi-circle of angry girls, but she didn't interrupt us.

"I'm never angry," Celine said, thoughtfully toying with the stitching on her pink skinny jeans.

"Maybe that's your problem," Tabitha snapped. She flicked whatever it was that she'd found in her teeth halfway across the room.

"And that was completely disgusting," Celine observed.

"Enough!" Kami scolded. "Merritt, can you tell us why you're angry?"

I stared at her. Let me count the ways.

Kami cleared her throat. "I find that I sometimes get angry instead of allowing myself to feel other emotions. Like grief, for instance." She paused. "Or guilt."

I bristled. Was she implying that it was all my fault? She'd never said what my parents had repeated a thousand times, over and over to me after Gran-Jo died, trying to get me to snap out of it: "Gran-Jo died in an accident. It was not your fault."

But Kami hadn't said anything like that, and she was a professional. Sort of.

"Oh, so you want me to feel guilty, is that it?" I shouted. I was angry, all right, maybe angrier than I'd ever been in my entire life. Hands clenched in fists, I dug my knuckles into the rug. "My parents are having a grand time at home without me, buying fancy running clothes and training for ultra marathons. Meanwhile you're telling them all this bullshit about how wonderful I'm doing when I'm actually completely miserable because you're right, everything that happened was really my fault!"

Kami nodded. "Was it?" she asked quietly.

I glared at her, breathing hard. There were so many things to sort through, all of it awful. But it couldn't all be my fault.

"The night before I came here I drank a lot of different things and took some random medicine. I walked out of the SAT. That was all definitely my fault. But Gran-Jo—"

I stopped short, realizing that Kami had set me up, yet again. This was my cue to admit that I didn't really believe Gran-Jo's death was my fault. It was an accident. Or maybe it was my fault. I didn't know what to think, I was just tired of Kami's mind games. The goal was to feel like we'd really accomplished something by warm brownies and movie time, but I wasn't going to give Kami that satisfaction.

"Let's walk out of the S-A-T. All those losers can fill in their a, b, c, d, e . . ." Amanda and Sloan sang in unison and giggled.

The holes in my lungs were bigger now, or more plentiful, or both. I couldn't breathe. Through the window I could see Red in a yellow stream of lamplight, waiting for me by the fence.

"I have to get out of here," I gasped and lurched to my feet, stumbling over Celine to get to the door.

18 | RED

I t was after dark but still the same day she'd clung to my neck and soaked my coat with tears. She walked up the hill with a saddle in her arms. I was waiting for her by my gate.

"I want to try something," she said.

I hadn't been ridden in months. Until Merritt came along, I'd decided that no one would ever have the guts to ride me again. I broke bridles, jumped fences that weren't meant to be jumped, lay down on top of people, galloped when I was supposed to walk and halted when I was supposed to gallop. I was the anti-horse.

Merritt might not have known all the details of my sordid past, but if she did, she didn't care. She seemed to be in a hurry. We were sneaking around, I guessed. And I was all for sneaking around.

I needed a thick foam wither pad for my sensitive shoulder, but she had only a dirty cotton saddle blanket. The bridle and bit were old and ill-fitting, with a drop noseband and a thick rubber snaffle—definitely not what I was accustomed to. Still, I let her tack me up with what she had, standing docile as a cow as she unbuckled and adjusted and readjusted.

Finally she pulled down the stirrups, walked me over to the fence, climbed up on the bottom rail, and mounted up.

It felt so strange to have her on my back that I froze. I stood still for a moment like a good horse is supposed to. Then I danced forward a few steps. She was more substantial than I thought, and she sat deep in the saddle. That was good. I never liked the way the jockeys used to perch up on my withers with their stirrups hiked up, all the weight in the front and none in the back.

Merritt had long legs that hung down on either side of the girth and sort of wrapped around my middle, making me feel secure, sort of like those thunder vests they give to skittish dogs. She held the reins on the buckle, loose as they could go, just letting us get used to each other. That was also a first. Normally when riders are scared of being run away with they just grab and yank, grab and yank. She was telling me that she trusted me, or wanted to trust me.

I wanted her to trust me, too. I stopped dancing and settled into a steadier walk.

My radio was on—it was always on. "Don't Feed the Reaper" by Blue Öyster Cult was playing again. At least I think that's what the song was called. They'd been playing it constantly for Halloween. I focused on the song's bonk-bonk-bonk-bonk cowbell beat and attempted to discern the lyrics as a means of calming myself down.

"The seasons don't feed the reaper . . . la la la la la . . ."

We walked around the perimeter of my paddock. It was a clear night, full of stars. I was on the alert, almost afraid of myself, because I was so used to doing everything wrong and I wanted to do everything right. After we'd walked along at a good clip for a few minutes, I felt nice and loose. Merritt shortened the reins just a little and squeezed her calves.

I stepped into a trot, sticking my nose out like I like to do, my knees barely bending. Once I get into a rhythm, it's like I'm floating over the ground—as well as a twelve hundred-pound animal can float.

She posted to the trot like a pro, helping me along with a little pressure behind the girth and light hands. We went around to the right twice, then cut across the diagonal and changed direction. Halfway around our second trip to the left she put her outside leg back and asked me to canter. I rocked back and stepped into it—one-two-three, one-two-three, one-two-three. She stayed up in two-point and let me stretch out my neck. One-two-three, one-two-three, one-two-three.

It felt great. I could canter like that forever.

She let go of the reins with one hand and patted me while we were still cantering. Then she said the words I loved so much.

"Good boy."

We cantered around and around and I thought I could feel rain on my neck. But it wasn't rain, she was crying. I slowed to a walk and she kicked her sneakers out of the stirrups and fell on my neck, hugging her arms around me and sobbing into my mane, like she'd done earlier. I stopped walking, aware that her position was precarious. If I tripped or stumbled in the dark she could fall off and be badly hurt. She wasn't even wearing a helmet.

"Romeo and Juliet . . . Don't feed the reaper . . ."

After a while her sobs subsided and she sat up.

"Let's try something else now." Her voice was shaky but resolute.

I'd already promised myself I'd do anything she asked. I'd even guess what she wanted and do it before she asked. Her wish was my command. She gathered up the reins and pressed me into a canter again, around and around, until we'd found a steady rhythm. I could do anything from that canter, anything.

Around and around again and then, without warning, she opened the outside rein and steered me directly toward the white clapboard fence that separated my paddock from the driveway.

I should have been having flashbacks to my first race. I should have doubted her sanity and mine. But I didn't doubt anything. I just kept the same canter and found my distance and jumped.

"Good boy!" She didn't just say it this time, she laughed it.

We kept cantering. The horses were all in for the night, except for the two gray ponies, but they were so old they barely even noticed us.

Merritt steered me toward the fence around the larger pasture. The fence rails glowed white in the moonlight. I kept my canter steady and even. Five, four, three, two, one and we were in the air again. This time she pressed me forward in a huge loop and back toward the fence once more.

We jumped out of the pasture and galloped across the driveway and up the grassy hill. Out of my good eye, I saw that an audience had gathered in front of the big log house. But we ignored them. Up and over my fence we jumped, back into my paddock again.

"Good boy," Merritt crooned, gently steering me in a tight circle. I slowed to a trot and then a walk. She let the reins loosen down to the buckle and threw herself on my neck again, hugging me. I was winded, otherwise I would have hugged her right back.

"Merritt?"

It was Kami. And Luis. And all the other girls. Yo, teacher, leave us kids alone.

Merritt didn't pull me up. We just kept walking. She knew I needed to cool down.

"You're a really good rider," one of the younger girls called out.

"You scared us to death," the tall blonde said. "Didn't she, Kami?"

"You are a good rider, Merritt," Luis agreed. "You're like, scary good."

"Can you do that again?" the fat one said. "Jump over the fence?"

"No, she can't." Kami sounded irritated. "She's not wearing a helmet or proper boots. If she got hurt we could be shut down. I could be sued." She pulled her cell phone out of her pocket. "Not that it wasn't impressive."

Merritt steered me over to the fence and halted. I felt sort of regal and majestic in the moonlight. I felt awesome. Merritt wasn't saying anything, but I hoped she felt awesome, too.

"Get him cooled off and watered and put Luis's tack away," Kami ordered. "Then go directly to your room. Don't get up for morning barn chores. Don't come to breakfast. Just stay put till I come get you."

Merritt stiffened in the saddle, but she remained silent. It sounded like she was in trouble. We both were.

"Come on, girls," Kami told the others. "Let's go start your movie. I'm bummed to miss *Frozen*, but I've got phone calls to make."

19 | MERRITT

got undressed slowly, my arms and legs already sore from riding again after so long. I could hear the other girls banging their doors shut and calling to one another as they changed into their pajamas and went downstairs to the kitchen to dish up their brownie sundaes. I'd seen *Frozen* once, which was enough, and I wasn't hungry, so I didn't care.

I stood face-up in the shower with my eyes shut tight, letting the hot water beat down on my cheeks. I could barely think I was so exhausted—emotionally and physically. I didn't even bother with shampoo. It took too much effort.

After drying off, I wrapped myself in my enormous red fleece bathrobe and went over to Beatrice's side of the room. Just like Beatrice, I was about to get kicked out of Good Fences—of that I was certain. Maybe the room was jinxed.

I was too hyped up to sleep. And with no TV, no phone, and no medicine cabinet or wine or liquor to entertain me, I didn't quite know what to do myself.

I switched on Beatrice's desk light and pulled open her desk drawer. It was empty except for a stray M&M and a misshapen heart faintly scrawled in pencil on the white wood. Inside the heart were tiny chicken scratch words: *Beatrice was here. So fuck off and die.*

Nice.

I went over to Beatrice's bed and lay down on the bare mattress. I put my hands behind my head and stared up at the bare white ceiling with its yellow circle of light from the desk lamp. I was pretty sure Kami was busy talking to my parents and Mr. de Rothschild right now. They were probably all on a conference call.

But what was the worst that could happen? Getting kicked out of Good Fences wasn't like being kicked out of an actual school. Everything would go back to the way it was before. I'd go back to Dowd and follow people on Instagram instead of actually interacting with them. I'd watch a lot of reality TV. My parents might insist that I go to therapy now, and I'd pretend to go—until I got caught and had to pay the consequences in some way that I was too weary to predict. Or maybe I would be sent away to boarding school like Beatrice. That would be fine, too.

No, it would not be fine, because Red wouldn't be there.

Or rather, I wouldn't be here with him.

I turned over on my side, curled into myself and closed my eyes, fighting back the tears that I knew were coming. It wasn't me I was worried about, it was Red. He'd stay at Good Fences, all alone with his stupid muzzle on, bored to tears, listening to those terrible classic rock songs and batting his deflated soccer balls around. No one would pay any attention to him because they were all too chicken. Eventually he'd get so bored he'd do something awful and probably hurt himself badly in the process. Or hurt someone else.

In a dramatic rush I thought of sneaking outside, tacking him up, and running away with him. But where would we go? We couldn't make it very far. People on horseback galloping down the parkway were not exactly an everyday occurrence.

I wept quietly, with my eyes closed, so achingly spent that I knew I'd be asleep soon. Red wasn't my horse. There was nothing I could do. At least I'd gotten to ride him the one time. And it was amazing, the ride of a lifetime.

My mother's voice woke me up. "Merritt? Can you open the door? I've got a bagel for you. And your riding clothes."

I was still lying on Beatrice's bare mattress, my skin clammy from sleeping in my oversized polyester bathrobe. I swung my feet to the floor, the muscles in my thighs and back screaming with soreness from last night's ride, and hobbled over to let her in.

"Merritt, you look awful," Mom said, entering my room in a rush. She was dressed for running, as usual.

"I'm sorry." My voice sounded hollow and strange. I felt bad for pulling her and my dad away from their marathon training or whatever it was they were doing. I just couldn't seem to stay out of trouble.

"It's okay. Quick though. Kami said to hurry. He'll be here any moment, and he's a very busy man. We don't want to keep him waiting."

I sat down on my bed and watched in confusion as she bustled around the room, placing my tall black leather riding boots on the floor and my breeches and riding helmet on my desk chair.

"And here's your breakfast," she continued, pulling a foil-wrapped package out from under her elbow. "A bagel really isn't the best thing, especially not when you're going to be exercising. We have protein bars in the car if you prefer." She stopped and frowned at me. "Merritt? Are you all right?"

"What's going on?" I demanded. "Who's a busy man? Why did you bring my riding clothes?"

Mom went over the dresser and pulled out a clean pair of socks and my favorite blue plaid flannel shirt. She tossed them on my bed.

"Roman de Rothschild, of course. Didn't Kami tell you?"

I shook my head. More of Dr. Kami's mind games. But this time I was grateful. If I'd known I was going to meet Mr. de Rothschild in the morning, I wouldn't have been able to sleep at all.

"Kami wants him to see you ride. Apparently you snuck a ride last night?"

I nodded. "I'm sorry. I was just so—"

"There's nothing to be sorry about. Kami and that nice boy Luis can *not* stop talking about what an incredible rider you are. Kami called us and Mr. de Rothschild here because she thinks you and that horse have something special. She wants us all to see." Mom raised the blinds and pointed outside. "Look."

"But there's no riding here," I stammered. I knelt on my bed and squinted into the sunlight. My parents' tan Prius was parked beside a shiny black Escalade. Out on the lawn a little group had gathered. My father, also in his running clothes, was talking to a gigantic man wearing a suit and tie. He towered over tiny Luis and squatty Kami, who stood at Red's head, trying to keep him quiet. Red was wearing Cinnamon's bridle and saddle. He jigged in place, as if eager to get going. Wherever it was we were going.

I turned back to Mom. "So I'm not in trouble?"

She sighed one of her quick, loud, impatient sighs. "I don't know, Merritt. Would you please just get dressed? We're all waiting. If this is your opportunity to not be in trouble you don't want to blow it, do you?"

I picked up my riding pants, glad I hadn't filled out too much in the last year. The faded green stains from Noble's grassy drool punctured a few more pinpricks in my already holey heart. My boots were tight and short—my feet and calves had grown—but I didn't care. It felt great to be wearing them again. Putting them on was like putting on a uniform. I was a rider now, no question. I pulled my hair back into a low ponytail, flipped the ponytail up, and eased my helmet on over it, fastening the chinstrap automatically.

My black Charles Owen riding helmet was my most prized possession. Gran-Jo had given it to me for my fourteenth birthday when I'd outgrown my old kid's helmet. I'd tied a piece of the royal blue ribbon she'd wrapped it with inside it for good luck. It was a fancy helmet, the kind professional show jumpers wore. It hugged my skull and gave me courage. If people jumped giant six-foot Grand Prix jumps wearing the same helmet, then I could jump a measly four feet, no big deal.

"You look great," Mom said, watching me appraise myself in the bathroom mirror.

I buttoned the top button on my shirt and tucked the shirttails into my riding pants. I never tucked my shirts into my pants normally, but when you ride you have to look neat and businesslike. It's kind of a code. Gran-Jo used to take me to horse shows whenever she could—Ox Ridge Hunt Club, Farmington, The Hampton Classic—and I'd noticed this. Some of the riders might have looked like cool, trendy teenagers when they got out of their cars, but as soon as they put on their riding clothes they were just riders.

"Here she is!" Dad cried enthusiastically when Mom and I stepped out of the Lodge. He rushed to greet me, arms open. "All ready to go!"

"Hey, Dad." I squinted up at him in the sunlight but made no move to hug him. He dropped his arms.

"That's quite a horse," Dad said as we walked toward Red.

Red's ears pricked forward. He nickered and stepped toward me, almost yanking the reins from Luis's hands.

"Whoa," Luis murmured.

Kami chuckled. "Someone's excited to see you."

I rubbed Red's nose and took the reins from Luis. I could smell Roman de Rothschild's powerful cologne—oranges and wood. I glanced up at him, huge in his suit, feeling stupidly terrified for no good reason at all. He rescued horses and adopted children and started places like Good Fences for girls like me. He was a nice man who did good things. There was nothing to be afraid of.

"Look at him!" Mr. de Rothschild's voice boomed like a cannon. Red rolled his eyes and shied away. "That horse was almost put down at the track. Professional jockeys were too scared to ride him." His voice ricocheted off the barn. I imagined the sound flying out over the treetops to the ocean. "And now look. She's made him her pet." He glanced at his watch and then nodded at me. "Go ahead, mount up."

No introductions. That was a relief.

Luis gave me a leg up and took Red's head. "This way," he said, leading us into the larger pasture. The small group followed us, keeping a safe distance away. "Kami and me, we built you a course. It's just hay bales and flowerpots and an old picnic table. I don't think we got the striding between them exactly right either. I don't know much about jumping. But you're so good, you'll figure it out."

I didn't know what he was talking about. I'd never jumped a whole course. Gran-Jo owned two sets of standards with which to put up two jumps. She'd raise them higher and higher if Noble and I were feeling frisky, and occasionally we'd jump a log in the woods, but that was about as far as it went. I was totally untrained, and now I was supposed to impress everyone with my amazing skill? If only it was dark out like last night so they couldn't see us very well.

Across the lawn I spied Celine, Tabitha, Sloan, Amanda—even Anton and Matthias—all lined up in front of the picture window in the Group room, watching. Tabitha gave me a thumbs-up. Even some of the horses in the barn had their heads over their stall doors, regarding us with great interest.

Mr. de Rothschild, Kami, Luis and my parents lined up by the gate. I asked Red to trot a circle to warm up, posting stiffly with his long stride. As we trotted I checked out the course. There were six jumps, two on one side set about six strides apart, two on the other side about four strides apart, and then a two-stride set at a diagonal in the middle of the ring. The in of the two-stride was the old burned door from the One-room Schoolhouse, leaning at an angle against two stacked hay bales. The out jump was a broken picnic table, wider than it was high.

If we missed the distance going in to the first jump, Red could put in two and a half strides and then decide not to jump the picnic table. And I'd go flying over his head and crash into it. Or worse, he'd try to jump it but leave long and not make it all the way over, catching his legs on the wood and hurting himself.

"Whenever you're ready, Merritt," my father called, not even attempting to hide the impatience in his voice. Dad had even less interest in horses than Mom. He'd much rather be training for his run. "No rush. But Mr. de Rothschild does have an important meeting in the city later this morning."

Mr. de Rothschild glanced at his gold watch. "Take your time, take your time," he boomed. Everything about him seemed to gleam: his carefully combed hair, his silvery tie, his tanned skin, even his pearly fingernails. He exuded luxury. Now I knew who'd picked out Beatrice's fancy satin pajamas.

All eyes were on us.

I urged Red into a canter. His neck was already patchy with sweat. I rubbed his withers with my knuckles as we circled, more for my own reassurance than his. He snorted his response, his big ears flipping back and then forward again. He seemed way less anxious than I was. I couldn't stop asking myself what all this was for. Red didn't care.

20 | RED

Merritt and I were perfect together. I was sure the big man could see it. Pure heaven compared to my ordeal with his hellish daughter. No vicious yanks on my mouth. No jarring knee jerks or heel jabs. And no shouting. All Merritt had to do was think about what she wanted and I was already doing it. It was the darnedest thing. I still couldn't get used to it—this feeling of wanting to please this girl, to be good for her, always. I'd finally been let in on the secret all the other horses knew except me: what it felt like to belong to someone.

We circled three or four times around the entire field, cantering, steady as she goes. Then Merritt held the inside rein open and steered me toward the smallest hay bale jump.

I popped over it without altering my stride. It was over three feet, but I jumped it like it was nothing.

"Very nice!" Mr. de Rothschild cried and clapped his hands together.

I'd forgotten how strong my owner's cologne was, as if he wanted to warn everyone of his presence before he arrived, or leave a lingering reminder long after he was gone. It made him more formidable somehow. As if he wasn't already formidable enough. Merritt patted me as I cantered on.

We did a figure eight at the far side of the pasture with an easy flying lead change, cantered solid as a rock toward home, and popped back over the jump the other way. I could feel my neck arch prettily with the effort, and my knees line up with my eyebrows. Merritt followed my head with her hands, taking just enough weight off my back to make it comfortable.

The little group by the gate applauded.

"Excellent!" Mr. de Rothschild called. His gold rings flashed in the sunshine as he rubbed his big hands together.

"Good boy," Merritt murmured under her breath.

Amazing how good those two perfect words made me feel. Unbelievable.

We continued to canter on steadily toward the long line set up on the outside. The first jump was a makeshift hay bale oxer decorated with potted geraniums, a little under four feet high. I jumped it like it was nine feet, hovering in the air for a good five seconds before landing lightly on the trodden grass.

"Whoa." Merritt sat back and steadied me. One, two, three, four, five easy strides to the next hay bale jump. "Good boy."

Now it was on to the other outside line. Each of the two jumps consisted of a simple white fence board balanced on top of three stacked hay bales. There was a lot of air between the board and the ground and no ground line, so it was difficult to judge just how high the jump really was, especially with my poor vision, but I would not back down.

Merritt's eyes were like tigers. She kept her hands up and steady, guiding me to the middle of the first jump, her legs firm against the girth. I got the message: no hesitation, we were in this together. Forever. That's the power of love.

I jumped the first jump huge and perfect, landed with my good eye focused on the second jump like I wanted to eat it, and one, two, pounce—boom, there it is!

We landed and I threw my head from side to side out of sheer hot-blooded exhilaration. I desperately wanted to buck and take

off running like a wild thing, but not with Merritt on my back. I couldn't do anything to hurt her. My shenanigans could wait until later when I was alone in my field.

"Whoa," Merritt murmured, leaning away and half-halting on the reins to steady me. "Two more jumps now. Pay attention, Red." She steered me across the diagonal at what looked like a shed door leaning against two stacked hay bales with a broken picnic table set directly behind it. I cantered toward the leaning shed door. It seemed to get bigger and scarier with every stride. I hesitated, slowing my strides so I was almost cantering in place.

"Come on, Red," Merritt growled, keeping her weight back and digging her calves into my sides.

All right then—if she said go, I'd go.

I sprang forward and in two break-from-the-gate racehorse strides I took off, sailing over the door. I landed, took one giant stride, gathered myself up and flew like an eagle over the picnic table.

"Good boy!" she laughed and patted my sweaty shoulder over and over.

I eased down to a walk and she let the reins go, hugging me around the neck as we made our way toward our little audience.

"Good boy," she whispered again.

If she repeated that all day and all night, I wouldn't have minded. I never got tired of hearing it. Love is a drug.

"Was that good?" Merritt's father asked. "It certainly looked good."

21 | MERRITT

"Beautiful." Mr. de Rothschild clapped his meaty, gold-ringed hands together once more. "Marvelous. Merritt, you have a gift, a talent. It's wonderful to watch. And my horse is pretty nice, too." He chuckled. "Finally he's found someone who can handle him."

"Thanks," I gasped, pulling up. I'd been holding my breath over every jump and I still hadn't gotten my wind back. "We left out a stride on all the lines and we're both not in very good shape . . ." I left the sentence hanging. *But it still felt awesome,* I wanted to add.

Luis took Red's head and scratched him behind the ears. He grinned up at me, his brown eyes shining. "You were having fun though, right?"

I grinned back. Fun didn't even begin to describe it.

Mr. de Rothschild walked around us slowly, appraising us. "Totally untrained," I heard him mutter to himself. "Sloppy. Dangerous. Babies, both of you. A huge risk."

Was he insulting us?

He glanced over at Kami and my parents. My father nodded at him, as if they'd been discussing something while I was riding and my father was just now giving his permission to let me in on it.

Mr. de Rothschild went to stand at Red's head. The scent of

his woody cologne was strong in my nostrils. "I want you to come down to Florida with me," he announced, his gleaming face serious and direct. "You'll stay in the staff condo and train with my trainer."

I was flabbergasted. "Me? Train for what?"

"You and the horse. You will train to compete in the hunters and equitation. The jumpers are more lucrative, but that horse is practically blind in one eye. Anything over four feet would be suicide. The jumps are lower in the hunters and I can still get a decent return." He was talking to himself again. "It's the only thing that makes sense." He focused on my face once more. "When we come back north in May you'll be ready to show on the East Coast summer circuit. You're going to win everything."

I stared down at him from Red's back, nervously fingering a hank of Red's thick coppery mane. "But what about school and here? I can't just—" I turned to my parents and Kami. They were smiling their heads off, like it was the best idea they'd ever heard.

"You're so good, Merritt," Kami said. "It's obviously your passion. I was just telling your parents, I've never seen you so animated."

"Don't worry about school," Mom chimed in.

"This is a much better option for you," Dad agreed.

And I'd always thought they thought school was so important. Silly me.

"Mr. de Rothschild has very generously offered to cover the expense," my dad added.

That explained part of it, at least. Showing horses was probably the most expensive sport on earth, other than maybe sailing yachts or recreational space travel.

"So, we are agreed," Mr. de Rothschild announced in his booming baritone. "Normally in business one has to make compromises, but there are no compromises here. We are all getting exactly what we want. Now if you'll excuse me, I have to make arrangements."

Speechless, I remained in the saddle while Mr. de Rothschild shook Kami's and my parents' hands. Then he came over to pat Red's neck one last time.

"How thrilling." He beamed up at me. "You two could be my best investment yet," he added. With that, he strode away to his shiny black chauffeur-driven car.

"Will I have my own room in Florida?" I called after him. I envisioned bunk beds and dirty boots for some reason. Hay in the shower.

Mr. de Rothschild turned and laughed loudly. "Oh yes. You'll see. The condo in Palm Beach is quite comfortable."

PART II
May

22 | RED

The word "horse" brings to mind certain livestock associations: manure, flies, dirt. Dusty hay. The stench of a farm. Such ghastly things no longer applied to me. I was a show horse now.

Every part of me was scrubbed clean, daily. My teeth, gums, and tongue were all plaque- and tartar-free. The insides of my ears and nostrils and even my eyebrows had been shaved. My body was new and improved, too. I was "seriously ripped," as the gym ads on the radio say. I looked like American Pharaoh, the Triple Crown winner. Plus, I still had that tattoo inside my lip from the old racehorse days—they could take the horse off the track but they couldn't take the track out of the horse.

I was sexy and I knew it.

I'd traveled the world and the seven seas, or at least to Florida. I had seen fire and I had seen rain. I'd seen palms trees, lizards, rolling waves, and sunsets you would not believe. I'd eaten hay grown in the Bahamas. I'd dipped my toes in the ocean. I'd rolled on the beach. I'd been turned out in paddocks beside million dollar jumpers with such exquisite European bloodlines their blood wasn't even blood, it was gold.

Merritt was ripped, too. Gone was the pale, haggard, angry girl she'd been when we first met. Now she was suntanned, sleek, and strong, a maniac out in the ring. We didn't compete in

Florida, but we schooled twice a day—in the early morning and the evenings, when it was cool, working hard on our technique until we were bulletproof, titanium, fire away. Yes, there was a radio in my stall in Florida, too. Pop songs, classic rock, disco—all music, all the time. Luis came with us as our groom, and little spotted Cinnamon as my companion. I lived in a regular stall, like a regular horse, and I never caused any trouble because I was happy, and happiness is the truth.

Merritt rarely left my side. After our morning lesson she gave me a cool bubble bath and then led me around the show grounds, stopping to watch a Grand Prix jump-off or a pony hunter class. We studied the horses and riders together, soaking up every last bit of information, learning as we watched. I rested my muzzle on her shoulder and dozed off, or she sat on the grass at my feet, shaded by my hulking, beautiful bod. We were an island in the stream. Sweet dreams are made of bliss.

Then, just like a dream, it suddenly came to an abrupt end.

23 | MERRITT

F lorida was a kind of magical, sun-drenched hallucination that was over much too soon. No more two-hour jumping lessons without stirrups while Red's coat was bleached a fiery copper color by the blistering Florida sun. No more slurping virgin pineapple daiquiris ringside during the Grand Prix. No more comical horse baths followed by sleepy grazing sessions beneath the palms. No more drifting on an inflatable raft in the condo pool, laughing privately at the thought of all my old Dowd classmates sitting in AP Calculus or running slushy relay races around the frozen reservoir in Central Park.

It was May now—showtime—the beginning of the East Coast summer circuit. Time for Red and me to earn our keep.

I don't think I'd slept more than three hours at a stretch since leaving Palm Beach and flying up north. It was only 5:30 A.M. and still semi-dark, but the Old Salem Farm show grounds in North Salem, New York, were mayhem. Little dogs roamed freely. Horse vans were parked at random. Grooms on cell phones led two horses at a time. Riders schooled over huge verticals set up at random in the muddy half-light. A long line had already formed behind the food truck. I caught a whiff of bacon, egg, and cheese sandwiches and coffee through the open car window and my stomach growled audibly.

I tried not to scratch the soft leather of the passenger seat with my nervous fingernails as Todd Olsen, my new trainer, parked his flashy electric-blue Porsche between an ancient Land Rover and a pickup truck. Todd was a great trainer but unconventional to the point of sketchy—another one of Mr. de Rothschild's "rescues."

My first morning in Florida, I looked out my bedroom window and spotted the passed out trainer lying half-in, half-out of his car. While I was watching, Luis came out of the front door of the condo and dragged Todd to the shade of a palm tree, placing Todd's trademark cowboy hat over his face to keep the flies off. Luis and I ate breakfast and went on to the show grounds. A few hours later Todd turned up, all freshly showered in a crisp pink shirt and white jeans. Totally unfazed by his wild night of partying, he built a complicated course in one of the practice rings and got straight to work. Todd was flamboyant, unpleasantly loud at times, and went out every night, but I could see what Mr. de Rothschild saw in him. Todd didn't care that Red and I had no formal training. He took great pleasure in jogging tirelessly alongside us while he smoked a Marlboro Light and explained the intricacies of a "turn on the forehand," or "shoulder in." He was a strong proponent of rigorous flatwork, believing that it enhanced a horse and rider's jumping technique: "How do you think all those little Olympic gymnast girls get so good at pointing their toes and keeping their posture when they're upside down? They friggin' take ballet!"

Todd pulled up on the parking break and skidded to a stop in the mud just inches away from one of the towering maple trees on Old Salem Farm's sprawling grounds.

"I'm going to check in with the steward and get our numbers and see if I can find that new boy from California." He grabbed his ever-present cowboy hat from the backseat and stepped out of the car. "You go find Red."

"Got it," I responded, trying not to sound as nervous as I really felt.

I headed toward the tented encampment of temporary stalls set up behind Old Salem's elegant white barns, on the lookout for the de Rothschild Farm colors—light blue with twin gold fleurs-de-lis on either side of a giant navy blue R. I'd seen it everywhere in Palm Beach: on their tack trunks, their horse vans, on the wine bottles from their vineyards in Southern France and Long Island.

Hip-hop music echoed down a row of stalls.

I spotted Red immediately, standing on crossties. A groom in ripped black overalls moonwalked down the aisle, backing toward him. An e-cigarette dangled from the groom's lips, the end glowing provocatively, like a tiny magic wand. Red stretched out his neck and nipped the groom on the shoulder. The groom whirled around, brandishing her cigarette.

"Seriously?" she shouted at the horse. "I dare you to bite me again."

I froze. It was Beatrice de Rothschild, my long lost roommate from Good Fences.

Red spotted me and pricked his ears. He whinnied shrilly, impatiently. Beatrice narrowed her dark eyes at me as she inhaled on her e-cigarette.

"Hello," I greeted her cautiously.

"Greetings," she said in a puff of steam. She yanked the cigarette out of her mouth. "I'm Beatrice, your new slave."

"But—" I knew Luis had decided to stay in Florida to work with the de Rothschild racehorses—who wouldn't choose to stay in Florida? But Beatrice? How could she be a groom? I forced myself to smile. Even if this was just a temporary situation, which I prayed it was, I didn't want to be on Beatrice the Bear's bad side. "Nice to meet you . . . again."

Beatrice ignored my awkward greeting and glanced back at Red. She laughed, dimples forming on her pale cheeks. "Check it out. He totally loves you. He's like, breaking the crossties to get to you."

I brushed past her and put my arms around my horse's neck. The three days it took for his drive up from Palm Beach was the longest time we'd been apart since we'd started training.

"Hey you," I murmured. "I guess you got here okay." I scratched behind his ears and looked him over. He was spotless, his red coat burnished and shiny. "You have to be good for me today. This is our first show. It's kind of a big deal." I glanced at Beatrice, blushing a little for being such a weirdo, talking to a horse.

Beatrice didn't seem to notice. She tucked her e-cigarette into her back pocket and began to roll up a pair of navy blue polo wraps, her hands working neatly and quickly.

"Just let me grab my helmet and—" I told Red, but Beatrice interrupted me.

"So after Good Fences my dad sent me to this boarding school in Switzerland. Huge mistake. It was basically a hospital for crazy girls with prescription drug addictions. They all pretended to be so innocent, and whenever anyone got in trouble they blamed everything on me. They put me on some kind of new medication too, so I felt like a zombie until they figured out the dosage. Anyway, I hated it, so I got myself kicked out. Then Dad said he would cut me off unless I went to work for him. He gave me three choices: work at the vineyard in France, work at his office in New York, or be a show groom."

She turned to give me a pointed stare.

I didn't know how to respond. "Wow, that's—" I began, but she interrupted me again.

"I chose to be your groom." She poked Red in the neck with

a blunt index finger. "This guy was my horse, for like five minutes. I know what a big jerk he is. And I grew up showing ponies, so I know what to do." She turned back to me. "Plus Dad said you and me might be friends." Her dark eyes flashed. "So that's the story. I'm your new groom."

I followed her inside the makeshift de Rothschild tack room, a temporary stall filled with light blue tack trunks adorned with the de Rothschild insignia. There was another smaller tack trunk that I didn't recognize, black with the letters CO monogrammed in neon green on the side.

Beatrice pulled Red's bridle and saddle out of a trunk and grabbed a white fleece saddle pad from the neat stack of them. If she had packed the trunks, she'd done a very professional job of it. Maybe she wouldn't be such a bad groom after all. She carried the equipment out into the aisle and began to tack up Red. I stood at his head, letting him blow big, steamy breaths into my face.

"So are you Mr. de Rothschild's only child?" I asked as she worked, still feeling awkward. Mr. de Rothschild had appeared now and then in Florida to observe my progress with Red, breezing in on his private jet, always standing at a distance talking on his cell phone. I knew no more about him than I had at Good Fences.

"Yes, but we're not related," Beatrice said. "My mom had me already when they met. Nobody knows who my real father is. My mother was a mess, but Dad had a thing for her, so he helped her. She's still a mess. She lives in this condo he bought her in Cannes and basically drinks pineapple juice and vodka and smokes cigarettes all day by the pool. She can barely hold a conversation, and she doesn't give a shit about me. She is pretty, though. You know, in an untouchable French movie star sort of way. I think Dad thought I'd grow up to be the functioning version of her. Like this brilliant fashion plate who looks good on a horse and in a couture dress." She sighed. "I'm such a disappointment."

I held Red's head while she adjusted the girth. "I'm sorry," I said sympathetically.

"Don't be." She picked up the bridle. "I'm not complaining. I had nannies. I had ponies. It's not like my life has been so terrible." She removed his halter and Red released his jaw to accept the rubber snaffle bit. That was one of Todd Olsen's pet peeves: If you couldn't control the horse in a plain rubber snaffle, the most comfortable bit for a horse, you shouldn't be riding at all.

"Good boy," I said and tucked Red's braided forelock beneath the bridle's brow band. I could feel Beatrice watching me as I smoothed out the white blaze that ran between his amber-colored eyes.

"I swear you're drugging him," she remarked. "This horse tried to kill me yesterday. He's like a piranha, always going after me with his teeth. But with you he's all happy and sweet."

I pressed my cheek against Red's smooth, coppery neck, unable to keep from grinning. Everyone in Florida had said the same thing. It was what everyone at Good Fences had said, too: Red was incorrigible, unmanageable, a menace, a killer. I kind of loved that I was the only one who could ride him.

"Seriously though," Beatrice went on. "I couldn't stay on his back like, ever. Not that I actually enjoy riding anymore. I hate it. It makes me feel fat and uncoordinated."

I shook my head in disbelief. "But you won on your ponies. I'm sure you're really good."

"No, I suck." She handed me the reins. "Dad says you're a prodigy. I can see the dollar signs in his irises every time he talks about you. Go ahead, get on. Show me what you got."

I felt my nerves come back. I fastened the chinstrap on my

lucky Charles Owen helmet and pulled the rubber overshoes off my fancy new custom-made riding boots—another gift from Mr. de Rothschild. Beatrice picked up a rag, squirted it with fly spray, and ran it over Red's face and ears. Then she tossed the rag on the floor and pulled her e-cigarette out of her back pocket.

"All set," she said. "Time to break a leg."

Inside the temporary stabling area it was quiet and calm. Out by the rings, the atmosphere was controlled chaos. Three jumping competitions were happening simultaneously: Adult Amateur jumpers, Equitation, and Children's Pony Hunters. Outside each ring was a warm-up area, where the competitors nearly collided over the warm-up jumps before trotting tensely through the gate when their number was called.

Beatrice led Red forward and I looked around nervously for Todd's cowboy hat.

"Carvin Oliver of Malibu, California, will be starting us off in the Maclay. Mr. Oliver is new to the East Coast circuit and is training with Todd Olsen of de Rothschild Farm," the announcer introduced the first rider in my class in the equitation ring.

That explained the strange tack trunk in the de Rothschild tack room. I'd seen Carvin Oliver ride a few times in Florida. He was impossible to miss—one of those semi-professional junior "catch" riders who didn't own a horse of his own, but would ride for trainers looking to rack up points for their horses. Carvin usually won. He was tall for a rider, with a freckled, surfer-handsome face, his green eyes accentuated by his neon green necktie. I watched him steer the gorgeous dappled gray mare he was riding to the first fence of the course, a huge three-foot, nine-inch plank vertical. They jumped it like it was nothing. Carvin looked almost bored.

Mr. de Rothschild had recruited Carvin to ride his latest acquisition, Sweet Tang, another "rescue," although she certainly didn't look like a rescue anymore. She was an Oldenburg from Germany that had been neglected and had almost died of dehydration before Mr. de Rothschild brought her to his Hamptons stable. Todd had told me Carvin would be riding her exclusively from now on.

Only when they cantered by the in-gate did I notice the intensity in Carvin's green eyes. His posture remained relaxed, his hands light. You'd think he'd been riding Tang forever, even though he'd never ridden her before today. Maybe it was the way his sandy brown hair poked out of his helmet that made him look so nonchalant, or the slightly irreverent color of his tie. His legs were so long, and so strong. I blushed, realizing I wasn't watching his jumping round at all. I was just watching him.

"Whoa." I heard Todd Olsen's gravelly voice. His cowboy hat loomed at the rail near the in-and-out where he stood growling at Carvin. "She's going to get there, don't worry. Eyes up." Trainers weren't really supposed to call out instructions while their students were competing, but many of them did. Todd couldn't help himself.

My stomach fluttered nervously. "I don't even know the course," I said under my breath. Beatrice grabbed my booted foot. I'd forgotten all about her.

"Just look at the jumps, not me," she commanded. "It's the big gray plank single, diagonal purple flowers in five, green skinny jump, coop broken line to green and white oxer in seven, outside yellow vertical four strides to the in-and-out, and then across the diagonal to the brown wishing-well oxer set at a funny angle." She pointed to the far end of the big ring. "Then the combination all the way down there. Three to the two to the one." She squeezed my foot again. "Got it?"

I nodded, repeating the course back to her as Carvin and Tang finished their round to Todd's gleeful whoops. My stomach fluttered again. I could hear Mr. de Rothschild's voice in my head: "You're going to win everything."

I still had no clue why he'd taken such an interest in me, paying for all my new custom-tailored show clothes and equipment. My riding boots alone had cost almost a thousand dollars. Red and I had worked hard, gradually getting better and better and more polished. No more hay bales and broken picnic tables. As far as Mr. de Rothschild was concerned, the reject girl and reject horse were now an A-circuit-ready machine, ready to compete and win.

I wasn't so certain.

"Riders, please be ready when I call your numbers," the equitation steward, a wiry woman in mirrored sunglasses and a white tennis visor, barked from the in-gate. "This is a big class. Let's keep it moving."

Time to earn our keep. Hopefully I wouldn't fall off.

"Okay, you got this," Beatrice said, giving Red's neck one last polish. She ran the rag over my boots and stepped back. "Time to warm up."

Todd strode over to us. Sweat ringed the underarms of his pink button-down shirt. He glared at me beneath the wide brim of his cowboy hat. "What are you doing just standing there? You should be warming up! You're competing in this class. Now. Let's go! Canter him on a loose rein and then pop him over the vertical. You're up in two. We don't have much time. Go!"

"Hurry before Todd has an aneurism," Beatrice giggled quietly.

Heart pounding, I picked up a long loping canter, praying my terror wouldn't transmit through the reins. I let Red take a good look at the chaotic surroundings as we circled the dusty warm-up ring, trying not to crash into the other fifty or so riders. A tiny girl on a huge white horse careened in front of me. I pulled up, glancing to the right and left. How could I possibly jump anything in this chaos?

"Get yourself together!" Todd screeched at me. Beatrice stood beside him in the center of the ring, calmly sucking on her e-cigarette as Todd continued his tirade. "You may be a newbie, but when you're on your horse, you have to be cool as a cucumber. I'm coming over there with my feather. I'm going to knock you off with it. Poof!"

"Sorry, I—"

"No time to argue. Canter now and pop over the vertical."

My heart thundered painfully in my chest as I got up in two-point. The collar of my ratcatcher shirt was too tight and the elastic on the hairnet keeping my hair in place beneath my helmet bit into my ears. Red stumbled and I nearly somersaulted over his head.

"Get him moving forward!" Todd shouted. "Heels down. Soft with your hands. We've covered all this, it should be second nature by now. Now the jump. It's showtime, girly. Pay attention. Where's the jump? And one, two, three—miss!"

I pressed my hands against Red's neck too early. He added a stride and then did his best to get us over the three foot-six inch rail, popping straight up into the air and landing on all fours with me in a huddle up on his neck.

"No big deal," Todd barked. "Recover, recover. And canter. One more time. Make it good. You're on deck."

24 | RED

t was all so strange. First, Beatrice—my least favorite girl in the world—was back. Not only was she back, she was my groom, the one who took care of me. Never mind how much I hated her loud voice, or the scent of her glowing smoke stick, or the way she never once patted me or sung my praises. At least Merritt was here now after a few horrible days of traveling and separation. Reunited and it feels real good.

Trainer Todd had an even louder voice than Beatrice, and his skin always gave off the same sickly, fermented fruit odor that I'd smelled on Merritt the first day we met. I didn't trust him.

Merritt smelled great now, but she was terrified, I could feel it. Normally she just left me alone to find the correct distance to the jump and adjust my stride accordingly. But she must have felt like she had to do something because so many people were watching. Problem was, everything she tried to do was wrong.

We came around to the practice jump once more and she jabbed me in the side with her heels and yanked back on my mouth on the approach. I knew what we were about to do was big and important and I didn't want us to mess it up. Another horse and rider got in our way, jumping the practice jump in the opposite direction when we were only three strides away, so we circled and came at it again. More jabbing and grabbing.

"Shit, shit, shit," Merritt swore under her breath.

Six strides from the jump she dug her heels into my ribs and shortened her reins so tight that I had to open my jaws to ease up on the pressure. Two strides away she threw the reins away and let loose an exasperated moan of defeat.

I couldn't take it anymore. I decided to dump her.

Half a stride from takeoff I pressed my front hooves down into the wet, sandy footing and put on the brakes, skidding to a halt just in front of the jump. Off my back she flew, somersaulting in slow motion. The back of her helmet clocked the top rail of the jump before she landed in a heap on the other side.

I stood beside the rail, very still. The reins dangled on the ground, but I knew not to move and get tangled up in them. I'd never stopped at a jump with her before. I hoped she was okay.

Todd strode toward me. He flipped the reins back over my head, pushed his mirrored sunglasses down on his nose and stared right into my good eye, his irises all blue and white and bloodshot red, puffing stinky fermented fruit breaths out of his nostrils. He wasn't mad, though. He was smiling.

"Smarty Pants. You're a better teacher than I am." He pushed his sunglasses back into place and turned to Merritt. "Come on, I'll give you a leg up. Beatrice went to ask the steward to give us more time."

Merritt wobbled over to us, shakily dusting the mud off the seat of her riding breeches. I saw that she wasn't okay. She didn't seem hurt or anything, but she was crying. I could smell her tears.

She stood at my side, but didn't pat me or talk to me. Todd boosted her up into the saddle and she took the reins in her shaky hands. I could smell her tears. I don't know what she was so upset about. Even Todd knew why I'd dumped her. She had to toughen up. A landslide couldn't bring us down.

As soon as she'd mounted up, we circled at the canter and went over the practice jump again. This time it was perfect.

Merritt held the reins loosely. The fall had taken too much out of her. She wouldn't fight me anymore.

"You're good to go," Todd told her.

Wrap it up, let's take it.

Beatrice strode over. I pinned my ears. "The steward said you're up next, after the bay."

Todd patted my neck as we waited. "Just do your thing. Pretend no one's watching."

I ground my teeth in warning as Beatrice went over Merritt's boots with her rag. "Go get 'em," she said and stepped away.

We trotted into the show ring and picked up a nice even canter. My ears were pricked and alert, my body coiled and ready for anything. The course was complicated, but I knew it now and I'd take care of her. We took off from exactly the right spot to the first jump and I squared my shoulders and lifted my knees up to my eyeballs. Up on my back Merritt felt perfectly balanced, looking straight ahead between my ears. We landed smoothly and cantered on to the next jump, not rushing, just taking it one fence at a time. Easy like Monday morning.

"That's it," Todd murmured as we circled past him. "Just like that."

I could feel Merritt relax and begin to enjoy herself. The next series of jumps was even better because we were in sync, guiding each other, like old friends. Me and my Bobby McGee. Our three-two-one combination was the bomb.

We cantered our closing circle to a chorus of Todd's whoops, Beatrice's wolf whistles, and thundering applause from everyone else. Ooh, it's so hot in here! Even the judge applauded, up in his box, although I don't even think that's allowed. It was a dead giveaway though. We'd won. We had to have won. We were the champions.

25 | MERRITT

"There's a long break before your next class," Beatrice said as I dismounted. She took the reins and waved me away. "I'll take care of him. You go get something to eat."

"Thanks," I replied shakily. "Want anything?"

"I'll meet you over there," she called, already leading Red back to the stabling area. I felt bad that she had to take care of both Red and Tang when we were competing in all the same classes. She'd be scrubbing the dirt off the horse's legs and bellies while I was eating breakfast. But Beatrice didn't seem to mind. Maybe her dad was smart to take her out of school and put her to work. Maybe, like me, she just needed something to do.

Carvin Oliver stood in front of me in the food truck line. We hadn't met, despite the fact that we were riding for the same barn, shared the same trainer, and now shared the same groom. I wanted to introduce myself and congratulate him. Instead, I slouched discreetly behind him, admiring the sharp contours of his shoulder blades. Riding clothes left little to the imagination.

The line inched forward in a cloud of bacon fumes. My stomach churned with a mix of hunger and nervous nausea. Carvin tapped away on his cell phone, swapping texts and chuckling to himself. I wondered who he was texting. That was one of the things I'd loved about Palm Beach. I was miles away from anyone I knew. And I didn't miss anyone. It was just me and Red. I didn't even carry a phone anymore. It wasn't like I wanted to check in with Ann Ware and ask how her career as a YouTube sensation was going.

Carvin kept on texting. Far off to my left I watched a palomino pony jump a course in the pony ring, his rider's beribboned braids bouncing off her shoulders.

"Congratu-fucking-lations, you guys!"

Before I knew it, Beatrice had grabbed me and Carvin in a sort of loose group hug, jostling me against him. "That was awesome."

She let go of us and grinned, her e-cigarette dangling from her lips.

Carvin extracted himself and glanced at me. He held out his hand. "Hey. I'm Carvin. Nice to meet you."

I'd thought Californians were supposed to be all sunny and friendly, but he was stiff and formal. He didn't even smile. "I'm Merritt," I said, shaking his hand.

He let go quickly and turned back to his phone, moving up in the line with his back to us. Beatrice scrunched up her nose and stuck out her tongue at Carvin's bony shoulder blades.

"You should have won that class," she told me.

I kicked at the grass with my toe. "Red was great. I was a big mess."

The Maclay, as it turned out, was a two-stage process. After the jump round, twenty riders were called back to test on the flat. I was called back on top, but I was still so inexperienced. The judge had asked us to "hand gallop" from the halt, and I had no idea what that meant. Neither did Red. The result was a disastrous bronco maneuver, a sort of half-rear into a very collected canter, like a failed break from the starting gate. We wound up in fourth place overall, only earning a ribbon because our score over fences had been so high. Carvin had won.

Beatrice took a big drag on her e-cigarette. It looked like a toy. "Listen, that was your first class at your first show. I used to tank at almost every show I rode in. I think I only got like two blue ribbons in eight years. My father just kept selling my ponies and finding me new ones. It wasn't their fault. I stank." She inhaled again. The tip of her cigarette glowed red. "That Sweet Tang horse is pretty amazing though, right?" she added. "Dad definitely knows how to pick them."

I nodded, blushing a little because I honestly hadn't paid much attention to Sweet Tang. What was wrong with me? I kept catching myself looking at Carvin. I was doing it even now. Of course he did happen to be standing directly in front of me.

"Dad says Carvin's going to become famous on her," Beatrice added, lowering her voice. "Straight to the top. He says they're going to win everything."

I bristled. That's exactly what Mr. de Rothschild had said about me and Red. Word-for-word. Carvin moved forward in line, examining the menu on the truck.

Beatrice stepped ahead of him and began to order. "Three bacon, egg, and cheese sandwiches with ketchup and three sweet black iced coffees," she said without even asking what we wanted. She smiled over her shoulder. "That's the classic horse show breakfast, you guys. You gotta try it."

I glanced at Carvin. He frowned back. "Whatever," he said. "I'm hungry."

A radio blared from inside the truck. "Next up is that catchy hit you heard here first," a peppy DJ announced. "This is Ann Ware singing 'F-ed up with the SAT.'"

I folded my arms over my chest and tried my best not to visibly react. No need to text Ann, after all. I knew exactly how her career was going. Forget YouTube. Her song about me was on the radio now.

"I don't need to prove that I'm smart . . . a, b, c, d, e—none of the above. What does it say about me?"

"That you're annoying?" I muttered.

I looked up to find Beatrice staring at me. She laughed. "No wonder they put you at Good Fences."

Was she trying to be funny or just plain mean? With Beatrice it was hard to tell. "I hate that song," I said defensively.

"Me, too. What about you, Carvin? Yay or nay to the song?" Beatrice turned to Carvin, but all he did was loosen his neon green necktie and scowl at the ground. Maybe he was grumpy because he was hungry. Maybe he was shy. Or maybe he was just a jerk.

"Whatever." Beatrice shot me a grin as she paid for our foil-wrapped sandwiches. I hadn't paid for a thing since I left for Florida. I unwrapped a corner of the foil as the three of us walked back to the stabling area and inhaled the delicious aroma of greasy bacon. Carvin had already demolished his sandwich. He probably could have eaten four of them.

"You know Carvin's father is like this famous surfboarder?" Beatrice remarked. "He does stunts for movies and has his own line of wetsuits. He was even in a commercial for Hawaiian Punch."

"Capri Sun," Carvin corrected her with his mouth full. He glanced at me, still chewing, and then strode ahead of us.

Beatrice snorted and slurped her iced coffee.

I took a small bite of my sandwich. "What's his deal?" I asked her.

"I guess he's just a huge asshole," she said. "And a total baby. You know his mommy homeschooled him? He has no social skills."

I took another bite of my sandwich. That makes three of us, I thought. But at least Beatrice seemed to have decided to like me. That was a relief.

The next three classes of the day were the junior hunters. Two jump classes back to back, and then the flat class. The courses were easier this time. I didn't need help memorizing them. Just up the outside line, down the diagonal, up the other outside line and across the other diagonal—then the whole thing in reverse for the next course.

I grew increasingly anxious as our start time approached, but Red felt completely relaxed and focused, not at all distracted by the activity around us.

"I know this sounds crazy," Todd told me as we stood outside the ring waiting to jump our first round. "But I want you to close your eyes on the approach. Just leave him alone." He patted Red's neck. The big horse's ears flicked forward and back, as if he were listening to every word. "He doesn't know what he's doing—he can't know, he's just as green as you are. But he's careful somehow. Like he's measuring the distance, trying to get there just right, trying to keep his balance and make you look good. Maybe it's his race training. Or maybe he's just talented. Anyway, you're better off not getting in his way. Just close your eyes and let him do his job."

I pursed my lips. Close my eyes? That was easy for Todd to say.

We trotted briskly into the ring and cantered our opening circle. As we headed for the first jump, I decided to try it. What was the worst that could happen? I'd already fallen off once today.

"Yikes," I whispered out loud as we left the ground, my eyes shut tight. I kept them closed as we approached the second jump, opened them to steer around the turn, then closed them again as we approached the next line. It was totally terrifying, but Todd was right. Red found the perfect distance every time. All I had to do was steer.

I opened my eyes for the closing circle. Todd's cowboy hat was in the air and Beatrice was wolf-whistling.

The announcement cracked over the loudspeaker: "In first place, Big Red, owned by Roman de Rothschild and shown by Merritt Wenner."

I couldn't believe it. My first show and we'd won a huge class.

"In second place, Sweet Tang, also owned by Roman de Rothschild and shown by Carvin Oliver."

The judge and the show steward stood in the center of the ring with the ribbons and prize checks. The steward flapped her hand, beckoning me to jog my horse into the ring for the judge's cursory soundness inspection—mandatory in all hunter classes—before the ribbons were distributed.

I stood beside Red, holding the reins. I couldn't move. I'd never won anything before.

"Go on." Todd pulled off his cowboy hat to scratch his thinning, white-blond hair. "Hurry up and get your ribbon before they give it to Carvin instead."

Carvin stood behind me, tapping his crop impatiently against the leg of his boot. I clucked to Red and tugged on the reins, feeling awkward and clumsy as I stumbled forward into the ring. Red trotted gamely after me. He'd never won anything either. We were total rookies.

"You ride him well," the elderly judge told me as she handed me my $300 prize check. "Good luck with him."

"Thank you," I responded hoarsely and tucked the envelope into my hunt coat pocket.

Back in the stabling area, Beatrice was all smiles. "And it's a de Rothschild sweep in the Junior Hunters," she proclaimed. She winked at me. "You know I hear the standard procedure is to give your prize checks to the groom?"

I'd won both jumping classes and placed second in the flat. I pulled the envelopes out of my pocket and thrust them at Beatrice. "Here, thank you."

"I was kidding—"

"Give those to Todd," a familiar booming voice interrupted. "He'll collect the prize checks after each show and mail them to your parents."

Roman de Rothschild, tanned and beaming in a blue double-breasted suit, strode down the barn aisle toward us. "I'm supposed to be up in Saratoga, but I had to stop in and see if I'm going to get my money's worth this summer." He laughed. I could see the gold crowns in his molars. "Looks like I am. I definitely am!"

"Hey Dad," Beatrice greeted him. She let go of Red's reins with one hand and reached out to give her father a limp side hug. "Yup. Once again you've made some very good investments."

"Hello Mr. de Rothschild," I said, trying to sound as respectful and grateful as I could to make up for her lack of enthusiasm. "Red was really good today. He jumped great."

Mr. de Rothschild kept on beaming happily as he patted Red's sleek chestnut neck. He glanced over at Carvin. "And the mare? You like her?"

Carvin nodded and began to unbuckle Tang's bridle without even looking up. "Nicest horse I've ever ridden."

Mr. de Rothschild laughed. He reached out and clutched the top of Carvin's black riding helmet with his tanned, gold-ringed fingers, shaking it back and forth and squeezing it like he was

testing a melon for ripeness. Carvin's face got very red, but he
didn't protest.

"Can you believe this boy?" Mr. de Rothschild crowed. "First
time riding that horse, ever. And he wins!" He waggled his bushy
eyebrows at me. "And Merritt. You've never even competed and
you were Junior Hunter Champion!" He stuffed his hands in his
suit pockets and bounced up and down in his shiny black shoes.
"You two better get used to those prize checks. It's going to be a
big summer for all of us!"

"What's up with the perfect behavior?" I asked Red once I'd
finished rubbing down his hind legs with alcohol and wrapping
them for the night. I stood up and scratched his withers in his
favorite spot. He flapped his lips and moaned happily. "You're
supposed to be a menace, remember?"

"It's all the tranquilizers you sneak into his carrots," Beatrice
joked from Tang's stall next door.

Carvin had already left without a word, driving away in a
trendy robin's egg blue Mini Cooper, complete with white racing
stripes. Todd had screeched off in his Porsche with a trainer
from another barn, to party the night away no doubt. That left
me to hitch a ride with Beatrice to our hotel, the Hampton Inn
in Brewster. No swanky condo until we went to Hits on the
Hudson, a series of big horse shows in Saugerties, New York.

"You get used to it," Todd had promised me. "Staying at
crappy hotels. Eating out of vending machines and drive-thrus.
It's actually kind of fun."

I latched Red's door and followed Beatrice into the tack room.

Her black denim overalls were grubby from the day's work
and there was a rip in one knee. With her short cropped black
hair and black combat boots she looked more like a roadie for a
band than a show groom. She wiped the last remnants of glycerin

soap from Sweet Tang's bridle and wrapped the throat latch in
a figure eight, tucking the reins neatly inside before laying the
bridle down in its place in the tack trunk. She closed the trunk
and sat down on the lid.

"You want to go see if we can get served in the hotel bar?"
Her big, brown eyes widened. They were actually sort of pretty.

I kicked the side of the tack trunk she was sitting on. "Not
really," I told her honestly. "I have to ride tomorrow morning.
Plus, I don't really do stuff like that anymore."

"No?" she asked. "Why not?"

I wasn't sure how to answer that. I'd never gotten drunk or
taken my dad's painkillers or anything like before Gran-Jo died.
And now that I was doing something I really wanted to do and
was relatively happy, there didn't seem to be any need for it. I
guess it was that simple: I didn't want to. Still, I also didn't want
to sound like a total goody-goody or worse, judgmental.

"I'm just not in the mood. I'll go with you if you want
though," I offered. Maybe this would be my new role, Beatrice's
wingman as she drank her way from horse show to horse show.
That could be sort of fun.

Beatrice wrinkled her nose. "Nah. Dad said I have to be on
my best behavior if I want to keep this job." She sighed. "And
it's not like I have a lot of other options."

While she finished up in the tack room I wandered back to
Red's stall. I watched him munch his hay, wondering why Beatrice
hated her father so much. Mr. de Rothschild seemed like nothing
less than a saint to me. He was certainly my patron saint.

All of a sudden I felt Beatrice tug out my ponytail and fluff up
my hair with her fingers.

I whirled around. "Hey."

"Hey what?" she asked, puffing on her e-cigarette. "Just
trying to get you to let your hair down," she said and laughed.

I tucked my sweat-dampened hair behind my ears and attempted a smile. Beatrice was standing very close to me. I could see the pores in her nose and on her chin and the dark mole beneath the thick curve of her left eyebrow. She had a widow's peak and wore two diamond earrings in each ear. Her neck was sunburned. I didn't mean to notice all those things about her, but she was only inches from my face.

"Um," I said and swallowed. My face flushed but I wasn't exactly sure why. "Don't we have to feed the horses?"

26 | RED

had three flakes of hay to get through, but I was exhausted. Merritt and that awful Beatrice were talking in the half-dark outside my stall. I watched them sleepily through my bad eye. My eyelids felt heavy. My whole body felt heavy. I considered lying down. Those temporary stalls were always so small though, and I was a big horse. A fly landed on my fetlock and I swished it off.

When I glanced up again, I saw that Beatrice was standing over Merritt, like a python ready to strike.

All of a sudden I was wide awake.

I threw myself down on the wood shavings and scattered hay, rolling on my back and throwing my legs around crazily, banging them up against the plywood walls. I pressed my head and shoulders into one corner of the stall, trying to wedge my hindquarters into another corner so I'd be stuck there and would need help. I was now what's called "cast." It could be very dangerous. It was possible that I'd panic and actually injure myself. I grunted and groaned, thrashed and kicked, trying to draw attention to my predicament. Won't you plee-ee-ase help me?

The girls peered down at me over the stall door.

"Red?" Merritt spoke to me in her sensible, quiet voice.

"Jesus." Beatrice yanked open the door and went to my head. She pulled on my mane and shouted into my face. "Get up!"

I pinned my ears and thrashed my hooves and bared my teeth.

Beatrice backed away. "Hey, Merritt. I sort of don't want to wind up in the hospital tonight. You want to get in here and try to stand him up?"

Merritt crouched by my head and slipped on my halter. She tugged on the lead rope and spoke to me gently. "You were too good today, weren't you? You had to do something crazy just so I'd know you're still you."

I was wearing wraps, so my legs were fine. I gathered them underneath me and stood. Then I shook myself and mouthed a bit of hay on the ground. I picked up my head and pushed my nose into her hair, chewing the hay and blowing out through my nostrils like it was all no big deal. Beatrice stood in the shadows outside the stall where she belonged.

Merritt patted my neck, checked my legs over, and took off my halter again.

All better, you better, you bet.

"He's okay, right?" Beatrice demanded. "Dad would go apeshit on me if he found out his big investment got cast and messed up his legs."

"He's fine," Merritt said and patted my neck again. "Idiot," she added, but I could tell she was relieved.

After all, I'd rescued her from the evil Beatrice. At least I thought that's what I'd done.

27 | MERRITT

"First place, how thrilling!" Mom shouted into the phone later that night. I don't know why she was shouting. The connection was fine. "Your first time competing!" My parents were at a lodge in the Chugach Mountains near Valdez, Alaska, about to embark on yet another endurance run.

"I'm so sorry we couldn't be home when you got back from Florida. We just really need to take advantage of our summer break to do the farther afield expeditions we can't do during the school year." She sounded like she was repeating something from a script, something Dad had told her to say.

"That's okay. I get it." I actually enjoyed not having my parents around. They'd only make me nervous. I definitely liked having a hotel room all to myself. I'd already showered and changed into my cut-off Dowd sweatpants and an old T-shirt. Show clothes were so hot and uncomfortable. I imagined this was how ballet dancers must feel when they take off their tutus and pointe shoes and put on pajamas.

"You know, now that I'm over the unconventionality of it, I think what you and your friend Ann are doing is just great. Especially in this economy." Mom was really pouring it on now. I guess she did feel guilty for not being there to cheer me on.

"I agree. It's wonderful!" Dad's voice suddenly chimed in.

"Am I on speaker?" I demanded.

"We were so worried about you dropping out your senior year, but now it makes sense," Dad went on. "You needed your freedom. Your cohorts are about to graduate and head off to college for four more years of school. But you and Ann took a different, more direct path. Why waste time on college? You've already begun your careers!"

This from a college professor. "Wait, Ann left Dowd?" I said, shocked. It was so unlike Ann. She was supposed to graduate from Dowd with honors and go to a fancy performing arts college.

"I think it's marvelous!" Dad crowed.

"Me too!" Mom chimed in.

"Me too," I said with the same false enthusiasm.

"Susan, we have that breathing seminar," Dad said.

"Yes, that's right. 'High Altitude Breathing Tips for Long Distance Runners.'" Mom sounded bored already. "We'd better go. Bye, Merritt. Good luck," she added before clicking off.

So Ann had dropped out of Dowd. Maybe I really had inspired her. Maybe her SAT song was sort of a compliment to me. Maybe she thought I was brave. But Ann was probably already making a living. She wasn't a star yet, but she seemed to be headed in that direction. Her song was inescapable. Meanwhile I was participating in one of the most expensive sports in the world and I wasn't paying for any of it. Yes, I'd won over $500 in prize money today, but that was far less than the horse transportation fees, the entry fees, and Red's board at the shows. Never mind all the custom-tailored riding clothes, the horse care, the hotel rooms. The expenses were endless. Or so I imagined. It wasn't like I'd ever seen the bills.

Back in Palm Beach Mr. de Rothschild had given me a credit card with the de Rothschild farm logo on it for "anything I needed," but I was too embarrassed to use it. I'd subsisted on the cash allowance of sixty dollars a week on a designated ATM card my parents had given me. Even that made me feel bad. Maybe I was taking a more unconventional path, but I wasn't exactly earning my keep.

I turned on the TV. There was nothing on except re-runs of *CSI* and *Glee* or the news. I could have used the pay channels and watched a movie, but again I felt guilty making Mr. de Rothschild pay for any extras. Besides, I was too restless. My body was exhausted, but my mind was racing. I could hear Beatrice singing loudly in the next room, but I didn't recognize the song. I pictured her jumping up and down on her bed in her cream-colored satin pajamas, screaming into her toothbrush. God she was weird.

I turned off the TV, picked up the stray quarters I'd scattered on the bedside table, and went out into the hall to use the vending machines. I stopped when I spotted Carvin, banging his fist against the snack machine.

"It's jammed," he said without looking up. He lifted up the front end of the machine and jiggled it, his freckled face turning red with the effort. His muscles bulged against the sleeves of his gray T shirt. His hair was longer than I'd expected, hanging over his forehead and sort of winging out around the tips of his ears. Aside from the T-shirt, he wore a pair of green plaid boxer shorts; nothing else.

"I just want a Coke," I stammered, blushing inexplicably. I brushed past him, stuck my quarters in the drink machine, and pressed the giant COKE button. Carvin continued to rattle the snack machine. He smelled like clean laundry. It was a nice scent. I pulled the plastic Coke bottle out of the machine. "I have an extra Snickers in my room if you want it," I offered.

He stopped pounding and straightened up. "Really?" Up close and in only boxers he seemed bigger and messier than he did in riding clothes. He smiled. "That'd be great. I'm starving."

I averted my gaze. Why could I not stop blushing? "Hold on." I scurried back to my room to retrieve the Snickers.

"Thank you," he said sort of formally when I handed it to him.

"No problem." I forced myself to look up and smile, but he was already turning away, walking stiffly down the hall toward his room. To save us both from further embarrassment, I turned and fled.

Beatrice poked her head out into the hall before my door had closed. "Hey, you guys having a party without me?"

I glanced down the hall at Carvin's retreating back. He went into his room and slammed the door.

"Not exactly," I mumbled.

"Can I come over?" Beatrice shoved her way past me and into my room, letting her door click shut behind her. "It's too boring in there all alone."

I wasn't sure where to sit. The queen-sized bed seemed too provocative, as if I might be suggesting some kind of girly intimacy by settling there—a pillow fight after which we'd do each other's hair and makeup, share a pack of Twizzlers, and giggle the night away. So I sat in one of the uncomfortable wooden armchairs by the window and hugged my knees defensively into my chest.

"I love hotels, but only the nice ones. This one sucks." Beatrice was wearing red fuzzy socks and the same cream-colored satin pajamas I'd seen on her bed at Good Fences. She looked like a celebrity lounging around after the Oscars, not a groom for a horse barn. "There aren't even any bathrobes. Did you ever stay at the Ritz in Paris?"

"I've never even been out of the country," I admitted.

Beatrice shrugged. I'd forgotten how different her upbringing was from mine—European boarding schools and luxury hotels.

Every July my parents rented the same house for the same week in Cape Cod, near their favorite sushi restaurant and their favorite quiet bay beach. Gran-Jo's house and Cape Cod. Those were the places I'd been.

Beatrice sprawled out on the bed on her stomach and tapped at the screen on her phone. "Do you know Anne Sexton, the poet? I did a project on her for school. She committed suicide—put on her mother's fur coat, poured a glass of gin, went down to the garage, and turned the car on with all the doors closed. And that was it. Boom. Dead."

She thrust her phone under my nose. "Press PLAY."

On the tiny screen was a video of Beatrice, dressed in her satin pajamas, reciting a bleak poem I couldn't really follow while she whacked a tambourine. It had been filmed in black and white and there were dark circles under her big, dark eyes. It was pretty bad, almost unwatchable. I didn't know what to say.

"That's how I managed to get kicked out of my last boarding school. I was supposed to write a paper, but instead I made that video. In the middle of the night." She rolled onto her back on my bed and began doing crunches, like it was perfectly normal to be exercising on someone else's bed in a strange motel room in your pajamas.

I tossed her phone on the mattress.

Beatrice kept crunching. "I love how she obsessed with death she is. Anne Sexton, I mean. And sex. The word sex is even in her name."

I hugged my knees to my chest even tighter. "Um . . . are you okay? You seem sort of hyper."

Beatrice laughed and sat up. Her cheeks were flushed and her short, dark hair stuck straight up. "It's late. My hyperactivity medication has worn off. Dad let Kami talk him out of medicating me while I was at Good Fences. That was part of the problem. I've been on medication since I was two. Then at the last boarding school they gave me the wrong medication. It's a delicate balance," she added with another shrug.

"Wow." I felt sorry for her. Sort of. Sorry, but also intrigued.

Beatrice snatched up her phone and tapped away again. "I'm Googling Anne Sexton. There." She threw the phone back at me. "Don't I look like her? With a little less hair? She was tall. I'm not that tall."

Beatrice was barely five feet tall and soft and curvy. In the photo Anne Sexton looked gangly and thin and extremely tall. Her hair was curly. Beatrice's was straight. Beatrice didn't look a thing like her. I chewed my lip.

She burst out laughing. "Okay, I totally don't look like her," she admitted. "I just wish I did. I'm fat, she's thin. I'm short, she's tall. And she wrote poetry! Anyway, she and this other poet, Maxine Kumin, were best friends. They wrote each other letters all the time and talked on the phone for hours." She went back to doing crunches. "Maxine Kumin is still alive, I think. She's really into horses. She wrote a whole poem about horse shit, called 'The Excrement Poem.'"

She laughed again, her satin pajama top billowing up around her pale, soft stomach. I didn't know anything about poets or poetry. All I could think of was the spice, cumin. Back in fifth grade my parents had gone to India to run in a cross-country race along the Brahmaputra River. They brought back a giant sack of cumin. I stayed with Gran-Jo. That was the first time she let me jump Noble.

Beatrice hopped off the bed. "I honor shit," she recited with a dreamy look in her soft brown eyes. She glanced at me. "That's how the poem goes. Something like that anyway. I have a whole stack of their books in my car." She sat back down again and yawned. "Okay, now I'm tired."

"Actually, I'm pretty tired, too." I faked a huge yawn. It was time for her to go back to her room.

Beatrice scowled at my bedside clock. "This whole grooming gig is great and all, but the hours suck. I have to meet the braider at five o'clock in the morning tomorrow. Jesus."

I yawned again. "Sorry but—"

A commotion outside my door cut me off.

"Todd? Hey! What the hell?"

It was Carvin, shouting. Carvin didn't seem like a shouter. Something was wrong.

I jumped to my feet and ran to open the door. Way down the long hallway Todd lay sprawled on the floor by the ice machine, his cowboy hat upside down beside him.

"Todd?" Carvin crouched over him. "Can you hear me?"

I hurried down the hall. Beatrice was right behind me.

"What happened?" I demanded.

"He threw up into the ice," Carvin explained, his green eyes huge and scared looking. "And then he just passed out."

I could smell the vomit. I put my hand over my mouth and nose. "Gross."

Beatrice chuckled. "It's okay, he does stuff like this all the time."

Carvin's eyes widened even more. "Seriously?"

Beatrice shrugged. "Why do you think he's working for my dad? Dad is a sucker for fuck-ups."

Carvin frowned down at Todd. "Damn."

I leaned against the wall, watching Todd's chest rise and fall. "I'm sure he'll be fine in the morning," I said, trying to reassure him. "He always is."

Beatrice squatted down near Todd's head. "We'd better get him into his room. He won't even remember this tomorrow. It's only ten-thirty. He'll be fine."

Carvin blinked at her. Then he sighed. "Okay, let's do it."

Todd's keys were on the floor outside his room. Carvin lifted him up by the armpits, Beatrice lifted his legs by the ankles, and I held open the door. Todd's untouched rolling suitcase stood on the floor beside the neatly made bed.

"So your dad knows about this?" Carvin grunted as he backed into the room. Todd's body swayed limply just above the floor. "He knows he . . . overdoes it sometimes?"

Beatrice rolled her eyes. "Of course," she scoffed. "On three. One, two, three."

They swung Todd onto the ugly orange bedspread. I picked up his cowboy hat and dropped it on top of his suitcase. Todd lay on his back, arms askew, still completely unconscious.

"My dad knows everything about everything," Beatrice explained. "He has people everywhere, digging up dirt, doing everything he asks. He only interferes if he's not getting the results he wants. Todd trains winners, so my dad doesn't care how he spends his downtime. Like, if I went to Harvard and was an Olympic show-jumper and swimsuit model but I was also shooting heroin, he'd be fine with that. Then he'd leave me alone."

Carvin crossed his freckled arms over his chest. "I don't believe that. Your dad's a cool guy. He definitely knows how to pick horses and . . . and the people who should ride them." He shot a glance at me and I felt my face heating up again. "Never in a million years would I be riding a horse as nice as Tang if it weren't for him."

"He got me out of Good Fences," I added.

Beatrice sighed. "My dad likes to feel like he's helping people," she said slowly. "But he always has an agenda."

The three of us stood in silence for a moment, looking down at Todd.

"So what do we do now?" I asked.

"Think it's okay to just leave him?" Carvin said.

"Sure," Beatrice assured us. "He just needs to sleep it off." She turned on the bathroom light and switched off the bedside lamps. Carvin and I followed her out into the hall, leaving Todd's key on the bedside table.

"Hey, you guys want to hang out for a little while?" Carvin asked.

For someone who was supposed to be a jerk he was being pretty nice. To my surprise Beatrice shrugged and nodded. None of us wanted to be alone.

"Sure," I agreed.

Carvin unlocked the door next to Todd's. "This way we can hear him if he needs our help or whatever."

His room looked like he'd been living in it for a month. Clif Bar wrappers and empty apple juice boxes were strewn everywhere. A bunch of bananas and a bag of apples sat next to the TV. On the floor was an unzipped duffel bag spilling over with ripped open cases of Clif Bars, juice boxes, bags of trail mix, and packages of dried seaweed. My parents would definitely approve.

Beatrice nudged the bag with her toe. "What is all this shit?"

Carvin sat down on the bed. "I'm from California, what can I say? My mom raised me to eat well, and I'm hungry like, all the time. I can't be without food."

"Seaweed is not food." Beatrice snorted and flopped down on her back on Carvin's bed. "Like twice a month I eat a salad somewhere. Otherwise I live on drive-thru, food trucks, or vending machines."

"That's kind of gross." I perched on the very end of Carvin's bed. "You're going to get scurvy." I yawned as fatigue kicked in.

We were all exhausted, and we had to be up very early. Carvin stretched out on one side of his bed and Beatrice on the other. I lay back in the middle of the bed, as far away from both of them as possible, with my legs dangling over the end. The three of us stared up at the dingy white hotel ceiling as if there was something to see there.

"I slept in the same bed with my Mom until I was ten," Carvin confessed out of the blue. "We called it 'the family bed.'"

"That's really nice." Beatrice nudged my ear with her toe and I fought to hold in a giggle. "What happened when you had sleepovers? Did your friends sleep with your mom, too?"

I pressed my lips together, grateful that Carvin couldn't see how hard I was working to control myself.

"I don't remember ever having a sleepover. I was home-schooled, so I never really had any friends my age. I finished all my high school work when I was about fifteen, and then I just rode horses for people and did the California circuit until Mr. de Rothschild offered to bring me out here."

"Wait, how old are you?" I asked.

"Eighteen in August. It's my last year as a junior rider. You?"

"I'm seventeen, too. My birthday was in November." It had come and gone in Florida without any acknowledgment except a birthday card from my parents, mailed from Vermont. *Here's to an exciting year for our special girl.* It was handwritten, but Hallmark might as well have printed it on the card.

"You guys are babies," Beatrice said. "I turn nineteen in September. I repeated sixth grade, and kindergarten, too, I think. That's why I'm still in school. Or was," she corrected. "I'm done with school forever now."

We stared at the ceiling in silence again.

"... *And you undid the bridle / and you undid the reins / and I undid the buttons, / the bones, the confusions* ..." Beatrice began to chant.

God, she was so weird.

"What is that?" Carvin asked. "A song?"

"It's a poem called 'Us,' by Anne Sexton. It's about sex."

"That's really nice," Carvin teased, imitating the way Beatrice had commented on his 'family bed.' We all chuckled. This was sort of nice, whatever this was.

Beatrice yawned hugely. "Oh wow." She yawned again. "I can't move."

We lay like that, not talking, for a long time. I continued to stare up at the ceiling, wondering if I should go back to my room.

My eyelids grew heavy and I felt myself drifting off. I could hear Beatrice's slow, noisy breathing somewhere above my head, off to the left. And then something nudged my right shoulder. It was Carvin's foot.

"Hey. You okay?"

My heart sped up, but I tried to sound like I was almost asleep. "Huh?"

"Why don't you slide up a little?" he whispered.

I pushed myself up on my elbows and slid backwards so that my head was up by the pillows. There were two pillows. Beatrice's head was on one and she was fast asleep. Carvin picked up his head and slid his pillow over toward me. Then he reached down, pulled his gray T-shirt off over his head and wadded it up to form a makeshift pillow for himself.

"There, that works." He switched off the bedside lamp.

I lay back with my head on his pillow, my body perfectly still and stiff. I'd never been in a boy's bed before—a boy I'd only just met that morning, who wasn't wearing a shirt. He was practically naked. I kept my eyes closed, hoping he would think I was one of those people who zonked out the moment my head hit the pillow.

Maybe he's gay, I thought, my heart pounding. It was a thing, gay guys in the horse world. Kind of like in ballet and figure skating. It wasn't the rule, but there were definitely a lot of gay guys around. Todd was gay, and I suspected that Luis might be, too. Nothing about Carvin seemed gay, but then again he didn't seem too bothered about lying next to me in only his boxers. He was probably gay.

The more I became convinced of it, the more I felt myself calming down. My mind wandered and I began to drift off. Then I felt his warm, apple-scented breath on my cheek. My eyes flew open and I turned my head.

"Hey." Carvin's face was incredibly freckly up close. It was like someone had drawn dots all over him with a brown marker that was running out of ink.

"Hey," I whispered back. My heart thudded in my chest. This is what it feels like to want to kiss someone, I thought. But he's probably gay, I reminded myself, so it was never going to happen.

His freckles moved as he smiled and then fell back into place. "Just wanted to say goodnight," he whispered. He lay back down on his shirt, clasped his hands behind his head, and turned his face up to the ceiling.

I tried not to look at the muscular outlines of his bare chest, but it was right there, only inches away, sort of glowing in the dim light.

"I'm glad you're here," he added.

I turned toward him, curled up on my side in a sleeping position with my hands tucked beneath my cheek, and closed my eyes.

"Me too," I whispered back. "Goodnight."

28 | RED

he next morning things were tense. Merritt was too quiet as she tacked me up inside my stall. Next door in Tang's stall Carvin was quiet, too. Only Beatrice was loud, as usual, sucking on her glowing pipe and singing along to the radio as she rerolled my standing wraps in the tack room doorway.

I love myself for hating you . . . !

See what I did there? I reversed the lyrics. Because Merritt and Carvin's freaky quietness was definitely all Beatrice's fault. Everything bad was her fault.

"Hey, losers, Todd just texted me!" she shouted at the top of her lungs, making us all jump. "He needs everybody up at the ring for the Handy Classic in five minutes. I told you Todd would be fine."

I could tell this class was important because of the way Merritt fingered the blue ribbon inside her helmet before she put it on. By the way she checked me over more than once before leading me out of my stall. By the size of the crowd near the ring. Also there was a scoreboard flashing neon yellow numbers beside the names of the horse and rider after each round. It reminded me of race day at the track.

I thought she'd ask for speed, but we jumped the course in slow motion, taking each fence squarely and making a nice, big, slow closing circle afterwards. As we walked out of the ring the board flashed our score. Todd waved his big hat in the air and whooped and Beatrice wolf-whistled.

Merritt dropped the stirrups and reins and threw her arms around my neck. "Good boy," she crooned, patting me over and over.

I was confused—we'd gone so slowly—but if she was happy, I was happy. At least she was talking to me now. Maybe the score wasn't about speed. It was about style and beauty. Well, we were beautiful and stylish. Fresh, exciting, and new. Delicious. Divine.

A little later on the same thing happened.

We jumped the most boring course in the most boring way, and I concentrated on being perfect and square and even. Afterward people came over to talk to Merritt and Todd and flashed their phone screens and patted my nose. They gave me mints and carrots and apple treats. And that's the way, uh-huh, uh-huh, I liked it.

The last course of the morning was more complicated. We had to stop and open a gate and trot over a huge water jump and even walk over a jump. Then we had to gallop out of the ring like it was on fire. I was on fire. I even opened the gate myself, with my nose. That made Merritt laugh.

The crowd stood up as she jogged me out first, ahead of all the other horses, and a lady in a long dress pinned a huge blue ribbon to my bridle. Merritt got another medal and another white envelope and kept patting me and hugging me. Todd took off his sunglasses and wiped away actual tears of joy.

Take a good look at my face. I was so not crying.

After a bath and lunch and my afternoon nap, Merritt brought me out again. This time the course was complicated, with lots of tight turns, and bigger jumps. She kept the reins short and my head up so I could land and respond, land and respond. It was like a dance—land and turn and loop the loop, circle back and jump and jump. Jump around! Jump around! Jump up, jump up, and boogie down!

Todd whooped and Beatrice wolf-whistled again. The crowd loved us. Sweet Tang and Carvin were the next to go, and they got even louder cheers. No wolf-whistling though.

After that, the judge called for the top two riders to switch horses.

At first I thought it was a mistake. Humans make way more mistakes than horses. But Merritt slid down from the saddle and held the reins out to Carvin. Too tall for a leg up, he swung into my saddle and I pranced nervously in place while he adjusted his stirrups. Out of the corner of my good eye I saw Todd give Merritt leg up on Tang.

Say what? I didn't like this. I hadn't prepared for this. Merritt and I were a team, and there were no other members. So whad'ja whad'ja whad'ja want?

Carvin urged me into the ring and asked for the canter, trying to get a feel for whether I wanted a loose rein or a tight one, or something in between. But I didn't care about any of that. I was hardly listening to him. I felt like I was losing my mind. All I wanted was for him to get off my back and for Merritt to get back on. He aimed me toward the first jump. I pretended to canter toward it gamely, but two strides before I slammed on the brakes and skidded in the dirt. Carvin flipped over my head and landed on his feet on the other side of the jump. The crowd gasped. I snorted and shook myself off. Another man bites the dust.

The expression on Carvin's face was almost comical.

He walked stiffly around the jump. "Guess you're not as

easy to ride as I thought." He tugged on the reins, but I pulled back, refusing to leave the ring. I wasn't going anywhere with him. "Come on," Carvin growled, his freckled face turning red.

Finally Merritt walked into the ring to help him out. I nickered at her and the crowd laughed.

"Adorable," I heard someone say as Merritt led me out of the ring without any difficulty.

"You've got balls, I'll say that," Beatrice told me when Merritt handed her my reins. Beatrice gave me a peppermint, which I promptly spat out.

Merritt got back on Tang and trotted into the ring, looking tiny and businesslike on the big gray mare. They completed the test in perfect form. The crowd gave her a standing ovation. I pawed the ground with my hooves.

Merritt beamed and the photographer snapped her photo as she collected another blue ribbon, another medal, and yet another white envelope. I was horrified. She'd abandoned me. But as soon as she dismounted, Carvin took Tang back and stormed off, and Merritt was mine all mine once more.

Back at the stabling area, Merritt pulled off my bridle and saddle and led me into the wash stall for my bath. She was probably more tired and sweaty than I was in all that riding gear, but she just threw her gloves on the ground outside my stall and took care of me first. She let the water run through the hose a long time before the temperature was to her liking. Then she poured a splash of liniment into a bucket and filled it up. The sea sponge danced inside the bucket.

She bathed me slowly, still quiet. Too quiet. She wasn't in a bad mood, just distracted—by something other than me, us. I didn't like it. I liked it when she talked to me nonstop. I kicked over the bucket full of liniment and water, just to hear the sound of her voice.

"Ugh, Red. What'd you do that for?"

Then Beatrice hurled herself into the wash stall in her black leather pants and swept Merritt up in a big bear hug. I reached out and tried to bite her shoulder blade but she jammed her elbow into my nose, hard. I was so surprised that I just stood there, dripping and staring. Finally Beatrice let go of Merritt and allowed her to breathe, but she was still standing so close—in Merritt's space, my space.

"Carvin is so pissed," Beatrice said, ignoring me completely. "He just threw Tang on crossties and stomped away with one of his granola bars." She threw her arms around Merritt again. "You were so awesome. You're a total rock star." She reached up and pulled off Merritt's riding helmet. "You must be cooking in this thing."

I shook myself off like a boxer trying to relax. Why'd she have to touch Merritt all the time? Couldn't she just text her? And why didn't Merritt seem to mind? I definitely minded—a lot. Merritt seemed to be getting used to it. Or maybe she was just too tired and too distracted by whatever was distracting her to even notice.

Beatrice's phone vibrated and jangled in the back pocket of her leather pants. She put the phone to her ear.

"Hey Dad." She smiled grimly and handed the phone to Merritt. "It's for you."

29 | MERRITT

"Do you know I was just offered a great deal of money for that wonderful horse that only you, my novice girl, can ride? Isn't it wonderful? I could be a richer man already!"

I clutched Beatrice's phone to my sweaty cheek, staring at Beatrice as her father's ecstatic praise boomed in my ear. Beatrice rolled her eyes, picked up a sweat scraper, and began to squeegee the water from Red's dripping hindquarters.

"Of course I'd be mad to sell him now," he continued. "You're a miracle team and this is only your first show. Nobody gets rich by being impatient!"

I'd never spoken to Mr. de Rothschild on the phone before. I was so intimidated I could barely think of a response. "Thank you for the opportunity," I managed awkwardly.

Beatrice gave a snort of disdain as she squeezed the water from Red's damp legs.

"Thank *you*," Mr. de Rothschild boomed. "The reporter from *The Chronicle of the Horse* was completely fascinated by my choice of riders—'Two gorgeous teenagers no one on the East Coast circuit has ever heard of.'" He laughed. "They asked me if you were boyfriend and girlfriend. I told them you only just met for the first time yesterday!"

Blood rushed to my face. Luckily Beatrice was squatting down at Red's hocks and couldn't see.

That morning I'd woken up on Carvin's bed at the hotel, alone. Beatrice had already gone to the show and Carvin had left a note on a piece of hotel stationery: *Out jogging*. I went back to my own room, showered, and changed into my show clothes, and then knocked on Todd's door, hoping he was up and could give me a ride. He opened the door right away, all buttoned into a clean white shirt, his freshly combed platinum hair still damp from the shower.

"Ready to go?" he asked brightly, with no sign of a hangover. I couldn't believe it.

Carvin was in Tang's stall when we arrived. I'd said "hey" and he'd said "hey" back, but that was all. We hadn't spoken since, not even after Red had dumped him.

"I think Carvin's kind of mad at me right now," I told Mr. de Rothschild. "Red wouldn't do anything for him when we had to switch horses during the Medal test. It was kind of embarrassing."

"Asshole," Beatrice coughed into her fist, and I had to suppress a giggle.

"Well, it's better that way than if you two were flirting with each other all the time," Mr. de Rothschild said cheerfully. "That could be very distracting."

"Carvin is gay though, right?" I blurted out.

He chuckled. "I stay away from my employees' personal lives."

Employees. Is that what Carvin and I were? I thought I was more like an adopted daughter. Plus, Beatrice had said her dad knew everything about everything. There was an awkward silence.

"Can I ask you something?" Mr. de Rothschild said after a moment.

"Sure," I replied hesitantly.

"I don't know how close she's standing, if she can hear me or not, but if you don't mind my asking, is my daughter a good

groom? Does she do her job well? I can fire her today if she's no
good. Send her to live with her mother in St. Barts or Nice or
wherever she is at the moment."

I reached up and brushed a few droplets of water away from
Red's bad eye. His ears were pinned flat against his head as Beatrice combed the braid out of his tail, her big brown eyes cast
down. I could tell she was trying to listen.

I felt torn. Things would be simpler without her there,
throwing herself at me, bouncing on my bed, demanding my
attention. And I knew Red didn't like her.

But I'd miss her. Without her, I wouldn't have a friend. Carvin
didn't count. He was too sensitive and moody. It was sort of
immature of him to storm off the way he had after the Medal
test instead of congratulating me. Plus, I still didn't want to be
on Beatrice the Bear's bad side.

"She's a great groom," I heard myself say, smiling at Beatrice
as I said it. She rolled her eyes again and gave me a thumbs-up.
"And she knows Red," I added. "He's not the easiest horse to
deal with, you know."

"Yes, yes. Well that's good to hear," Mr. de Rothschild said.
"But be careful. She's not the easiest girl to deal with either. And
if she tries any funny stuff or starts acting crazy, I want you to
tell me immediately. Don't feel like you owe her anything. In
fact, you owe me."

I wasn't sure what to make of that, so I didn't say anything.

"I mean, I'm her father. I need to know what's going on."

"Yes, of course," I agreed, desperate for him to change the
subject.

Beatrice frowned suspiciously at me. "*What's he saying?*" she
mouthed, but I ignored her.

"Congratulations again, my dear," Mr. de Rothschild said,
wrapping it up. "Hits on the Hudson is next, yes? They do a

very nice job with the shows there. You'll like it. Now pass me back to my daughter, please."

I handed over the phone.

"Thanks for checking up on us, Dad," Beatrice said, then abruptly clicked off and stuffed the phone into her back pocket.

After his bath I led Red out into the sun to dry off and graze on the long grass behind the stabling area.

"Hey, Merritt Wenner. Nice job in the Medal today," a girl's voice rang out behind me.

I knew that voice. I whirled around. Nadia Grabcheski and Amora Wells from my class at Dowd Prep were walking toward me, leading two sleek, fat ponies. They looked exactly the same as when I'd seen them last, at the SAT, only now both girls were dressed in jodhpurs and short boots, their long blonde hair braided with big bows on the ends. It was the show attire of much younger riders.

"Hey," I grumbled. I knew I was going to run into these two at a horse show at some point. I'd forgotten seniors got out early at Dowd. I thought I had more time.

"So we didn't even know you rode," Nadia said with a fake smile. "And now here you are at Old Salem, winning everything?" She cast a longing look at Red. "Your horse is amazing. You're so lucky. I still have my large pony. My dad refused to get me a horse because he wanted me to focus on my early admission to Brown." She sighed and tucked a few stray wisps of white-blonde hair behind her diamond-studded ears. "And you have those amazing Italian boots and that cool helmet. Amora, see? Those boots are totally custom fitted. And that's the exact Charles Owen helmet I've put on my Christmas wish list two years in a row."

I glanced down at the helmet, dangling by its harness from

my wrist. I used to think of it as a luxury item, too, like a cashmere sweater or a nice watch. Now it was just a necessity.

"You are so lucky!" Nadia cried again.

I was tempted to explain to Nadia and Amora that Red wasn't really mine, and that I hadn't even paid for my fancy riding boots or even gone to the store to buy them. A little old Italian lady had come to the condo in Palm Beach and taken all of my measurements. A week later my boots, several pairs of breeches, ratcatchers, hunt coats, and a beautiful leather belt were delivered to my room. I decided to just let them envy me.

"My lease runs out on this guy next month," Amora said, glancing at her fat bay pony without a hint of regret. "I'm way too big for him. And anyway, my mom wants me to focus on my tennis this summer so I can play for Yale—"

"Wait," Nadia interrupted. "Oh my God. Shut up, Amora. Merritt, that boy you ride with? Carvin Olivier or whatever his name is? He is so cute!"

"Totally," Amora agreed. "You must be dying looking at him all the time."

I considered telling them that Carvin was gay, but then again, I didn't really know that for sure. "He's okay, I guess."

"Okay?" Amora repeated.

"Oh my God, what is wrong with you?" Nadia squealed.

Red continued to crop the fresh green grass, completely oblivious.

"How was graduation?" I asked, only because I felt like it would be rude not to.

"Totally amazing," Nadia gushed. "I can't believe you and Ann Ware both missed it."

Weird that Ann and I were now aligned in our classmates' and parents' minds. We were the rebels, the ones who'd left school our senior year. Maybe one day we'd even be friends again.

"Graduation was—" Amora started and then stopped. Both girls looked at each other and screamed shrilly.

Red looked up, startled. Their ponies kept on eating.

"So where are you showing after this?" Nadia asked when she'd composed herself.

I was starting to enjoy the new awestruck tone she used to address me.

"Hits in Saugerties for three shows," I replied, running through the busy summer show schedule in my mind. "Then the Saratoga Classic. Then Lake Placid. Then Devon. Then Hits again for two more shows. Then the Hunter Derby Finals in Kentucky at the end of August."

I didn't share that I had no idea what would happen in September. Would I go back to school? Back to Good Fences? Keep showing Red? If my parents and Mr. de Rothschild had a plan they hadn't let me in on it.

The two girls stared at me.

"Wow," Nadia said after a moment.

Amora scowled and tugged on her pony's lead rope. "My parents would never let me show that much."

"I know, it's a lot," I admitted.

"Nobody shows that much unless they're trying to win as much money as possible," Nadia declared. "Or they need to get their horses seen because they're trying to sell them."

I knew she was jealous, but she didn't have to be rude. If Mr. de Rothschild were trying to make a quick buck he would have asked me and Carvin to show Red and Tang down in Palm Beach this winter.

"I'd better get him back to his stall," I said and began to lead Red away. "Good luck," I added for no good reason at all.

• • •

Back in his stall, Red lay down and rolled in the deep pile of clean shavings. I shook my head at his utter disregard for cleanliness or composure. He wanted to roll, so he rolled. Back on his feet, he shook himself and began to pull mouthfuls from the flakes of hay that were piled in the corner. I loved watching him. All was well in his world as long as he had a cool stall to relax in, enough hay, and a bucket of fresh water.

"I miss you, too," Carvin's voice sounded from Tang's stall. I stiffened. I hadn't even realized he was there. I stole a peek into the stall. Carvin was sitting on the shavings, talking on his phone while Tang munched her hay.

"I'm sorry I didn't call before. Okay, I will. Love you, too, Mommy. Bye."

I turned away so he wouldn't catch me eavesdropping, but I was too late. He stood up. "How long have you been standing there?" he demanded, glaring at me through the metal bars.

"I—I'm sorry," I stammered. "I think it's cute that you call your mom 'Mommy.' My parents are just plain old Mom and Dad. Pretty boring. You must miss home, being so far away . . ." My voice trailed off. I should have stopped talking a long time ago.

Carvin didn't say anything. He walked around Tang, checking her wraps.

"Tang was great today. You both were," I went on, unable to shut up.

Carvin continued to ignore me. He knelt down to rewrap Tang's right hind. I wanted to tell him about Mr. de Rothschild's call and my annoying classmates from school. I wanted to ask him for a ride to our next show. But we'd only met yesterday, and Carvin seemed to have changed his mind about me. He didn't want to be friends. We were rivals really, competing against each other in all the same events. He didn't like it when I won? Well then, he was going to be pretty unhappy all summer long.

I slipped quietly out of Red's stall. I could get a ride with Beatrice, help her pack up and load the horses and set up when we got to Hits. That would be more fun anyway.

Beatrice was right. Carvin was a spoiled, conceited jerk with no social skills. And a big baby. And probably gay.

PART III
June

We were all good at our jobs. I didn't even have to wear a muzzle anymore. I gave so much of myself in the show ring I was too exhausted to stir up trouble at night in the barn. Hunter class after hunter class, it was as if I couldn't not win. There were more blue ribbons, medals, and white envelopes than we had room for in our tack trunks.

I suppose I could have not won. I could have dumped her in front of a jump like I did in the warm-up ring at our first show. I could have tried not to be so perfect so she'd stop taking me for granted. But I liked winning. I didn't want negative attention anymore. I was like one of those spoiled movie stars who get to guest DJ on the radio. I needed the applause, the cheers, the wolf-whistles. After all, that was what made Merritt happy.

And Merritt was happy—laughing all the time, hugging and kissing me in that new offhand, affectionate way of hers. It was the offhandedness that got to me. I wanted all of her.

The best I could hope for was that Beatrice would just . . . disappear. She'd disappeared before, why not again? And maybe there was something I could do to make her disappear. I was pretty industrious for a horse. I'd think of something.

"Be good," Merritt always said after she switched on my fan and turned up the radio and left for the night.

But I was beginning to think we might be better off if I was bad.

30 | RED

hated sharing her. It was partly a herd animal thing. As a colt in the field with all the other mares and colts I had to kick and bare my teeth to claim my little patch of grass or some other colt would eat it. But mostly it was the person I had to share her with.

Beatrice was always hovering around Merritt, in the way. Sometimes I thought about how to get rid of her. All right, not sometimes, all the time. I thought about it when she held my head for the braider. I thought about it when she came into my stall with a pitchfork to pick it out. I thought about it when she brought me my meals, when she filled up my water buckets, when she sprayed me with fly spray. I went after her with my teeth or my hooves whenever I had the chance, but Merritt was with her most of the time, and going after Beatrice wasn't something I particularly wanted her to see. I didn't want to be her beast of burden.

Hits on the Hudson in Saugerties, New York, was luxurious and hit-tastic. Our accommodations were first class, in a permanent barn with larger stalls than at Old Salem, perfect for a big horse like me. Because we'd be staying there for many weeks, Beatrice had installed fans inside our stall doors to keep us cool. I slept with my face in the whirring breeze, trying not to think about how much I hated her, even if she was good at her job.

31 | MERRITT

t was early, the morning of the $25,000 Hunter Stake, our last event at Hits before we went on to Saratoga. Red lay dozing in the large, comfortable stall piled deep with fresh cedar shavings, his white face near the whir and wind of the fan.

"He looks like a foal, doesn't he?" I asked Beatrice. We watched him sleep for a moment, his large nostrils flaring in and out with each breath.

"*Your nostrils open like field glasses and can smell all my fear,*" Beatrice recited, quoting Anne Sexton, I guessed.

"It's so creepy when you do that," I said, but secretly I was impressed. I could never quote anything, except maybe that stupid Ann Ware song.

Beatrice slurped the enormous iced coffee she'd picked up at McDonald's. "I can't help it if I'm better educated then you are."

It was our third week at Hits. Mr. de Rothschild had rented two condos in Saugerties very close to the show grounds—one for me and Beatrice, and one for Todd and Carvin. There was a pool and a hot tub, with gorgeous views of the Catskill Mountains on one side and the Hudson River on the other. Horse showing de Rothschild-style was like being on an endless five-star vacation, except for Beatrice's terrible eating habits.

Todd consistently roared in drunk in the wee hours of the morning and then appeared totally fine in the warm-up ring only a few hours later. Carvin continued to ignore me, which was fine, because I had Beatrice. Most of the time we were at the show grounds, but in the time we had off we'd gone to a rundown shoe store in the town of Saugerties where Beatrice had tried on every pair of white nurse's shoes they carried, pretending to deliberate and bargain with the salesman because the ones she "wanted" had a tiny scuff mark on the heel. We'd followed Carvin and Nadia Grabcheski to the movie theater—apparently she'd asked him out—and Beatrice and I sat behind them, wearing hoodies and sunglasses, trying not to giggle audibly while Beatrice periodically threw popcorn at their backs. Beatrice short-sheeted my bed and egged Carvin's car. She put fake spiders in my boots and taped a whoopee cushion to my saddle. Sometimes I got annoyed, but most of her antics made me laugh. There was never a dull moment with Beatrice around. No time to sulk, or get sad, or even watch bad TV.

"We better get him ready," I said. "We don't have much time." Carvin had beaten me to the show grounds that morning. He was already warming up.

Beatrice unlatched Red's stall door, then hesitated. "I'm not going in there while he's fast asleep like that. He'll kill me." She handed me his halter. "You wake him up."

The leather slid through my sweaty fingers and dropped to the floor. It was humid and I was tense. Carvin wanted to win this class badly, and so did I. I picked up the halter. "Come on, Red. Rise and shine."

A rumble of thunder sounded in the distance. Red startled awake. I stood to one side as he rose and shook himself.

"Hey, you," I murmured, strapping on his halter. "Let's go. We're already late."

Beatrice's phone bleeped as I led Red out of his stall. She held it to her ear.

"Jesus. You have to listen to this," she said. "It's hilarious."

"Who is it, Todd?" I asked. Another rumble of thunder sounded, louder this time. Red started, but I held his head down and clipped him into crossties.

"I'll go get his tack." Beatrice said. She handed me her phone. "You gotta hear this."

I put the phone to my ear. "Beatrice," a woman slurred in a thick French accent. "I don't know where you are. I don't even know where I am some of the time. But you are precious to me, like a pink diamond. My little girl. That is all. Kisses. Big hugs, too."

Beatrice returned from the tack room with Red's saddle and bridle and I handed back her phone. It was her mother, I guessed. And it wasn't funny, it was sad. It made me feel guilty for not missing my parents. They were in Montana now, or Utah. I couldn't keep track.

Thunder rumbled directly overhead, followed by a bright crackle of lightning.

Red rolled his eyes and pawed the cement floor of the barn aisle. Storms made him nervous. Heavy rain began to patter on the barn roof.

Beatrice walked down the aisle and stood in the wide doorway leading outside. "Hello, people? Everyone is still riding around and jumping in the warm-up ring like it's not pouring rain and their horses aren't miserable and covered in mud. Like this show has to keep happening no matter what. Seriously, I don't get it."

I reached for Red's bridle. I didn't mind the rain.

The announcer's voice rang out over the loudspeaker. "Good morning. As you can see we're experiencing some weather, but it is due to clear up later on. We will postpone this morning's classes and keep you updated as to start times once the heavy rain stops and we have raked the rings. Stay tuned. Thank you."

"Never mind," I told Red. I unclipped the crossties and led him back to his stall. "You can go back to sleep."

Rain-soaked and breathless, Carvin jogged Tang into the barn's back entrance. The mare's gray coat was so drenched she was almost black. Her legs and belly were caked in mud.

"I'll take her," Beatrice called, striding toward them with impressive efficiency. "She needs a warm bubble bath."

"I can help," I offered, happy to pitch in now that the show was postponed. The tension that had been building inside me all morning was suddenly gone. It would be fun for us all to give Tang a nice long bath.

Carvin didn't even glance up from undoing Tang's bridle. His freckled nose was running. "That's okay, I got it," he sniffed. "I'm all wet anyway."

Beatrice stopped in the aisle and put her hands on her hips. "Fine," she turned to me and rolled her eyes at Carvin's rebuff. "Want to get out of here?"

I glanced at Carvin again. He was busily removing Tang's soiled girth. His tall black riding boots, beige breeches, and navy blue riding coat were streaked with mud. Even his black helmet was spattered with it.

"Sure," I agreed. We had time to go to Starbucks or a diner. Now that I was riding so much I was always hungry. "Maybe for a little while."

I was about to ask Carvin if he wanted anything, but then thought better of it. He'd need to go back to the condo and change before the show started up again. He could grab something to eat on his way.

I dashed out into the rain to Beatrice's black Volkswagen Beetle.

"Not so fast!" she shouted behind me when I reached out

to open the passenger door. She shoved the car keys into my hand. "You're driving."

I handed them back. "But I don't drive." I knew she knew that, and I didn't have the patience for one of Beatrice's practical jokes. We were getting soaked.

"Just go get in behind the wheel," Beatrice insisted, her brown eyes huge and bright. "Hurry up, it's crazy out here."

"Fine." I ran around the car and got in the driver's seat. A plastic daisy—an accessory that came with the car—bobbed cheerfully on the dashboard despite the dreary weather.

"Okay." Beatrice shoved the keys into the ignition. Water dripped everywhere. We were both drenched. "First things first. Adjust the seat and then the mirrors."

I snorted. "Only you would decide to give me my first driving lesson in a tsunami."

Beatrice ignored me. Once she got an idea into her head it was impossible to change her mind. "You're seventeen. This is a basic life skill. Plus, everyone drives like ten miles an hour in bad weather. It's the perfect time."

I stared through the windshield at the deserted rain-soaked show grounds. "This is a basic life skill." Those were the exact words Gran-Jo had used, half-serious and half-joking, when she'd taught me to use a can opener to open up a can of chicken noodle soup, when we'd made chocolate chip cookies from the recipe on the back of the chips packet, when we'd made microwave popcorn, when she taught me how to use a corkscrew to open a bottle of wine. Teaching me how to drive was on the list. She'd promised to teach me the summer after I turned sixteen, but she'd died that spring.

My parents never taught me anything. I was just someone who lived in their house. Someone they didn't get. Gran-Jo always got me; she taught me everything.

"The seat adjuster thingy is on the left side of the seat. Your legs are longer than mine and I like to sit high like a truck driver so I can see over the dash. You probably want to lower the seat and scoot it back." Beatrice fiddled with the rearview mirror. "Look here. Do you feel like you have a clear picture through the back window?"

I looked. All I could see was a sheet of water. "I guess."

She reached down to rearrange the books on the floor beneath her feet, then pointed to a paperback. "Watch my foot. Maxine Kumin on the left is the brake." Next to it was a thick hardcover. "Anne Sexton is the gas. Put your foot on Maxine and turn the key."

I drove at a crawl around the muddy show grounds, learning how to start and stop and turn and park. After twenty minutes of me clutching the wheel at nine o'clock and three o'clock she convinced me to venture out onto the road, which was almost completely deserted.

"Left turn signal. This is the turn for Starbucks," Beatrice instructed me in a calm voice.

"Oops. Sorry. Whoa," I said frantically as I stepped harder on the gas pedal instead of the brake and we whizzed past the turn.

"Never mind. We'll hit the river soon," she said.

"Wait! What?" I demanded, imagining us plunging off a cliff to our deaths. "Should I pull over?"

"No, you're doing great," she reassured me. "There's a Dunkin' Donuts this way."

I made the turn for Dunkin' Donuts and maneuvered through the drive-thru. Ordering went fine. Paying, not so much. I rolled down my window, but I'd pulled up much too far away. Without thinking, I unlatched my seatbelt and leapt out into the rain to pay. Unfortunately I'd put the car in neutral, not park.

"Hey!" Beatrice shouted from the passenger seat as the car started to roll toward the main road. "We're still moving here!"

"Shit!" I tossed our bag of donuts and coffee through the open car door and lunged behind the wheel, shutting the door and strapping on my seatbelt while we were still in motion.

"Hello, stunt driver woman," Beatrice crowed. "That was awesome!"

By the time we reached the scenic overlook on a clifftop above the Hudson, the rain had stopped. Sun poked through the breaking clouds and a spectacular rainbow hung over the Rip Van Winkle Bridge way off to our right. We sat on the hood of the car and watched the sailboats and birds, origami shapes crisscrossing the glimmering highway of water. It was mesmerizing.

The Manhattan apartment I'd lived in my whole life had a view of the Hudson River, too, but it wasn't as pretty as this. I squeezed my jelly donut and licked the sweet pink stuff oozing out of the hole in the side.

"So where exactly did you grow up?" I asked Beatrice.

"Me?" she responded with her mouth full of chocolate glazed donut. "At first, a crap neighborhood outside Paris. My mom was a high school dropout. She did some modeling and had a portfolio and everything, but then I ruined that. She met Roman de Rothschild when I was like, not even two. He moved us to his chateau in this little village in the South of France. There were no other kids around and he was always either traveling or dealing with her problems—like hiring more staff for her and me. My mother was totally hopeless at motherhood. Eventually he left her in France and moved with me to the Hamptons and the nannies raised me."

I nodded and turned back to the river. My parents may have been selfish and self-centered and totally annoying, but at least they were around. Well, until recently anyway.

Beatrice sighed. "As soon as I was big enough I rode ponies all the time. I barely even went to school. I lied to you when I said I sucked. When I was little I was really good. I wintered in Florida and spent the summers doing the show circuit you're on now. I had a sort of business going with my dad. He would find a pony, I would show it and win everything, and then he'd sell it. I learned not to get attached. Then puberty hit and my body turned against me. The judges turned against me. That's when I started to suck."

I shot a quick glance at her. "Your body did not turn against you," I remarked.

She smiled. Her eyes were the same color as the chocolate on her teeth. I turned back to the river.

"Once I decided to quit riding my dad sent me to boarding school, but I kept getting kicked out. Switzerland. Massachusetts. England. Then Good Fences. Then Switzerland again. So I guess I didn't really grow up anywhere. I'm like, homeless." She stuffed the rest of her donut into her mouth and chewed it thoughtfully.

I was finished with my donut. The sun was warm on my face and on the hood of the car beneath my seat. I was dry now. I closed my eyes and let my head fall lightly on Beatrice's shoulder.

"Me too," I said and it felt like it was true. Yes, I did have a home, but I'd never belonged there.

We sat like that for a while. Then Beatrice's phone rang loudly from inside the car. She jumped off the hood and retrieved it from the passenger seat.

"Oops." She tapped at her screen. "It's Todd. The show started. We're kind of late."

"Shit!" I leapt off the hood and threw the keys at her. I felt like I could hear my heart pounding inside my head. All the sugar from the donut and the caffeine from the iced coffee wasn't helping. "Hurry, you drive. Come on, hurry up!"

Beatrice started the engine and backed onto the road. "Relax. We're fine."

I kicked at the books at my feet. Anne Sexton stared coldly up at me from the cover of one of them, brandishing her cigarette.

"Uh oh," Beatrice said as we rolled to a stop at the next intersection. "South along the river, or west?" She peered up at the rearview mirror. "Or maybe we went south and we need to go north?"

"Shit!" I opened the glove compartment. That's where my parents kept their maps. A sheaf of papers fell out onto my lap. Many of them featured Mr. de Rothschild's letterhead with the giant blue R. Some of them bore the name Soar Farm and Vineyard in green cursive with purple grapes nestled between the words and a single gull flying over them. There was a page with a red stamp on it that read: DRAFT COPY. DOCUMENT NOT LEGALLY BINDING.

I glimpsed the word "Thoroughbred" on one document and the name "Sweet Tang" on another.

"What are you doing?" Beatrice lunged at the sheaf of papers and stuffed them back into glove compartment. Behind us a car honked.

"What is all that?" I demanded.

"I'll tell you later," Beatrice grumbled. "Right now you really need to go on Google Maps or something and get us back to the show. I have no clue where we are."

"Fine." I stabbed at the screen on her phone to bring up the maps app and locate us via GPS. I couldn't help but blame her for making us late. It was her idea to teach me to drive, her idea to get donuts, and her idea to stop at the scenic overlook to eat them. Now we were lost. If I missed Red's start time for the Hunter Stake it would be all her fault.

• • •

When we returned to the barn, Red was already tacked up and on crossties with his halter on over his bridle. Carvin had gotten him ready for me.

I went to his head and unhooked his halter from the crossties. "Sorry, buddy. I'm here now."

Red stamped his feet one at a time—right front, left front, left hind, right hind. He swished his tail, shook his head again, and snorted explosively through his nostrils.

"Can you put fly spray on him?" I barked at Beatrice. "He hates flies. He won't go well if he's worried about flies."

Beatrice came out of the tack room with a bottle of fly spray. "Yes, dear. I'm aware."

Red pinned his ears back as Beatrice circled around him, spritzing out a cloud of potent spray.

"Watch his eyes," I warned. "Don't get it in his eyes. They're really sensitive."

Beatrice flung down the bottle and picked up a rag. "I think I know what I'm doing." She wiped the rag over Red's face and ears.

He ground his teeth and stamped his front hooves in annoyance. I fastened the chinstrap on my helmet and pulled on my black leather gloves. "Hurry," I said impatiently. "Todd said I go in five and I still have to warm up."

Beatrice handed me the reins. "All set." She put her hands on my shoulders. "Hold on." I stood very still while she tucked a few stray hairs into my helmet. She put her hands back on my shoulders and ducked under my visor to kiss me on the cheek. First near my eye, and then again on the other side of my face, sort of near my mouth. "You know you're going to win again."

I pulled away, flustered. What the hell? It felt like a real kiss, not just a friendly sort of kiss. But I was late. I didn't have time to ask her what she meant by it. God, Beatrice was infuriating.

32 | RED

Merritt backed toward me and wiped Beatrice's slobber off her cheek. "I have to go warm up." She sounded as angry as I felt.

It was about time, too. She and Beatrice had spent all morning together. And I didn't like it. I didn't like it one bit.

Cuz she don't love you like I love you.

"Hold on, I'll give you a leg." Beatrice crowded forward and Merritt backed up another step, using me for shelter.

Helter-skelter.

Beatrice didn't get the hint. She took another step toward me. I'd had just about enough of her. I exploded, lunging forward and snapping my teeth. I caught the soft pale skin of her upper arm.

"Hey! Fuck you, horse!" Beatrice shouted and elbowed me hard in the muzzle. I sat back on my hind legs, eyes rolling, snorting in anger, surprise, and pain. She didn't mess around when she lashed out. She wanted it to hurt.

Merritt whirled around to quiet me, her hands on my neck. "Hey, hey. You're all right. She didn't mean to hurt you."

"Oh yes I did." She showed Merritt the angry red circle on her upper arm. "Look at what he did to me."

"You scared him!" Merritt was trembling. "What is wrong with you?" she demanded. "I know he can be sort of a jerk, but I would really appreciate it if you wouldn't abuse my horse."

Beatrice glared at her and rubbed her arm. "He's not your horse."

"Whatever," Merritt snapped. She took the reins and led me outside to the mounting block.

As we jogged through the mud to the warm-up ring there was a slight twinge in my hock. It wasn't much, just a little stiffness, but it gave me an idea. If I went lame now and we couldn't show, Merritt would be furious with Beatrice, so furious she might even send her away—for good.

Whoops, there it is.

"Earth to Merritt!" Todd shouted from the center of the warm-up ring where he stood at Tang's head. The gray mare was sweaty and winded.

Carvin squinted at me from her back as I jogged by. "Does he look off to you?" he asked Todd. Oh yeah. Tell him something good.

"Keep trotting," Todd instructed Merritt. He took off his cowboy hat and squatted down in the mud. "Change direction. Post on the wrong diagonal."

"He's favoring his left hind, isn't he?" Merritt asked as I trotted past them once more.

"Looks like it," Carvin agreed.

"Dammit," Todd said.

Merritt halted me in front of them and Todd bent down to feel my hind leg.

"It's a little hot. Take him back and ask Beatrice to hose it for a good ten minutes, then rub it with alcohol before she wraps. He has to ship to Saratoga tonight. I'm sure he'll be okay in a couple of days."

I waited for Merritt to tell him that my injury was all Beatrice's fault, but Merritt didn't say anything. She just slid off my back and pulled the reins over my head. Her whole body was shaking. She was so angry at Beatrice she couldn't speak, not even to me. Time to tell Jane to go her own way because she's playing a game she just can't win.

33 | MERRITT

Todd turned back to Carvin and Tang. "You're still showing, kid. Keep her moving. I don't want her to get stiff."

Carvin glanced at me. "What a bummer. Sorry, Merritt," he murmured as he gathered up his reins. He nudged Tang into a trot. The mare's coat was spotless now. Her gray dapples gleamed prettily in the summer sunshine. The humidity was all gone and the air felt cool and fresh after the rain. It was perfect horse show weather. But I wouldn't be riding in this horse show anymore, thanks to Beatrice.

"Sure you're sorry," I fumed, not loud enough for Carvin to hear.

Todd raised the rails on the practice jump. "Take her over the oxer on an angle and then roll back and do it the other way," he called out to Carvin.

I led Red through the mud, back to the barn. I hated that Carvin and Tang were probably going to win today. And I hated myself for being such a bad sport. It was just one hunter stake. There would be others.

There was litter in the mud-caked grass. The row of Porta-Johns gave off an unbelievable stench. Someone's Jack Russell terrier would not stop yapping. I thought I heard Ann Ware's song somewhere off in the distance. *"Let's walk out of the*

S-A-T. All those losers can fill in their a, b, c, d, e none of the above, thanks, it's not for me . . ."

"Did Carvin go yet?" someone shrieked at me. "I promised him I'd watch him go!"

Nadia Grabcheski hurried past in her sneakers and jodhpurs. Now that school was out she and Amora were staying at Nadia's summer home in Rhinebeck to be closer to the shows. I'd tried to avoid them, but they were unavoidable.

Back in Red's stall, I hurriedly removed his tack. "Poor guy." I rubbed his nose and looked around for Beatrice. "I'm sorry it hurts."

Beatrice stomped out of the tack room with her ear buds in her ears and her e-cigarette dangling from her lips. "What's up? I was about to come out and watch you guys go."

I glared at her. This was all her fault. I should have told Mr. de Rothschild to fire her when I'd spoken to him on the phone back at Old Salem. She wasn't a good groom. She was unreliable and unpredictable and I didn't want her around anymore.

"He's lame," I spat. "Thanks to you." I yanked off my helmet and tossed it in the aisle. The piece of blue ribbon tied inside it was limp and stained with perspiration.

Beatrice tucked her e-cigarette into her back pocket and pulled out her ear buds. "Oh no. Merritt, I'm so sorry." She squatted down to run her hands over Red's legs. "I didn't think—"

"No," I snapped, cutting her off. "You didn't. Todd wants the leg hosed. It's the left hind. And he said to put alcohol under his wraps."

"Of course." Beatrice began to unbuckle Red's bridle. "I'll take care of him. You go watch Carvin. I hope he falls off."

I stared at her with my mouth open, my fists clenched at my sides. She really didn't get it. She didn't get anything. No wonder her father was always shipping her off to different boarding schools. She was impossible to deal with. Totally impossible. "You always have to push things one step too far," I hissed.

Red's head went up and his ears flicked back, startled by my angry tone of voice.

Beatrice didn't respond. She pulled off the saddle, clipped a lead line onto Red's halter, and undid the crossties. Then she led him down the aisle toward the wash stall. "I'm going to hose his leg and give him a warm bath and blow-dry so he's all nice and clean for Saratoga," she called with her back to me.

"He might not be sound for Saratoga, thanks to you," I replied even though she was too far away to hear. I unbuttoned my hot wool jacket, tossed it on top of my helmet, and stalked away to the show ring.

In the short time I'd been inside the barn the sky had clouded over once more and the air had thickened.

"Folks, if we can keep it moving it looks like we'll have just enough time to finish up here before it rains again," the announcer called over the loudspeaker. "Riders please be ready when your number is called."

Todd's cowboy hat flew up into the air as I drew close to the hunter ring. Carvin and Tang had just won the class. Of course they had. Nadia Grabcheski jumped up and down near the in-gate, squealing and clapping her hands. I stood at the rail as Carvin jogged the pretty gray mare back into the ring to accept the blue ribbon. The jelly donut swam queasily in my stomach.

Carvin led Tang out of the ring and handed Todd the prize check.

"I'll mail it to your parents from Saratoga," Todd said, tucking the white envelope into the back of his Levis. "I'm going to head up there now. Check into the hotel, pick up your numbers from the show office. Nice job today. You guys need anything?" he asked, addressing us both.

I shook my head, wondering if I should complain about Beatrice to Todd. Or maybe I should call Mr. de Rothschild.

"I'll check on Red once he gets there, too," Todd assured me.

"See you up there," Carvin called.

I watched Todd's cowboy hat bob away toward the parking lot beneath the ever-darkening sky, the white envelope flapping from the back pocket of his jeans.

Carvin pulled off his helmet and swiped the sleeve of his hunt coat across his sweaty brow, his green eyes fixed on the ground. He didn't look happy about winning. He didn't look happy at all. Maybe he was in a fight with his mommy.

"Way to go, Carvin!" Nadia appeared at his side, all shiny blonde hair and lip gloss. She rubbed Tang's neck with her usual annoying zeal. "You were so amazing!" she gushed.

"Thanks," Carvin said without looking up. He came around to Tang's left side, near where I was standing, and loosened the girth. Then he turned around to face me. "Merritt, do you want to walk with Tang and me while I cool her off?"

Was he actually speaking to me now?

"Sure," I agreed. Any excuse to stay out of the barn and away from Beatrice for as long as possible.

"See you at Saratoga, Carvin," Nadia called after us.

We walked in silence down the well-trampled path that skirted the parking lot. The grounds were even more chaotic and crowded now as grooms and trainers hurried to wrap and load their ponies and horses before the rain returned.

"Hey, would you mind giving me a ride to Saratoga?" I asked.

"Of course," Carvin agreed with a smile. "As long as you don't mind stopping at Whole Foods on the way."

34 | RED

Beatrice led me into the wash stall and dropped the lead rope while she adjusted the hose. That may have been careless of her, but it was not unusual. Grooms rarely use crossties in the wash stall. Most show horses are so well trained they'll stand still for a bath or to have their legs hosed down with cold water without being tied up. There's nothing more relaxing or refreshing on a hot day than a cool bath. Most horses would stand still and enjoy it. But I was not most horses.

My rear end faced the entrance to the wash stall. Just outside it, on the cement floor of the barn aisle, was one of those horse vacuum cleaners that the grooms used to vacuum our coats or to blow dry us by attaching the vacuum hose to the vent so that it blew air out instead of sucking it in.

I stood quietly while Beatrice ran cold water over my "sore" leg, the left hind. Her headphones were in her ears and she was gnawing on her fake cigarette. My ears were the only thing that moved, flicking back and forth, reading the signs. I didn't have a plan, but I had her alone and I wanted to take advantage of it.

From out of the phone in her back pocket came the repetitive beats of a French hip-hop song. That was her favorite kind of music, so I hated it. I took a tiny, almost imperceptible step backwards, and then another one. I kept backing up until I could feel the hard, cold coil of the hose against the back of my right hind hoof. I backed up once more so that I was stepping directly on the hose. The water belched and sucked and then stopped flowing all together. I could feel the surge of it beneath my hoof.

"Hey!" Beatrice shouted. The fake cigarette fell out of her mouth. At the same time a bolt of lightning flashed and a clap of thunder sounded, so close and so loud as to seem like it was coming from within the barn. I bolted forward, toward the back of the wash stall, then spun around and jigged in place, assessing the situation.

Beatrice was soaking wet now, having taken the full force of the water gushing from the hose when I shot forward. The overhead light in the wash stall had gone out. The air smelled smoky and electric. Sparks shot out of the electrical outlet where the vacuum cleaner was plugged in. She bent down and picked up the gushing hose. Why she picked up the hose first and not my lead rope, I don't know. The lead rope hung down from my halter and dangled on the cement floor of the wash stall so that I was still free to move around as I pleased.

Water pooled and circled toward the drain. Beatrice swiped at the lead rope, but I swung my head to the side, trailing it just out of reach. She lunged at it once more and I swung away again. She was close to the sparking electrical outlet now, the hose still spouting water in her hand. I knew about the dangers of electricity from the fence in my paddock at Good Fences. I knew the power of an electric current and what it could do to a horse. I had some idea of what it could do to something much smaller.

"Cut it out, Red," Beatrice growled at me.

Another flash of lightning, another clap of thunder. Ever since my first race lightning had scared me. I felt it in my bad eye, in my shoulder, and in the part of my jaw that had been hurt in the race. I reared up in response, whinnying and lashing the

air with my front hooves. I was bad to the bone, and Beatrice
was in my way.

What happened next happened very quickly.

Beatrice staggered backwards out of the wash stall, away
from my lashing hooves, and tripped over the vacuum cleaner.
The spouting hose in her hand sprayed the sparking electrical
outlet with water and puddled water at her feet. I heard a sizzle
and she fell. My nostrils flared with the odor of singed hair.

Beatrice didn't get up.

I cowered in the back of the wash stall, waiting for Merritt.
I was bad, so bad.

Would she still love me after what I'd done?

35 | MERRITT

The storm began again while Carvin was putting Tang back in her stall. I waited in the barn aisle while he threw a flysheet over her and checked her water buckets. Beatrice would give her a bath and wrap her when she was done with Red.

Carvin latched Tang's stall door. "Ready? Come on. Let's get out of here." Grinning playfully, he grabbed my arm and pulled me toward the barn entrance. It was pouring. We paused in the doorway, preparing to sprint.

Rain pelted our faces and thunder boomed overhead as we dashed across the slick grass from the barn to his car. I splashed through the puddles, laughing. We were both filthy with mud and completely soaked.

This time I was definitely not driving. I dove into the passenger seat and slammed the door. My clothes and hair were dripping wet. "This is crazy," I gasped giddily.

Carvin flung his bag in the backseat and turned the key in the ignition.

"Oh gosh, sorry." He reached across my legs to gather up the Clif Bar wrappers and empty juice boxes littering the floor at my feet. One by one he tossed them behind us. Then he reached up and pulled out my seatbelt. I could feel his warm breath on my wet cheek. "There," he said, snapping the buckle into place. "It catches sometimes."

"Thanks," I murmured, heat creeping up my neck to my hairline.

Carvin grinned at me. "All set?"

I nodded, furiously trying to remind myself that he was gay. He rested his free arm on the back of my seat and began to back up. A motorcade of ambulances and fire trucks trundled in behind us, blocking our way, their flashing lights and sirens somehow muted by the rain.

"Something must've happened," Carvin observed, his eyes on the rearview mirror. "I hope no one got hurt."

Saratoga Springs was only an hour away, or should have been. Traffic was slow because of the storm, and unlike Todd or Beatrice, Carvin was a cautious driver. I wanted to complain about Beatrice, but decided to let Carvin concentrate on driving in peace.

We arrived at the hotel and checked into our rooms. It was a luxurious hotel. Mr. de Rothschild would be joining us there, so of course he'd made sure to book the best. I took a long hot shower and wrapped myself in one of the white hotel bathrobes. Then I dialed the front desk to find out which room Todd was in. I wanted to know if Red had arrived and if he'd had a chance to check on him.

Todd didn't answer.

I watched the last half of the movie *Avatar*, just because it happened to be on TV. I called the front desk again and asked for Beatrice's room number. It was next door. I knocked on the door. No answer. I called Carvin's room, but the phone was busy. A little while later there was a knock on my door. I opened it.

Carvin stood in front of me looking pale and shaken.

Something was wrong. He walked into the room, sat down on the bed, and stared at his knees.

"What?" I demanded. "Oh my God, what?"

He looked up. "I just got off the phone with Mr. de Rothschild's assistant," he explained hoarsely. "Remember all those fire trucks and ambulances?"

I nodded.

"There was an accident. Two accidents. One at the show and one on the road. Mr. de Rothschild is on his way to Saugerties now, by helicopter."

I felt sick. It was Red. Something had happened to Red. I hadn't even checked on him before I left, still too annoyed with Beatrice to risk bumping into her again. But why hadn't she called me? If it was anything serious she knew I'd want to know.

"Please, just tell me what happened," I begged.

Carvin stared straight ahead. "Beatrice is dead. She was electrocuted in the wash stall. And Todd has been arrested."

What he said didn't register. I was still convinced that something had happened to Red. "What about the horses?"

Carvin blinked at me. "The horses are fine. They're being shipped here now. Mr. de Rothschild wants me to drive back down to Hits with you to pick up Beatrice's car. He wants you to drive it here."

"Her car?" I repeated stupidly. "But I don't have my license. I barely even know how to drive."

"You were driving this morning." His voice was slightly accusing. "Anyway, I don't think Mr. de Rothschild cares. I asked if we could do anything and that's what his assistant said. You can follow me. I'll take the back roads and I promise to go slow."

"Now?" I gasped. I could hardly breathe, let alone drive somewhere.

"No, tomorrow morning so you don't have to drive in the dark. Mr. de Rothschild will meet us here when we get back and tell us what to do." Carvin stood up. "I'm sorry," he said woodenly. "I have to go now. In case someone calls my room."

As soon as he closed the door, I fell onto my bed and hugged my knees to my chest. Beatrice was dead. She was the only friend I'd had since Gran-Jo. We'd argued and then she died. Just like Gran-Jo and I had argued before she died. I was like a girl in a horror movie. When I got angry, the people I cared about died.

I woke up where I'd fallen on the bed, still wearing the white hotel bathrobe. Sunlight streamed into the room. Everything was pleasant and bright, which was all wrong. Beatrice was dead. Todd was in jail. I picked at the encrusted drool on my cheek and stared at the rose-patterned wallpaper until Carvin knocked on my door.

"We should go soon," he called. "Are you ready?"

It was only eighty miles to Hits from Saratoga Springs. It took a little over an hour to get there with Carvin in his car. But the return trip was arduous and awful. Once again I found myself behind the wheel of Beatrice's black Volkswagen Beetle. The plastic daisy bobbed on the dashboard as I gripped the steering wheel with white knuckles, my eyes fixed on the taillights of Carvin's car. Every time someone approached from the other direction, I nearly swerved off the road. The upholstery smelled like Beatrice—a mix of French fries and milky iced coffee. Anne Sexton's haunting image stared up at me from the passenger-side floor, flaunting her long bare arms and glamorous cigarette.

No, Beatrice didn't look anything like her. Beatrice was Beatrice, totally unique. And she was my friend. She drove me crazy, but I still cared about her. Not that I ever told her that. And now she was dead.

By the time I pulled into the hotel parking lot in Saratoga Springs I was shaking all over, a permanent lump stuck in my throat. I couldn't even get out of the car. I just put it in Park and sat there with the engine still running.

Carvin knocked on the window. I rolled it down.

"You did it. You can get out now."

I stared straight ahead.

Carvin reached carefully across me, turned off the ignition, and removed the keys. Then he opened the door and undid my seatbelt. His freckled hand gripped my shoulder. "Hey, everything's going to be okay. Come on, let's go inside."

He took my hand and helped me out of the car. On any other day I might have focused on his hand, on his nearness. I might have gotten excited about how nice he was being to me. But he was a liar. Everything was not going to be okay. And right now all I could think about was whether or not the hotel had a bar and if so how stringent they were about checking IDs. I dropped his hand and headed for the entrance.

"I really am so sorry about Beatrice," Carvin said as he followed me inside. "You guys were close."

There was a sign over a doorway across the lobby: TAVERN. I walked toward it, past the reception desk, and into the cool, dark, wood-paneled room. It was one o'clock in the afternoon. The place was completely empty. The bartender looked like he'd been keeping bar for over a century.

"What can I get you?" he asked.

"I'll have an Old-Fashioned," I said without hesitation and took at seat on a swiveling barstool.

Carvin entered the bar and looked around. He sat down on the stool next to mine and cleared his throat. The bartender set my drink down and raised his bushy white eyebrows, waiting for Carvin to order.

"Um. Do you have apple juice?"

Carvin swiveled around to face me. I looked down at my drink.

"I'm sorry," he said again. "You know if there's anything I can do, please just ask me." His hand wavered in the air near my ear, like he wanted to touch my hair or pat me on the shoulder. Then he let it drop. "I'd be happy to help with . . . anything."

I sipped my drink in silence. The ice-cold bourbon was a familiar medicine. It tasted awful, but it was just what I needed, what I deserved. Carvin nursed his juice. I knew he was waiting for me to say something. Instead, I finished my drink and signaled the bartender for another.

Carvin pushed away his glass. "I guess we should talk about Todd. He stole my prize money from yesterday. To buy drugs. He's been stealing all our checks. I'd be surprised if any of them were mailed home."

So that's why he'd been arrested. I found it hard to care. My friend had died and it was my fault. I didn't want to talk to Carvin. I didn't want to talk to anyone. I just wanted to be alone.

"If we're going to keep showing we're going to need a new trainer," Carvin persisted. "I'm sure Mr. de Rothschild—"

"Keep showing?" I demanded. What was wrong with him? Beatrice was dead. Red was lame. Todd was in jail. It was over, all of it. Time to leave. Not that I had anywhere to go. I didn't even know where my parents were.

Carvin turned away from me and toyed with the ice in his glass. "Yeah, I guess. I mean these are some pretty big shows coming up. And they're not our horses. It's why we're here."

I took another swig of my drink. The ancient bartender had made the second one much too weak. He was nowhere in sight. I knelt on my barstool, grabbed the bottle of bourbon from behind the bar, and topped off my glass.

"It's why *you're* here," I said. "I'm done."

Carvin swiveled toward me again. He put his hand on my back, up high near my shoulder blades, and left it there. I guess he was trying to comfort me. I stayed facing the bar, not looking at him. I didn't understand why he was being so nice. We barely knew each other. I thought of telling him that if he valued his life he'd better stay away from me, but explaining why would require a lot of energy and tears. It would involve raving like a lunatic. Instead I just stared straight ahead and sipped my drink, which was now extremely strong.

"If you need a break, to take some time to think or whatever, now is the perfect time," Carvin said quietly, his hand still on my back. "Just like you said, Red is off. So let him hang out during this show and get better while you rest. Then we'll go back to Hits with whatever trainer Mr. de Rothschild has found for us and you can start over again. Or, if you want, I can try to ride him for a while until you're feeling up to it."

I snorted. "Go ahead. Good luck."

Carvin dropped his hand and swiveled back to face the bar again.

There. I'd done it. He'd stop trying to be friends now.

"Hey guys!"

I spat a bourbon-soaked ice cube back into my glass. Nadia Grabcheski—queen of perfect timing—sauntered into the tavern from the lobby. She wedged a space for herself against the bar between Carvin and me and stood on tiptoe in her frayed denim short-shorts, pretending to check out the liquor.

"Oh, they have Absolut Coco. I love Absolut Coco!" She turned to me and lowered her voice. "So you know that girl Beatrice? I heard she tried it before. Is that true?"

I glared at her, my eyes burning holes in her lacy white tank top. "Tried what before?"

"Suicide," Nadia clarified lightly, as if we were talking about shopping or the weather. "This time it just . . . I don't know . . . worked?"

Carvin scooted his stool back to give us more room. "Careful Nadia. Better not talk about something you don't know shit about. It was an accident. Enough said."

Nadia batted her clueless eyelashes at him. "I'm just saying I heard it might not have been." She pulled Carvin's glass toward her and took a sip. "I guess we'll never know." She made a face. "Ew. Is that apple juice?"

I knocked back the last of my drink in silent fury. I hadn't eaten anything all day. My stomach roiled and churned. The Beast was back.

"I have to go," I croaked. "Tell him to charge the drinks to my room."

I would never have dared to charge drinks to Mr. de Rothschild's credit card before, but I wanted to prove to him that I didn't deserve to ride Red ever again. I was done. For good.

"Hey, wait up," Carvin called as I staggered off my barstool. "I'll walk you to your room."

"No, no, I'm fine," I called without turning around. "Please, just stay here and get the check."

"She's a mess," I heard Nadia say. "Like, seriously disturbed."

"No one asked for your opinion, Nadia," Carvin snapped.

But she's right, I thought as I hurried out of the bar.

•

36 | RED

I f I were to pick a song to illustrate exactly how I felt, it would be "Rudderless," or "She's Not There," or "Horse with No Name."

I used to feel like this all the time. Like life was a state of limbo in which nothing really mattered. I would sleep so hard and so long on the floor of my stall I couldn't tell if it was tomorrow or yesterday. I was always waiting for something to happen, and I'd been waiting forever.

That's how I felt before I met Merritt.

Horses are not simple companionable creatures like cats or dogs, but we do need companionship. We're herd animals. We need to belong.

Before I met Merritt I had no one.

With Merritt I was truly happy. Until I messed everything up.

I never meant to hurt Beatrice. Not really and truly. All right, there's no point in lying. I did want to hurt her sometimes. Fine, all the time. Jealousy will do that to you. I wanted to bite and kick her. But mostly, I just wanted her to go away. To disappear. I never planned on killing her. I didn't have a plan. I just saw the window of opportunity and leapt through it. It just *happened*. The same way Merritt and I happened. It was an accident. Merritt and I were the happier accident. The other thing was an unhappy accident, a miserable one. But accidents do happen. They always will.

I admit the moment Beatrice fell in the wash stall and didn't get up, I was elated, just for a fraction of a second. I was so big and so powerful and lightning struck at just exactly the right time. It was so easy. Then the horror of it hit me and I became afraid. Beatrice was dead and it was my fault.

Then Merritt didn't come. And didn't come. And there wasn't any sunshine when she was gone.

Where was she? Two days had passed since the storm, since the end of Beatrice, since Tang and I were shipped to this new horse show. Two days and no Merritt. This was definitely *not* what I wanted. With Beatrice gone we should have been together all the time.

Without Merritt I wasn't myself, at least, not my best self. I was my *old* self. I hated everyone and everything. My head hung pathetically. I refused to touch my grain. When they trotted me out I limped worse than ever. The vet stuck a thermometer up my rear end, shone a bright light into my eyes and ears, took blood and x-rays. The farrier removed my shoes, trimmed and filed my hooves, then put on lighter shoes lined with soft foam pads. They could try, but I needed Merritt. No one else could fix me.

I watched Carvin bring out Tang, all spruced up and braided. A white-haired groom from another barn had done the braiding and sprucing. He tuned my radio to the classical station so we could listen to the New York Philharmonic perform *Don Quixote* by Ludwig Minkus, in its entirety. Dramatic strings mimicked the turning of windmills, the loss of sense. It was enough to drive anyone insane, but I had already lost it.

I paced the four walls and chewed on the door. Over the frenzied cacophony I could hear the announcer summoning riders and horses and calling out time faults and scores. Flies landed on my eyelids, but I didn't bother to shake them off.

Someone threw me a few flakes of hay and I ate them slowly, one strand at a time, chewing and chewing. Pacing and chewing.

Carvin returned to give Tang a drink and change her saddle pad. I watched without seeing. Casually he reached into my stall and scratched my muzzle. I didn't respond. Someone threw me more hay and I ignored it.

Carvin and Tang disappeared again. Minutes, maybe hours later, they returned. Tang was sweaty. A giant blue ribbon was pinned to her bridle.

"We won, buddy," Carvin told me. "Tang was flawless."

As if I cared.

That night they strapped on my muzzle again. I dreamt Merritt was jumping, but not with me. She was back in Florida, riding other horses. I awoke in a panic, eager to demonstrate that I was no longer lame. Maybe Merritt hadn't come because she thought she couldn't ride me.

The next morning when Carvin came, I nickered at him, pawed at my stall door, and demanded his attention. He fed me carrots and watched me dance in place. *Let me out*, I told him with my whole body. *I'm fine. I'm more than fine.* He opened my door, took off my muzzle, and led me out of the barn to graze.

"Bet you miss her, too, huh?" he said as he watched me crop a patch of grass with all the energy of a completely not-sick horse.

I wanted to show him that nothing hurt. I was good to go. Get on up! I pranced and danced and snorted and flexed my neck. See? No limp, nothing wrong at all. I could canter all day and night and jump mountains.

"*Whoa.*" Carvin shortened the lead shank and patted my

neck, paying no attention at all to my fancy footwork. "She'll be back soon," he said. "She just needs some time."

But I want her to want me. I need her to need me.

I nipped at his shirt and butted his chest. *Tell her*, I urged him silently. *Tell her.*

37 | MERRIT

I t was the second day of the Saratoga Classic, but I wasn't in Saratoga Springs. I was back home in New York. The details were fuzzy after more bourbon from the mini bar, but I'd ignored Carvin's knocks on my door and numerous phone calls, passed out, and slept a solid twelve hours.

When I woke up the next afternoon, I took a cab from our luxurious hotel to the Saratoga Springs train station, hopped on a New York City-bound local train, and then took another cab from Penn Station back to the apartment. I used Mr. de Rothschild's credit card for everything, including the bar tab on the train.

It was after eight in the evening when I arrived.

"We weren't expecting you," Salvador, the doorman, greeted me as he pulled open the lobby door. "I've been misting the ferns and bringing in the mail. Newspapers are in a pile just inside the door."

No one was home. The apartment was like an oven. The blinds were down and the kitchen counter was covered in a film of dust. I pulled up the blinds. Our Hudson River view was ablaze with streaks of pink. The last time I'd looked at the river was with Beatrice, two days ago, eating donuts on the hood of her car.

I stood at the window for a long time, watching the sun disappear behind New Jersey, wondering what to do now that I was home and completely alone.

Beneath the window in the dining area were two open cardboard boxes filled with bottles of wine—a red and a white—with the de Rothschild logo on them. Gifts from the de Rothschild vineyard on Long Island.

The white wine had a screw top. The label said "Serve Chilled," but I filled up a coffee mug with it anyway and sat down at the dusty kitchen table with the bottle and the mug and the home telephone. I dialed mom's number.

It rang six times followed by buzzing static.

"Hello, this is Susan. Who is this?" The connection was terrible. My mother's voice was broken, the syllables cut off at the ends.

"This is your daughter. Remember me?"

"Merritt? I'm sorry I can't hear you very well. Where are you, Lake Placid? Mr. de Rothschild's assistant emailed me an itinerary for all your shows this summer, but I don't have Internet right now."

"Actually I'm back at home. I just got here. Where are you?"

"Home? Why are you home? We're in Kulusuk. Eastern Greenland. At a training kennel for sled dogs. We came here from Alaska. I'm even thinking about fostering a dog or two. Wouldn't that be fun? Sled dogs in Manhattan! Oh, here's your dad. I'll put us on speaker."

More static, jostling, and thumping. I held the phone away from my ear and took another gulp of warm white wine.

"Hello, daughter!" My dad's voice was beyond loud. "Alaska was stupendous. Greenland is a trip. How are you? How is that magnificent horse?"

"She's at home. Riverside Drive." My mom's hushed tones crackled sharply in the background. "Did we leave out any wine?"

"Keep out of the wine!" Dad boomed into the phone.

"Michael, this is serious."

"Whoops," I said and took another gulp.

"Why are you home?" Mom demanded. "Is someone there with you? Mr. de Rothschild's daughter? What's her name?"

"Red is lame. Beatrice is dead. Todd's in jail."

The line crackled and wavered.

"What? We didn't hear anything." Dad's voice was more cautious now.

"If something was wrong I'm sure Mr. de Rothschild would have contacted us," Mom agreed.

They didn't believe me. And maybe they were right, maybe I'd hallucinated the whole thing.

"I drove a car. I drove it all the way from Saugerties to Saratoga Springs." As soon as I said it I realized it sounded like even more of a fabrication.

"Whose car? You don't have your license. You don't even know how to drive." Mom was using her impatient voice now.

"Beatrice taught me. It was her car. She was my friend. We had a fight. Then she got electrocuted in the wash stall. It's possible she did it on purpose. I don't think so though."

There was another crackly silence and the sound of them whispering sharply to each other. I heard Mom say the words "relapse" and "Good Fences."

I refilled my mug as I waited for them to respond.

"Who's in charge over there?" Dad demanded. "I'd like to speak to the person in charge."

"Um. Me, I guess? Since I'm the only one here?"

More static and jostling. "Give me the phone, Michael," Mom commanded sharply. "Hello? Merritt?" I was no longer on speaker.

"I'm still here." I stood up and opened the flaps on the box of red wine. I pulled out a bottle of red zinfandel with the giant unmistakable *R* on the label.

"You stay right there. Sit tight," Mom said, now using her bossy, reassuring voice. "We'll call you back when we have a plan in place."

"Okay." I had a lot of wine to get through and no plans to be anywhere. I put the bottle of zinfandel on the kitchen counter and rooted around in the drawers for a corkscrew.

"Merritt? Merritt, are you still there?" Mom demanded over the crackling line. "I have to go. It's feeding time. The dogs eat raw reindeer." She must have thought I'd want to know that. "I'm going to make a few calls. Help is on the way. You just stay put."

"Sounds good. Bye," I said, and hung up.

I wished I'd never called. I just wanted to hole up in my room and stare at the television without anyone there to bother me.

After maiming the cork with both our corkscrews, I found a menu for Hunan Delight and ordered spicy sesame noodles, shrimp fried rice, and General Tso's scallops, using the de Rothschild credit card.

Waiting for the food, I sorted through the pile of mail on the kitchen counter, looking for envelopes from Todd with my prize checks in them. There were only two, one with two checks for $150 and another with a solitary check for $175. I'd won almost $7,000 so far. I knew it was wrong for Todd to have taken it, but I didn't really mind. I wasn't in it for the money.

I wasn't in it at all.

The food came. I pulled out the container of sesame noodles and poked the congealed clump with a pair of chopsticks. They looked and smelled terrible.

I left the rest of the food in the bag on the counter, picked up my mug of red wine, and wandered into my room.

The remote was in its spot on the bedside table. I clicked on the TV and flopped down on my bed. Nearly every channel was running marathons of shows that had aired over the winter. That was fine with me. I could catch up on *Survivor*.

My old cell phone lay on my desk, unplugged and uncharged. I got up, found the charger, and plugged it in. Maybe I'd text Ann Ware and we could go to a movie or something tomorrow. I could help her write her next hit song, or we could lie out and get suntans in Riverside Park like we used to do in seventh grade. My tan needed evening out. Only the lower half of my face and the top of my neck were brown. The rest of me was winter pale.

I lay down on my bed again, indulging in the softness of my lavender-colored comforter and the smell of the laundry soap they used at the drop-off place on Broadway.

This season of *Survivor* was called "Blood vs. Blood" because the teams were made up of family members. My über-fit parents would totally rule on *Survivor*. They'd be the last ones standing. But first they'd have to form an alliance and get me voted off. I'd only bring them down. Or I'd get mad and people would die. No one was supposed to actually die on *Survivor*.

I watched three episodes back-to-back without moving from my bed. The fourth was just beginning when my cell phone bleeped three times in quick succession. I got up and looked at the screen.

They were text messages from Ann Ware, sent nine months ago, the day I'd walked out of the SAT and left my phone—this phone—on the New Haven line train. It was the first time my phone had been charged since. I wasn't allowed a phone at Good Fences and Mr. de Rothschild had supplied me with a new one in Florida that he paid for and I rarely used.

Hey. Are u ok?

I talked to ur mom.

The SAT stank. U were smart to leave.

I began to reply, smiling as I typed, thinking how surprised Ann would be to hear from me after all these months.

hey Ann, its Merritt. long time no hear.

i'm back at home. r u around??

I hit SEND. Seconds later my phone beeped as it received Ann's reply.

Thank you for contacting Ann Ware.

For more information about her upcoming

debut album and tour please contact

Jimi Jones at Hit! Management.

jimij@hit!management.co.uk

or check out her fan site at annwarefan.com

Thank you. You know Ann loves you. xxoo

Of course Ann had a manager now, a British one. She probably had numerous cell phones and a stylist and an assistant to update her social media. I went over to Instagram and a stream of pictures appeared. At the top was Amora Wells's most recent post from Saratoga. It was a picture of Carvin and Tang, posing with their medal and blue ribbon from today's equitation class.

Guess who's going to win the finals? Amora had written beneath the picture, along with a flurry of hearts and air-kissing smiley faces.

Carvin wasn't smiling though. In fact, he looked pretty grim.

I flopped down on my bed again and turned up the sound on the TV, staring at the screen without actually seeing it.

What was Red doing right now? I wondered. Would Carvin feed him carrots? Who was he training with now that Todd was gone? Not that I cared. But someone should be feeding Red carrots.

• • •

The next morning I lay in a bathtub full of cold water, trying to cool off. I kept my eyes closed so I wouldn't have to look at my pale skinny legs, my ragged toenails, my muscular arms, my calloused hands and dirty fingernails. Somehow in the course of the year my body had transformed from Upper East Side schoolgirl to Depression-era farmhand.

The trill of the downstairs buzzer interrupted my damp trance. It rang and rang. I lay there, listening to it, as though it were a signal for other people, the kind of people who moved and functioned. Then the doorbell rang. I stayed where I was, eyes closed. Then I heard the apartment door open and a familiar bossy voice call my name.

"Merritt, where are you, honey?"

I sat up with a splash. It was Kami. "Dr." Kami, from Good Fences.

"Merritt, are you awake?"

"Merritt?" Kami was outside the bathroom door now. Her voice was still bossy, but there was a note of fear in it, too. "Please answer me."

I got out of the tub and put on my mother's weird purple stretchy zip-up robe. I opened the bathroom door.

"Hi," Kami greeted me, dressed in her favorite warm weather uniform of pleated khaki shorts and pink Crocs. She seemed relieved to have found me alive. "How're you doing? You okay?"

I fiddled with the zipper on my mother's robe. "Why are you here?"

"Your parents called. I'm taking you back to Good Fences," she said firmly.

I folded my arms across my chest. "What about Red?"

Kami shook her head. "Red is in Saratoga. I don't know the details, but I imagine they're going to keep showing him."

A mean little smile crossed my lips. *Good luck with that*, I thought.

Kami pushed her glasses up on her head and frowned at me. "Mr. de Rothschild asked me to fix you up quick so you could get back to riding again." She sighed and shook her head, as if she thought that was a terrible idea.

I stared evenly back at her, guessing that this was some sort of Dr. Kami Challenge. If she told me I was hopeless then I'd do my best to prove her wrong. I'd go back to Good Fences and share myself silly and feel wonderful and empowered afterwards and in no time at all I'd be back with Red, winning blue ribbons and smiling for the camera.

"Beatrice is dead," I told her. "We had a fight and now she's dead."

Kami nodded sympathetically and opened her arms, inviting me in for a hug. I stood where I was, arms crossed, glaring at her. I didn't have any choice about going back to Good Fences— she wasn't going to leave without me—but I could choose not to hug her.

She dropped her arms and stuffed her hands into the puffy pockets of her pleated shorts. "Why don't you go get dressed and get a bag ready? I'm double-parked downstairs."

38 | RED

Days passed and still no Merritt. Days that felt like weeks. Somehow by getting rid of Beatrice I inadvertently got rid of Merritt, too. This morning Carvin led me out of my stall just after sunrise, groomed me quickly, and put on my tack. He led me to the indoor ring where one of the petite blondes Merritt hated waited beside a weather-beaten woman with a smoker's cough who I'd seen at other shows.

What happened to Todd? I wondered. Then again, nothing was the same anymore.

"Just take it slow, Amora," Carvin advised. He gave the blonde a leg-up into the saddle. He sounded nervous, like her riding me was not his favorite idea. It wasn't my favorite idea either.

Amora was compact—her legs barely made it halfway down my barrel—and she radiated confidence. Her confidence came from being small and blonde. It had nothing to do with her ability to ride. Groove is in the heart.

"Just walk him around on a loose rein and let him get used to you," Carvin said.

Amora huffed impatiently, squeezed my sides with her short little legs and tightened the reins. "Candace?" she asked her trainer, whose face looked like a worn out saddle. "This is so boring. May I please trot?"

"Go ahead," Candace croaked. "Trot on."

Amora poked me with her heels and I picked up the trot. As we trotted by him, I noticed Carvin watching me with a sort of knowing dread. He knew I didn't follow orders from just anyone. I belonged to Merritt and no one else. I wasn't up for grabs. No way was I going to let these people just take over. She belonged with me. I belonged with her. She was my whole heart.

I've never liked indoor rings in the first place and the green fluorescent lights on the ceiling of this one were messing with my bad eye. I could feel a migraine coming on.

This is how I do it.

At the far end of the ring was a cutout diamond-shaped window that opened onto a bright field of green grass. When we reached the window I stopped, snorted, and pawed the ground.

"He's going to roll!" Carvin shouted.

"Kick him!" Candace croaked hoarsely.

Amora jabbed me in the ribs with her heels, trying to get me moving again. I went backwards.

"Get up there, Red!" Carvin cried, striding toward us and waving his arms.

"Kick him!" Candace croaked again. "Hit him with your hand!"

Amora kicked me a few more useless times. I pawed the ground and refused to budge. She reached behind her and slapped my hindquarters with her hand. She flapped the reins. She kicked me again and again. I snorted and bolted forward, as if I'd been spooked by something outside in the field. The girl shot backwards in the saddle, landing *behind* it, on my slippery smooth hindquarters. I thought another one was about to bite the dust, but miraculously she stayed on.

"Guys?" she wailed. "What do I do now?"

"Hold on." Carvin walked toward me with his hand out. He was only a few feet away, but he didn't want to startle me.

"Steady, big guy. You're not making it easy for us, are you? 'Course you're not."

Irritated that I hadn't yet gotten rid of runty Amora, I let my knees buckle and crumpled down in the dirt.

"No!" Carvin stood to one side, watching helplessly, as I rolled that girl right off me. I'm not the horse you want, babe. I'm not the horse you need.

"Emergency dismount!" Candace yelled.

Amora shrieked and rolled away from me. Her nice clean riding clothes were filthy now. The old roll-on-the-girl trick. Worked every time.

Candace led the whimpering Amora out of the ring. I stood up, shook myself off, and looked around as if to say, *Who's next? Anybody stupid enough to try?*

"Not so fast, Red." Carvin took my reins and I rubbed my forehead against his upper arm, nearly toppling him over. "Cut it out," he growled with a businesslike tug on the reins. He lengthened the stirrups as far as they could go and mounted up, his long legs wrapping around me in a soft, controlling vice.

"Gallop," he growled, urging me forward. "Come on. Let's gallop."

Candace came back to watch. "That's it," she said when we passed her at a gallop for the umpteenth time. "Get all his sillies out."

Carvin rode me as if I were a dolphin or something equally slippery and he had to keep me balanced and coursing through the water at an even pace or we'd wipe out and drown. I'd like to see him surf, I bet he's very good. I knew I could make him look good in the show ring, too, if I wanted to behave. I thought it over as he slowed me to a canter and turned me toward a jump.

The three-foot course was simple—outside line, diagonal

line, outside line, diagonal line. Carvin shifted his weight back and tried to keep me straight to the first jump but I closed my good eye and veered drastically to the right. Carvin dangled off my left shoulder like a very large decorative epaulette. Then I changed my mind and corrected myself. *Why not let Carvin ride me?* He was perfectly capable and seemed like a decent guy. Plus, Merritt was competitive. If she found out that Carvin and I were winning, she wouldn't be able to stand it. If I couldn't be with the one I loved, I could love the one I was with. At least for a little while.

Carvin readjusted himself just in time and I jumped the first jump squarely. Then it was onto the next one in six even strides. I floated over it and breezed around the turn. Easy, easy. Two more jumps. One. Two. Now everybody clap your hands.

"Good boy." Carvin patted me as we cantered our closing circle. He brought me down to a walk and patted me again.

"What the hell was that?" Candace croaked, obviously impressed.

"I guess he changed his mind," Carvin chuckled, still patting me.

"Do it again," Candace instructed. "Other way this time. I need to be sure that wasn't a fluke before I tell the show steward you're riding him."

I cantered on pleasantly, resolved to be good for Carvin from now on.

I'd let him win so often she couldn't keep away. She'd have to come see what all the fuss was about. Sweet child been holdin' out too long. She goin' miss me.

PART IV
July-August

39 | MERRITT

"Why don't you go on up to your room while Celine's at lunch?" Kami suggested as we pulled up to the Lodge in the van. "Unpack. Get yourself reacquainted with the rules."

"Celine?" I repeated, confused. What did Celine have to do with anything?

I got out of the van and slung my duffle bag over my shoulder. Good Fences looked exactly the same as it had last October except the leaves were greener and the burnt door of the One-Room Schoolhouse had been replaced with a shiny red one. Up on its lonely hill, Red's old run-in shed stood empty. No classic rock or affectionate nickers resounded from within.

"Come," Kami said, slamming her door. "Follow me."

She led me upstairs to my new room, right next door to the room I was supposed to have shared with Beatrice. There were two beds in the room. One was made up with the standard Good Fences white sheets and white cotton bedspread. The other was made up with a hot pink and white striped comforter pulled tight with severe hospital corners. Beneath that bed was a pair of neatly lined-up hot pink velvet slippers. A pale pink nightgown was folded neatly on the striped pillow. Sitting upright and staring at me with its beady black plastic eyes, was an overstuffed pink panda bear.

"Oh God," I gasped and whirled around. "Please don't make me room with her," I pleaded. "Please? What about Tabitha? I'll room with her."

Kami stood in the doorway, barring my way. Her face was resolute.

"Tabitha went home. I'm sorry Merritt, but your coping strategy is avoidance. You want to be alone so you don't have to talk to anyone or see anyone or deal with anything you don't want to. Well, I'm sorry, but unless you're a painter or a poet not a whole hell of a lot can be accomplished alone."

"But Celine?" I argued. "Why does it have to be Celine?"

Kami pushed her glasses up on top of her head and then put them down on her nose again. "You've both just lost someone close to you. Lacey, the horse Celine always worked with here, colicked one night not long after you left. We tried everything. Pumped her stomach, walked her and walked her. Celine stayed up with her for forty-eight hours, walking and talking to her. But Lacey was twenty-six years old. She just didn't have the strength to fight it."

"I'm sorry." I'd never really gotten to know the horses at Good Fences, only Red, but it was sad when any animal died.

"And you lost Beatrice," Kami went on. "I know you two were close. Her father was super nervous about her grooming for you, but it was my idea. I thought you'd make a good team. And you did."

I blinked at her. "Until I got mad and she died."

Kami took a deep breath and smiled grimly. "You want to talk? Let's talk. The sooner you get it out of your system the better. Normally I'd take a more roundabout approach and let you get there when you're ready. But we haven't got time for that. Mr. de Rothschild wants you back for some big show in Lexington, Kentucky. My job is to get you ready."

I glared at her back as she retreated into the hallway. "And what if I don't want to go to Kentucky?" I demanded.

She turned, hands on her hips. "You have five minutes to get settled. Then I want you down at the barn. You and Celine are both working with Arnold, the big draft horse."

40 | RED

wasn't at all sure I could do it—behave myself, I mean. But I had to try. I had to try and *win*. So Merritt would find out, get jealous, and come back for me.

We were still in Saratoga. Carvin was anxious about competing on me, with good reason. He carried his hands high as we cantered our opening circle, preparing to jump the giant brush on its own at the far end of the ring. Some riders pretend to understand the whole "it's a partnership" thing, but I sensed that deep in Carvin's California surfer heart he was a control freak. He liked to manhandle his horse around the course, steering her with his knees and ankles and shoulders and elbows. He wrestled his horse like he wrestled a surfboard, which is an inanimate object.

I decided not to let him get to me and just do my job. We jumped the brush with style and I turned across the diagonal, jumping the left side of the logs and striking out with my right foreleg for the bending line to the right and over the spooky beer barrels in-and-out with the gray rabbits running across the standards. I don't think I've ever jumped so roundly or so squarely. I could see the pearly white teeth of the judge, who was smiling at us in the periphery of my partially blind eye.

Carvin seemed to get more and more anxious as we went. His hands remained high and he kept his weight back, as if he was waiting for me to somersault over a jump and dump him in the dirt on his head. Guess I'd traumatized him, poor kid. I cantered the turn with as much grace and rhythm as I could muster with his hands so high. One, two, three. One, two, three. Up and over the planks, land, and five, four, three, two, one down over the bizarre dangling platform water jump that vaguely resembled the Brooklyn Bridge.

No sleep in Brooklyn!

The boom-boom-clash beat of the classic Beastie Boys song reverberated inside my head—and the final two jumps were like those little blips you feel when you're on a long journey on a smooth highway and there's a crease in the tar. Before you can say "perfect round," we'd soared over the single birdhouse oxer, landed, and pirouetted a flashy, rhythmic circle in front of the grinning, mustachioed judge. Oh yeah, I'm doin' it, doin' it, doin' it so well.

Forgetting, I listened for Beatrice's trademark wolf whistle. Then Candace coughed out a throaty "Woo-hoo!" and I remembered: no more Beatrice. The scoreboard flashed an array of numbers and the crowd went nuts. We were in the lead.

Carvin leaned over my neck and rubbed the top of my poll. "You've been holding out on me," he murmured. "What am I going to tell Tang?"

I shook my head and snorted. Not my problem. There were two more horses to go, but the first refused the water jump and the last was adequate, but not flawless like me. I may have made a wrong turn once or twice, but not today. Today I was perfect.

If only she could see how high her love kept lifting me.

I stood still and handsome for the photographers, the blue ribbon flapping from my bridle. Carvin kept patting me, probably more relieved that I hadn't killed him than excited that we'd won. I was capable of both killing *and* winning. That was the dark secret I'd have to carry around for the rest of my days, my handicap.

"You two make a great team," the judge told Carvin as he handed up our medal.

Not so fast, buddy. There were only two members of my team and one of us was missing.

41 | MERRITT

Now that it was summer, Mall Day had been replaced by Beach Day.

I piled out of Kami's van along with the rest of the damaged Good Fences crew and tiptoed gingerly across the hot sand of Hammonasset Beach. The beach looked surprisingly nice and clean despite being so close to I-95 and New Haven.

While the other girls ran on ahead to claim a good spot, I slowed down, clutching my towel to my chest. I felt exactly the way I had on Mall Day—like an alien on a field trip. On the drive there "Dr." Kami had proclaimed that vitamin D was good for depression. She was wrong. Being around all these carefree people enjoying the salt and sun just made me want to dive under the covers and reach for the remote.

"Who wants to go boogie-boarding?" Sloan yelled from the front of our group. She sprinted toward the water with the only boogie-board stashed beneath her skinny, freckled arm.

"I call the board second!" Amanda shouted and took off after her, trailed by the three new thirteen-year-olds who'd been in a school bus accident in Darien and were suffering from post-traumatic stress disorder.

"You two hold down the fort while I go buy some water," Kami instructed Celine and me.

I squinted into the sun and watched the younger girls gallop happily into the waves. "What's their deal anyway?"

"Who?" Celine unfolded her towel and stretched out on top of it, nose to the sun, eyes closed, obviously very serious about tanning. Her shoulder bones, hipbones, and ribcage jutted out so sharply I had to look away.

"Sloan and Amanda. Why are they here?"

Celine propped herself up on her elbows and squinted up at me. "It's sort of crazy actually. Sloan is a pathological liar. You honestly can't believe anything she tells you. And Amanda claims to have this big secret that she can't tell, but it involves Sloan somehow. It's all they talk about, privately, with each other. They were driving their parents crazy at home, so they sent them here. Kami can't get it out of them either. And they love it here because they get to be together all the time. They're never going to give up their secret."

I squinted at the two girls wading in the surf. They were all smiles and laughter and seemed perfectly harmless to me. "Maybe there is no secret. Maybe it's just another one of Sloan's lies."

Celine settled back down on her towel again. "Maybe," she said doubtfully.

It occurred to me as I sat there that I hadn't given much thought to why I was at Good Fences—for the second time. Since I'd arrived over a week ago, I'd avoided Kami's many attempts to revisit SAT day, the day Beatrice died, and other touchy subjects, preferring to treat the place like some sort of witness protection program or spa, where nothing was required of me except breathing, eating, sleeping, and barn chores.

"I hope you're wearing sunblock," Kami said when she returned. She began to unfold her beach chair. "I have SPF 70, if you need some."

"I'm good," Celine murmured without opening her eyes.

Kami had brought a portable radio with her, the exact same one we'd used in Red's shed. She turned it on and tuned it to the classic rock station, the only station that came in at Good Fences.

"This okay?" she asked me.

I nodded. Obviously this was another one of her not very subtle attempts to mess with my mind. As if the first few bars of "Jack & Diane" would make me miss Red so much I'd take the plunge, blurt out everything that was troubling me, and be instantly healed, just like she and Mr. de Rothschild wanted.

"It's fine." I crossed my arms and stared out to sea. "Jack & Diane" segued into "Mellow Yellow." There was a line about "electrical bananas" in the song. At least I wasn't as messed up as that singer.

"Oh, I almost forgot." Kami reached into her pink and green L.L. Bean canvas tote, pulled out a sheaf of papers, and handed them to me over Celine's prone form. "Your emails. Sorry. I was in such a hurry this morning I didn't have time to print them out and give them to you at breakfast. I thought you could read them here at the beach."

I took the papers. Kami turned down the radio and sat back in her chair. "No deeper, girls!" she shouted at the others. "I need to be able to see you!"

I pulled my towel out from under me and put it over my head, creating a makeshift tent so I could read in semi-shade and privacy.

With a mix of eagerness and trepidation I examined the thin stack of papers. The first email was from my mom. It was very short, which annoyed me. What was wrong with my parents anyway?

Dear Merritt,

I'm sorry I haven't been in touch sooner, but internet access is very patchy here. I wanted to go home and check in on you, but your dad talked me out of it. Kami has been keeping me posted, and it sounds like you're where you need to be right now. I hope you feel that way too. I just sent a letter of condolence to Mr. de Rothschild. What a terrible tragedy.

This trip has been so exhausting. Your dad and I have been working on our own issues, which I won't get into here. The big news is I might bring a sled dog or two home with me. How cool is that?

Kami says you have Beach Day every Sunday—I hope you're enjoying the sun. Most of all we want you to feel better soon.

Your dad sends his love.

Love,
Mom

Briefly I wondered what she meant about her and Dad "working on their own issues." What issues? They'd always seemed like they were perfectly compatible—two college professors who liked to run. I shuffled the papers beneath my towel. Sweat beaded on my upper lip. The second email was from Mr. de Rothschild.

Dearest Merritt,

First let me apologize for not writing to you sooner. Losing Beatrice so suddenly was a big blow. I have been in France with her mother, grieving. This morning we held a small service for her and laid her ashes in the family plot with her grandparents, on the hill behind our chateau in

Saint-Rémy-de-Provence. I know you were there, too, in spirit. Beatrice was not good at keeping friends, but you were a good friend to her. She was lucky to have you.

Todd, your talented but unruly trainer, is at a program in Kentucky. It's a working farm and he is a big help to them. I hope, in turn, they can help him.

I hope you will take advantage of Good Fences and let Kami do her good work so you can finish up the summer circuit with Big Red. I heard from his new trainer yesterday that Carvin rode him in the final round of the Hunter Classic at Saratoga and they were champions! Carvin also won both equitation classes and was reserve champion on Sweet Tang in the Junior Hunter division. He is a fine rider, but you provide him with some much-needed competition!

The horses have been shipped to Lake Placid where it is nice and cool. Carvin will ride Red there, too. Then they will go to Devon in Pennsylvania for the East Coast National Championship. It is a very big important show and it was you who rode Red well enough to qualify. If you must miss it, so be it, but let that be the last show you miss.

Meanwhile I will remain in France to help Beatrice's mother with her grieving. In time all of us will heal.

I hope to see you in Lexington. Your horse is waiting. We are all waiting—with open arms.

All my best wishes,
Roman de Rothschild

I reread the letter. I'd forgotten how nice Mr. de Rothschild was. He wasn't trying to be pushy. He actually cared about me, more so than my parents it seemed.

And Red was being good for Carvin. He didn't need me after

all. He would go on winning, and Carvin would probably go professional when he turned eighteen and have a long, illustrious riding career.

I stuck the note in the back of the pile and turned to the third email, expecting it to be from my parents again. But it was from Carvin.

> *Dear Merritt,*
>
> *I know you were mad that I stayed at the show and kept riding after what happened. I still don't know if it was the right thing to do. I couldn't face going home to California though. We never really talked much, but my mom's super-clingy and my dad's gone pretty much for good, so home is not a happy place for me. I hope you can understand.*
>
> *It's been very quiet around here. I think about you all the time. I hope you're OK.*
>
> *I've been riding Red—yeah, I know, right? He actually lets me. At first he was awful, but I guess he changed his mind. Maybe you sent him a text? My mom has this little Yorkshire terrier named Toast that she loves and whenever she has to leave him at home she'll check her phone to see if Toast has sent her a text. Now you think I'm crazy. Anyway, Red has been pretty amazing. I try to talk to him like you always do but I get the feeling he'd rather just listen to his music. We both miss you.*
>
> *That's all, I guess. Just wanted to say hey.*
>
> *Take care,*
Carvin

I reread the note three times. The little story about his mom and her dog was exactly the sort of thing Carvin never would have mentioned when Beatrice was around. Beatrice would have made fun of him. Red was being "amazing," and they were winning, but Red missed me. And Carvin said he missed me, too.

I threw the towel off. Sweat streamed down my face. My T-shirt was plastered to my skin. The bright sun blinded me. Celine had turned over onto her stomach. She looked like one of those wooden models of dinosaur skeletons. I could see every one of her vertebrae. Her shoulder blades jutted out like shark fins.

"Water?" Kami offered.

I nodded and she tossed me a bottle. I opened it and gulped the entire thing. Kami had to have read all the emails, since she was the one who'd printed them out.

"You want to talk about it?" She reached into her bag, pulled out an enormous floppy white sunhat, and put it on, as if preparing to listen.

I shook my head. Sweat dripped off my chin and beaded on my eyelashes.

"Well, you look like you could use a swim."

I stood up and sprinted toward the water. I wasn't wearing a bathing suit and I didn't bring a change of clothes, but the cold water felt like a healing balm on my ankles. I waded out to deeper water, fell on my knees, and dove in face first.

42 | RED

It's a common misconception that horses are colorblind. We're not. Grass is green. The sky is blue, except when it's gray or black. Plus we can see sideways—peripherally—if we're getting technical. We have far better night vision than many other animals, including humans. While you bumble around with your car headlights on, we can gallop through a field at midnight and not take a wrong step. Which is why we prefer to be turned out at night. Grazing on a summer night is the bomb.

I guess it was my reward for putting in not one, not two, but three spectacular rounds at Saratoga.

After leaving there we traveled for a few hours and arrived at a cooler place called Lake Placid. I was turned out in my own little grass paddock with a view of the mountains but no evidence of a lake.

Even though it was well past sunset and a new moon, I could see Tang grazing in the paddock next to mine. I could see the night watchman standing in the barn doorway a quarter of a mile away. I could see a little field mouse running across the grass, fleeing the slither of a garter snake. I could smell the pines, and maybe even the lake, and I wished Merritt was there to smell them, too.

My double vision got the best of me, because when I tried to remember that day, the last day we were together, all I saw was darkness and confusion, the way it must be for humans at night in the dark.

What happened that day in the wash stall haunted and tormented me, but not in the way you'd think. I didn't miss Beatrice. I was glad to be rid of her. But I regretted what I'd done. Because Merritt was gone now. And even though I was winning with Carvin it felt like the DJ was playing a constant loop of dead air, or that song, "Comfortably Numb," on repeat.

How could she just disappear like that? Didn't she love me? Didn't she care?

43 | MERRITT

Celine was so sunburned she couldn't walk, talk, or eat. Not that she ever ate much anyway.

"Okay for me to come in?" I cracked open the door to our room. When I'd left for dinner she'd been soaking in a cold oatmeal bath. Kami had sent me up with a vanilla milkshake and some aloe spray.

"It hurts," Celine moaned.

I opened the door all the way. She was lying on her back under her pink striped sheet. "I would have said something, but you have so many products, I just assumed you'd put on sunscreen."

"I wanted to tan," Celine said grumpily.

I went into the bathroom to brush my teeth and change into the green and yellow Ox Ridge Hunt Club T-shirt I liked to sleep in. Then I lay down on my bed. The room was dark, except for a faint light coming in through the open windows. Every now and then one of the ponies out in the pasture let out a low, contented snort as they cropped grass and bathed in the moonlight.

I lay still, listening and thinking about the emails I'd read on the beach. I'd been thinking about them all day. I'd wanted to hear that no one could ride Red like I could, but that wasn't the case. Red and Carvin were winning. So what was Mr. de Rothschild's hurry to have me back? He didn't need me. Carvin was doing a great job all on his own.

"I've never had a boyfriend, have you?" Celine's question cut through my thoughts.

I shook my head in the dark. "No."

"What about a girlfriend?" Celine asked and then giggled.

I kicked away the sheet uncomfortably. If I turned on the light and started reading Celine would stop talking to me. I didn't think she was expecting an answer. She was just trying to be funny. But the question wasn't funny to me.

"Beatrice tried to kiss me once," I confessed. "At least, I think that's what she was trying to do. I got mad at her. Not just about that though. About how she treated Red, too."

I heard Celine's head thump against her headboard. "Wait. So you guys were . . . *Ew!*" She thrashed around in her bed. "Ouch, my sunburn."

I didn't want Celine to go on thinking whatever it was she was thinking. "I was pretty freaked out," I admitted.

"When she died, you mean?"

"No, when she kissed me. She just did it. And then I got mad at her." I winced. *And then she died.*

"Beatrice was so weird," Celine said. "At least she was nice to you. She was never nice to me."

"Being nice to you is a challenge," I quipped, trying to lighten my mood.

"Hey, thanks. No wonder your parents are in Greenland or wherever—as far from you as possible."

"Oh, that was a nice thing to say. No wonder your parents are always sending you here."

"Hey, don't take your stuff out on me. Nobody sends me here. I come here voluntarily. Unlike some people."

I sat up, my blood boiling. I looked around in the dark for something to hurl at Celine's sun-sizzled body. A book was the nearest thing. It was a hardcover.

"Hey! Ow, ow, ow!" Celine cried as the book hit the wall and then crashed down on top of her.

Her enormous pink panda bear flew across the room and hit the window over my bed. I tossed it back.

"My blisters," Celine whimpered.

Still furious, I got up and grabbed her treasured kit of travel-sized beauty products off the dresser and hurled it across the room. The little plastic bottles hit the wall and rained down on the floor.

"Stop it!" Celine yelped.

Our bedroom door opened and the overhead light came on.

"What the hell is going on in here?" It was Kami, wearing a hideous camouflage-print bathrobe. She looked like the warden of a prison for duck hunters.

I squinted at her in the bright light. "I told you this wasn't going to work," I said flatly. "Maybe I should just go sleep in the Schoolhouse."

Celine got out of bed and began to pick up the travel-sized bottles scattered all over the floor. She zipped up the little cosmetics case and put it on the shelf over the bathroom sink. Then she went back to her bed and sat down, crossing her legs primly in her short pink nightgown. Her skin was pinker than the fabric. She took a deep breath and exhaled. "We weren't really fighting."

I glared at her, but she smiled back. I swallowed. Okay, maybe I'd overreacted.

Kami patted her bathrobe pockets and pulled out a chocolate chip cookie. "Do either of you want a cookie?"

We both shook our heads.

"What's this?" Kami picked up the book I'd thrown. It was Beatrice's book of Anne Sexton poems. She turned it over and read the back. "You know Anne Sexton committed suicide." She took a bite of her cookie. "She had two daughters. It's very sad."

I nodded. "It is sad." But something about Kami and her cookie was making me smile.

Kami put the book on the dresser and took another cookie out of her pocket. She took a bite. "Normally," she said, chewing and talking at the same time, "I'd confiscate that book for being inappropriate. A bad influence and all that." She took another bite and kept talking. "But since it belonged to Beatrice I think it might be comforting to you. A memento. Okay?"

I hadn't really read any of the poems, but I liked having the book. I nodded, trying not to smile because really there was nothing funny about this situation. If Kami kept talking with her mouth full of cookie, I was seriously going to lose it though.

Kami shuffled back to the door and took another cookie out of her pocket. "Have you two calmed down now?"

I glanced at Celine. She was holding her pink panda bear over her face, her blue eyes huge. It looked like she was about to lose it, too.

"Hello?" Kami said with her mouth full.

Both of us burst out laughing. Actual tears streamed down my face. Celine snorted, loud and unladylike. I tried not to look at her.

Kami wiped the cookie crumbs off her mouth with the sleeve of her robe. "Good night," she said and flicked off the light and closed the door.

"Oh, my sunburn," Celine moaned.

I slid under the covers. "I'm sorry it hurts."

As I drifted off I thought about Carvin's email again. The cute story he'd told about his mom's dog. The way he said he thought about me all the time and that he missed me. I remembered that first night at the Old Salem show when I'd fallen asleep lying next to him on his hotel bed. I felt myself blush in the dark and reminded myself for the hundredth time that he was probably gay.

44 | RED

The grounds at Devon were classy. I was stabled in a neat brown barn with white trim, bordered by carefully landscaped flowerbeds. There were no smelly food trucks or Porta Johns. The food vendors operated beneath cool green and white tents and the bathrooms were in an actual odorless building with walls and doors.

My stall was plastered with blue ribbons.

People came to admire me. They snapped pictures of me, and took selfies with me. Even Sweet Tang—who did beat me sometimes, but only rarely—regarded me with a sort of reverence now, as if she were proud to share a stable with such a notorious beast. I was pretty fancy, but you already know.

I imagined there was gossip about me. I could picture the discussion on a radio call-in show.

"I heard he was cloned from Secretariat's freeze-dried manure."

"I heard he eats only kale by the baleful."

"I heard they sprinkle actual gold dust into his bath water."

"I heard he killed a girl."

Which was actually true.

All the attention didn't make me miss Merritt any less. It was as if I was traveling farther and farther away from her, both of us becoming harder to find. But I still loved her. I still needed her.

It was like that Fleetwood Mac song "You Can Go Your Own Way," or the Indigo Girls song, "Closer to Fine." Or maybe it was the opposite of those songs—I could never make sense of most of what I heard. But it didn't matter what the words were. Any song about love gone wrong reminded me of her. And my aim was true.

The last day of the East Coast National Championship, the day of the Handy Hunter round, Carvin wouldn't leave me alone. He'd already taken out half the braids in my mane and rebraided them. After that it was my tail he was unhappy with.

"Hey, Carvin." It was one of the blondes. Amora or Nadia. I couldn't keep them straight. Carvin stayed where he was, separating the long strands of my thick tail. "I just wanted to wish you luck today. You're totally going to win. I also came to say goodbye. We're leaving for Maine."

"Uh-huh," Carvin murmured. I don't think he was even listening.

Amora or Nadia—whichever one it was—unlatched my stall door and came into the stall. She walked around me without even looking at me. "So goodbye," she said, standing very close to Carvin and very close to my left hind leg. "You ride him so much better than Merritt. You'll totally win."

I swished my tail and took a step back, catching the side of her foot with my hoof. She was wearing flip-flops.

"Hey!" she yelped. "That hurts!"

"Red," Carvin growled and shoved my hindquarters away.

I moved sulkily aside and Carvin led the limping blonde out of my stall.

"See you around," he said. "And you're wrong, by the way. Merritt rides him way better than I do. I'm just winning because Red feels like it. Any day now he could change his mind. Besides,

Merritt's coming back. Mr. de Rothschild wants her to ride at Lexington."

Amora or Nadia ignored what he was saying and stood on tiptoe to kiss him on the cheek. "Good luck. Not that you need it."

We watched her leave the barn and then Carvin went back to detangling my tail. "Better not change your mind today," he muttered.

I just kept repeating what he'd said before: *Merritt's coming back*.

A horse's life is all about the person he belongs to. I belonged to her. She belonged to me.

She was coming back.

45 | MERRITT

It was Sunday—Sucky Sunday—the day we all got to speak to our parents and have Intense Group. I'd been at Good Fences a whole month now and my parents were in Canada, taking a break from the dogs to compete in a cross-tundra ultra marathon. This time they spoke to me separately.

"Good to hear you're feeling better!" Dad boomed cheerfully, even though I hadn't said anything about how I felt.

"Your father and I have been arguing," Mom explained when Dad got off the phone. "About you."

"Really?" I said bitterly. But I was at Good Fences, taken care of. Why waste precious energy discussing me?

"Mr. de Rothschild wants you to ride at that big show in Lexington, Kentucky in a couple of weeks. Your dad thinks that's a fine idea, but I don't want you to do anything you're not ready for. There will be other shows. Other horses even."

I didn't say anything. Every time Kami brought up showing at Lexington or riding Red again, I changed the subject.

"Merritt?"

"I have to get off the phone, Mom." There wasn't much time between my phone call and Group. "Good luck in the marathon."

"Oh, right. Thanks." Mom blew out a long, frustrated-sounding breath. "Have a good week."

• • •

Another email printout was waiting on my pillow when I went upstairs to change. I brought it down to Arnold's oversized stall and sat in the corner to read it while he munched his lunchtime flakes of hay.

Dear Merritt,

Devon was great. Red was Junior Hunter Champion and Tang was Reserve Champion, so that was pretty cool. After the show I went to Hershey Park and rode on some of the rides, but amusement parks aren't that fun on your own. I was hanging out with Amora Wells and Nadia Grabcheski a lot this summer, don't ask me why. They both left for Maine, which makes me happy. Wish you were here to hang out.

Now we're back at Saugerties for Hits V and VI. Red was Champion in the hunters and Tang was Reserve again today. We're beginning to see a pattern, folks. Mr. d R told me the rivalry between you and me got a lot of good press and he wants you to come back. He says I can't ride both horses in the same class at Lexington either. It's against the rules.

I want you to come back, too, but not because of that. I'm secretly hoping you'll just turn up one day. That would be amazing. You're an awesome rider and Red misses you so much—he told me to tell you that ;) Plus, Mr. d R rented a condo in Lexington with a pool and a hot tub and everything. It'd be sweet if you were there.

Love,
Carvin

"What are you doing?" Celine poked her head over Arnold's door. "Is that from that boy?"

It was no secret that Kami had recruited Celine to try and motivate me. All Celine knew was that there was a boy riding Red now, a boy Beatrice hadn't liked much, and everyone wanted me to ride at Lexington. Everyone except me—and Mom, apparently.

She unlatched Arnold's stall and came inside. "Read it aloud to me," she commanded bossily. After the Kami-eating-cookies-out-of-her-bathrobe-pockets incident things had changed between us. We still engaged in the same antagonistic banter, but it was with the understanding that no harm was meant. I guess that meant that we were friends.

I glared up at her, then took a deep breath, cleared my throat, and began to read Carvin's email aloud.

"Oh my gosh," Celine gasped when I was finished.

"What?" I looked up and fanned my hot face with the note.

"We have to talk to Kami," Celine gushed. "Come on. Get up." She unlatched Arnold's door.

"About what?" I folded the note carefully and followed her out of the stall.

"Kentucky," Celine said, as if it were obvious. "You totally have to go."

Group had moved into the new and improved Schoolhouse. It was cozier than the old Group room and more private without the big picture window. Plus, it had a free-standing portable air-conditioning unit on wheels that you could aim directly into your face to blast yourself with cold air.

Sloan and the three younger girls, Kristyn, Charlotte, and Emma, were already sprawled all over the purple beanbag chairs. Amanda commandeered the air-conditioning unit.

"Kami's on the phone," she told us. "She'll be down in a few minutes. We're making mini pizzas in the toaster oven. She said we could."

I sat on the floor and hugged my knees while Celine arranged herself on a large white upholstered armchair, like a queen settling into her throne.

"Merritt has big stuff to discuss," she announced. "So when Kami gets here don't go interrupting her and whining about going to Cold Stone Creamery for ice cream, or complaining about how there's no swimming pool and all the other crap you pull all the time. Okay?"

The other girls nodded respectfully. Celine could be very intimidating when she wanted to be. But I wasn't afraid of her.

"Actually I really don't have anything to discuss."

"Yes, you do," Celine insisted.

I shook my head. "No, I don't."

The toaster oven dinged and the girls jumped up to get their snack. Kami pushed open the door. She looked hot and frazzled. "There had better be a chair for me, and I want the AC aimed directly in my face."

Celine jumped up to give Kami her chair and did her best to fold up her long stick legs on the floor beside me, like an enormous cricket. The tiny shed was crowded but cool. I pressed my back up against the wooden shed wall beneath the only window. I was used to hiding during Group as much as possible, listening to the other girls talk and complain, maintaining a mildly engaged face. But Celine wasn't going to let that happen today.

"Merritt wants to talk," she told Kami. "Don't let anyone else talk before her, okay?"

"No, it's fine," I protested. "Go ahead and talk."

Kami arranged herself on the white armchair and swiveled the air-conditioner around. "Ah," she breathed, closing her eyes. "That's nice." She opened her eyes and glanced at me. "Go ahead. Don't mind me," she said before turning away and closing her eyes again. I knew this was one of her tricks—pretending not to listen so I would talk.

The other girls stared at me expectantly.

I looked down at the floor. Good Fences was supposed to be a nurturing, low-pressure place. Why couldn't they just leave me alone?

"Okay, I get it," I began. "Everybody wants me to go back. And I miss Red. I miss showing, I really do. But—"

"Don't forget about Carvin," Celine put in.

"Quiet!" Kami roared. She was looking at me intently now. "Go on, Merritt. But what?"

"Who's Carvin?" Sloan demanded.

I blushed.

"He has a hot name," Amanda observed.

"Totally," Celine agreed. "That's why she has to go to Kentucky."

Kami swiveled the air-conditioner away. "Whoa, whoa, whoa. I don't know about that. If this is all just about a boy, then you're definitely not going." She pushed her glasses on top of her head, and then pushed them down onto the bridge of her nose again. "I was just talking to Mr. de Rothschild and your mom about this. We had a conference call."

I sat up straight. "You did? Just now?"

"Yes. The International Hunter Derby in Lexington, Kentucky, starts on September fourth. So you still have time to get down there and get ready." She frowned. "Mr. de Rothschild has been tracking your progress and he thinks you'll be fine. I just don't know how comfortable I am sending you down to Kentucky on your own. What if you revert back to your old habits?"

Exactly, I agreed silently. *Which is why I shouldn't go.* Not that I didn't want to go to Kentucky. I did. I was just . . . terrified.

"I'll go with you," Celine piped up. She turned to Kami. "As her chaperone. In case she's tempted to do something bad."

Kami furrowed her brow and nodded. "I suppose that could work. Merritt's mom said she might meet you down there. And Luis will be there. Mr. de Rothschild asked him to come back and groom."

"Luis?" I perked up. "Really?" It would be fun to see Luis again.

All of a sudden I felt like a decision had already been made, regardless of how I felt. I was going to Kentucky.

"I'll have to hammer out the details. Get you both plane tickets," Kami went on. "And remember, this is just for the finals."

I nodded. I couldn't think beyond Kentucky anyway.

"Can *we* talk now?" Amanda complained.

Kami smiled wearily across the circle at me and Celine. "I don't say this often, but I am really going to miss you guys."

PART V

August–September

46 | RED

The sun shines bright in My Old Kentucky Home, 'tis summer, the people are gay! When you think of Kentucky you think of Thoroughbreds. The moment I stepped off the ramp of the horse van and sniffed the sweet, humid air, I knew: this was where I came from.

Very few of my horse show comrades had the same experience. Most of the fancy hunters and jumpers and dressage horses these days are warmbloods from Europe—Hanoverians, Holsteiners, Oldenburgs, Trakehners, and Wesphalians from Germany, Selles Français from France, Dutch warmbloods from Holland, Swedish warmbloods from Sweden, Belgian warmbloods from Belgium.

Apparently the warmblood is more athletic and energetic than the cold-blooded draft horse, sturdier and more even tempered than the fine-boned, hot-blooded Thoroughbred or Arabian. I did have a quick temper. Was it because my blood was so hot? I'm hot-blooded, check it with sticks. Got a fever of a hundred and six!

Yeah, I know. That's not how it goes.

Kentucky was hot. Like melt your feet hot. Like flies' wings sizzling and dropping out of thin air hot. Like get all lathered up with sweat just standing still hot. Like don't even bother with a bath because ten minutes later you'll need another one hot.

My water buckets were full of warm soup. My nostrils and ears were sweaty. My hindquarters rubbed together. The girth chafed. Even my cannon bones were sweaty and they were just bones. The Kentucky Derby is run in May, not the end of August. Not sure what the organizers of this show—the International Hunter Derby—were thinking. Kentucky in August is brutal.

Kentucky was its own peculiar planet. The air, the grass, the water, the people, the cars, the scents, and the sounds were different from anywhere else. Even the dogs were different. Jack Russell terriers were more popular than children. They were everywhere—yipping and yapping, peeing on the hay and feed buckets when no one was looking, napping in the sun, ignoring their shouting owners and eating scraps from the garbage. Watching the dogs' antics while I listened to Dixieland jazz on my radio was like watching an old silent film.

Candace was delighted to even be at the finals. She'd never trained horses as talented as me and Tang, so she'd never qualified. And Carvin kept doubling back to check on me. The day after we arrived they turned me out with Tang in a small grass paddock and leaned against the fence to watch us.

"He better not bite her," Carvin said when he unbuckled my muzzle.

"It's too hot to bite anyone," Candace complained. Her face was so leathery it probably didn't sweat.

But she was right. Even though it was still morning, Tang and I were both sluggish from the heat. I sniffed the blue grass and closed my eyes, trying and failing to rouse sweet memories of my Kentucky foalhood. There were other scents in the air though. Fried dough. Barbecued chicken. Rain. And something else, something that was emanating from Carvin, a sort of nervous excitement.

Anticipation.

"You think he knows?" Candace asked.

"He knows," Carvin said with a great big smile on his face. "He may not know he knows, but he knows."

And that's when I knew: Merritt was almost here.

47 | MERRITT

exington was green and hot and completely dedicated to horses, even at the airport, where a store called The Paddock Gallery sold framed pictures of famous racehorses. Not that anything I saw actually registered in my brain. I was in a sort of self-induced coma. I was going to see Red again. I was going to ride at a huge show. And Carvin would be there.

Thank goodness for Celine. She got us on the plane. She found our bags and picked up the rental car. She drove.

"Look, Merritt, *horses!*" Celine pointed out the window as she followed the GPS's directions to the de Rothschild condo. Endless white fence rails guarded undulating green fields of Kentucky blue grass dotted with sleek Thoroughbreds. Broodmares and foals. Galloping stallions. Bands of yearlings. "Look! *Look!*"

"I'm not blind," I growled, my stomach a fluttering mess of nerves.

"Just trying to wake you up," she said. "You haven't said a word since we got here."

But I couldn't talk. I could barely breathe. If Beatrice were there she would have slapped my face and poured ice over my head, but I'm not sure that would have helped either. I was excited, but I felt guilty for being excited. I was scared, but felt stupid for feeling so scared. Most of all I just wanted to see Red.

"You have reached your final destination," the GPS announced as we pulled into the condo complex. Behind us was a golf course with cascading water fountains. To our right, a shimmering pool and tennis courts. To our left was yet another horse farm. The condo buildings themselves weren't quite as opulent as the condos in Florida had been with their white marble, pink flamingos, and palm trees. These were white-shingled and prim, their tranquil views of grazing Thoroughbreds almost dreamlike.

Our condo door was unlocked. Carvin was already at the show, but evidence of him was everywhere. Running shoes by the door. A case of power bars on the kitchen counter. A fruit bowl full of apples. An empty juice box on the coffee table.

Celine wheeled her bag inside and headed upstairs to check out the bedrooms.

"It's super nice!" she called down. "Oooh, Carvin has a picture of you in his room."

"He does not." I dashed upstairs, following the sound of her voice. The bedrooms were decorated with thick cream-colored carpets that felt luxurious underfoot. Carvin's room had a king-sized bed with a brown leather headboard and a navy blue and gold paisley bedspread that was straight out of a Ralph Lauren catalog. Enormous windows faced out onto a sea of blue-green grass dotted with grazing broodmares and foals.

"See?" Celine shoved a magazine clipping at me. It was a picture of me and Carvin at Hits earlier that summer, when Red and I had won the Hunter Derby and Carvin and Tang were Champion in the Junior Hunters. We sat side by side on our horses, holding up our ribbons and smiling our heads off. Beatrice stood in the far background between the horse's rear ends, grimacing comically and holding up two fingers in a symbol of peace.

"That was a fun show." I tried to sound nonchalant, but my voice stuck in my throat. I handed back the clipping. "Put that back where you found it. We shouldn't even be in here."

Celine giggled. "The bed's big enough."

I scowled at her. "Can we just hurry up and go to the show?"

It was only ten o'clock in the morning and the US Hunter Jumper Association's International Hunter Derby Final wouldn't begin for another four days, but the horse park was bustling. Horses and riders and grooms and trainers were everywhere, preparing for the big event. There were jumping lessons in the warm-up rings, grooms lunged horses in the smaller corrals or lathered them up in wash stalls, horses napped in the sun-drenched paddocks or stood with their heads over their stall doors, drowsily observing the activity around them.

Celine and I walked up and down the aisles in the stabling area until I spotted the row of light blue tack trunks emblazoned with the navy blue de Rothschild *R*.

"There's no one here," Celine said.

Red's old grazing muzzle hung from a hook outside his empty stall. His radio was on, tuned to some sort of hyperactive jazz with lots of brass instruments. I could imagine Beatrice dancing the Charleston to it with her e-cigarette dangling from her lips.

"Come on," I said, turning away.

Celine followed me to the end of the barn aisle. "Hey, there's Luis. Is that them?" She pointed to a ring where a boy jumped a chestnut horse with a white face over a series of low gymnastics. Luis stood by the rail holding a pretty gray mare.

My heart slowed almost to a standstill and then sped up again. "Yes, it's them. Come on."

Carvin cantered Red over a bounce, bounce, three stride, in-and-out combination as we approached. They were both concentrating hard. Red took the bounces perfectly, rocking back on his hindquarters and lifting his hooves up around his ears. But in the middle of the three-stride he stopped and whirled around like a cutting horse. Carvin had to hug him around the neck to keep from falling off.

"Don't let him get away with that! Get him over the next jump!" A leathery blonde shouted at them from the ground. She had a voice like gravel, a smoker's voice. This was our new trainer, I guessed. "I don't care if you trot over it, make him finish!"

But Carvin couldn't do anything with Red. The big horse was staring right at me, head high, ears pricked, trembling all over. He let out a loud, pealing whinny that echoed throughout the horse park and trotted toward me.

"Aw, he like, *smelled* you," Celine gasped. "That's so cute!"

"Hey," Carvin pulled Red up by the fence, swung his feet from the stirrups, and hopped to the ground in one easy, athletic motion. Sweat dripped from the unruly golden brown strands that poked out of his helmet, streaking his freckly, overheated, smiling face. His teeth were white and perfect—I hadn't noticed before. "I'm glad you're here," he said. It was the same thing he'd said that night in his hotel room right before I fell asleep.

My insides were doing something weird. "Me too," I said, unable to wipe the goofy smile off my face.

Red whinnied, his whole body vibrating with the sound like a giant bell. He pawed the ground impatiently.

"I'm glad to see you too," I laughed. Ducking under the fence, I threw my arms around my horse's neck and pressed my cheek into his shoulder. I closed my eyes and breathed in his scent, the scent I'd missed so much. Red butted his head against my back. "Good boy," I murmured into his fur. All my doubts about going to Lexington were forgotten then. I was right where I belonged.

I opened my eyes to find Carvin taking in Celine's pink tank top, pink short-shorts, and pink flip-flops. He stuck out his hand in that oddly formal way of his. "Hey, I'm Carvin."

Celine giggled, leaving her hand in his for a moment too long. "I know. I've heard a lot about you."

I would have to kill her later.

Red dipped his nose down and rubbed his whole head against me. "Easy, boy." I steadied myself with a hand on his sweaty neck. "Don't knock me over."

"You must be Merritt," the trainer with the ashtray voice spoke up. "I'm Candace." She looked like one of those gourds used to decorate the table at Thanksgiving—weathered and tough, her bright blue eyes peeping out of sunken, suntanned sockets.

"Hi." I swayed comically, trying to keep my balance as Red kept up his affectionate performance.

"Look at him," Candace growled. "I've never seen that horse do anything but try to bite and trample people. Look at him, look at him!"

I laughed and pushed away Red's big head, but he swung it back to nibble the buttons on my polo shirt. "I wish I'd worn my riding clothes," I said wistfully.

"You want to get on? Get on!" Candace waved at Luis. "Would you mind running down to the barn and grabbing Merritt's helmet out of the trunk?"

"Hold on." I shoved the reins back into Carvin's hand and ran over to hug Luis.

"You made it." Luis wrapped his arm around my shoulders and gave me a squeeze. "What's the bitchy blonde doing here?" he whispered in my ear. "I thought we hated her."

"It's okay, we're friends now," I assured him as Celine walked up behind me. "She's still sort of bitchy though," I added loudly.

"Hey! I heard that." Celine air-kissed Luis on both cheeks. "I'm here to make sure Merritt behaves herself." She giggled as Carvin led Red over to us. "Although I'm not sure I want her to."

"I'll give you a leg up," Carvin offered.

"I really shouldn't ride in shorts," I protested.

"Like you care?" Celine chided me. She took Tang's reins so Luis could retrieve my helmet. "She has Lacey's coloring exactly," she gushed, stroking the mare's elegant gray face.

I gathered up Red's reins and lifted my left foot. "On three," I told Carvin. He cupped my left knee in his hands. I tried not to blush or react in any way as he boosted me onto Red's back, but my cheeks were on fire.

Red sprang forward as I settled into the saddle. "Whoa. Easy, boy," I crooned, reins slipping in my sweaty grasp. "Wait for my helmet."

Candace helped shorten my stirrups. Then Luis returned and handed up my beloved Charles Owen helmet. Gran-Jo's mangled blue ribbon was still tied inside. I tucked in my ponytail and fastened the chinstrap. The helmet felt right as ever, a perfect fit.

Carvin pulled a Clif Bar out of his back pocket and tore open the wrapper. He took a bite and looked up at me as he chewed. "How do you feel?"

I shortened the reins, adjusted my posture, and flexed my heels down. "Good." I couldn't stop smiling. Celine giggled again for no apparent reason until I realized that Carvin and I were staring at each other. I forced myself to look away. "What should I do with him?" I asked Candace.

"Just walk him around," Candace instructed. "Let him look at everything. Get acquainted with the show grounds. I'll give you and Carvin a jumping lesson tonight when it cools down a bit. We've only got four days to get you ready."

48 | RED

knew she was coming, I just didn't know when. And I'd grown impatient. A moment before she showed up I'd decided I'd changed my mind about being good. It was time to shake things up. Time to roll on Carvin, kick Candace, let Tang out of her stall—whatever chaos I could manage. But as soon as I smelled her and she was there, speaking to me, petting me, I was a horse again—a good horse, her horse. Luis was back, too, which was nice. But she didn't seem all that interested in anyone else. Only me, us. Paradise.

Carvin gave her a leg-up and Candace opened the gate. Then we just walked and walked. We walked around the show rings where they were building courses. We went behind the grandstands and around the parking lots. We found a trail and took it to where it ended at a fence beside the highway. Then we turned around and found another trail and got lost for a little while. We didn't mind.

While we were walking she lay down on my neck and hugged me and talked to me. "You're going to be good for me, aren't you boy? And I'm going to try to be good too. I'm a little rusty. Sorry about that. You won't mind though. That's my *good boy*."

I swear, wild horses could not have dragged me away.

We came out of the woods behind the food tents. The show hadn't started yet, so most of them were closed, but there was a man selling ice cream bars from a little cart and Merritt bought one and ate it, still on my back. She let go of the reins and I just wandered free, following strains of music on various radios, munching grass where I could find it. I was finding it hard to believe. I was in heaven.

I wished we could have wandered right out of the show grounds and run away together because it was just so perfect, the two of us hanging out like that. These were the good old days. It was so nice. And I knew from experience that nice things never last.

49 | MERRITT

Roman de Rothschild had arrived in Lexington a few days before Celine and me. He was staying with fellow European billionaire friends at their Thoroughbred breeding farm outside of town and had yet to set foot on the show grounds, but he'd arranged to host a poolside dinner outside our condo in honor of my return.

"If it's a pool party do we wear bathing suits?" I mused aloud when I emerged from the shower. I could hear Calvin banging around in his room. It sounded like he was doing jumping jacks.

Celine sat on her own bed, painting her toenails. "You're wearing that." She pointed to the navy blue halter dress spread out on my bed. I held it up. There wasn't much to it, but I was short enough that it might cover up most of the tops of my legs. "I might not go to dinner," she added.

I wondered if this was some kind of ploy. She would stay in the room and pretend to be sick. Carvin might come up to check on her and she'd have him all to herself.

"I'm pretty sure Carvin's gay, you know." I wasn't sure I believed that anymore, not after the way he'd smiled at me from Red's back when we first saw each other that morning, but I said it anyway.

Celine looked up from her toes. "Really?"

I pulled the dress on over my head. It was form-fitting and

short, but comfortable. My legs were as tan as my face now that I'd been to the beach and spent more time wearing shorts. "It seemed like you were flirting with him before."

She rolled her eyes and went back to her toes. "You're impossible. Merritt, you know I would never . . . Okay, forget it. I am going to dinner after all. I'm supposed to be keeping tabs on you anyway. I also need to thank Mr. de Rothschild for being so awesome and renting us the best condo ever."

The sun was low in the sky, casting long shadows over the swimming pool. Candace, Luis, and Mr. de Rothschild were already seated at one of the poolside cocktail tables, drinking tall iced teas. Mr. de Rothschild looked like he'd lost half his body weight and aged twenty years. His hair was black the last time I saw him. Now it was light gray. His cream-colored linen suit was too big all over, having been tailored for a much larger man.

"Merritt!" He stood up to greet me and I gasped to see how shrunken he really was. He opened his arms and smothered me in linen and the citrus-wood scent of his cologne. "Candace was just telling me how happy Big Red was to see you today." He patted my hair and took a step back to smile down at me. His brown eyes were sad. "I'm so glad you're here. It makes everything better."

I didn't know what to say. He'd lost his daughter. I'd lost a friend. Like an old injury, some days I thought of Beatrice often, and some days not at all. Was that wrong? It seemed wrong.

Celine coughed delicately. I remembered my manners.

"Mr. de Rothschild, this is my friend, Celine."

"Thank you for being so generous." Celine shook his hand. "It's beautiful here," she added, turning on the charm.

I couldn't help remembering how Beatrice had always acted

around her father, rolling her eyes and grimacing whenever anyone complimented him. It had always baffled me.

"And here is Carvin," Mr. de Rothschild announced.

Carvin strode down the flagstone walkway from the condo to the pool. His freckled legs were very pale in a pair of red Bermuda shorts and black flip-flops. His damp hair was combed and parted so neatly I had to smile.

"Good to see you again, sir," he said and shook Mr. de Rothschild's hand.

"My savior," Mr. de Rothschild replied sincerely. "Without you, Carvin, everything would have fallen apart. And so much success—beyond my wildest hopes!"

I considered this while they chatted. Carvin had really kept it together the day Beatrice died. And afterward too, riding two horses and winning everything. Meanwhile, I had totally fallen apart. So had Mr. de Rothschild, apparently.

"We're expanding. We have big plans," Mr. de Rothschild was saying, but he was speaking to Celine and I didn't catch all of it.

The caterer had set up a wood-fired grill and was grilling pizzas to order. I noticed that there was no alcohol in evidence, probably for my benefit.

I sat by the edge of the pool between Celine and Carvin, our feet dangling in the water, while Luis, Candace, and Mr. de Rothschild supervised the creation of their pizzas.

"Thanks for your emails," I told Carvin, my eyes on the sun-dappled water.

"No problem," Carvin said, staring at the water too. "This is weird," he added quietly. "I mean *he*'s being weird. Everything's weird." He bit his lower lip and glanced at me. I had the feeling he wanted to say more but he didn't feel comfortable talking about it when Mr. de Rothschild was standing so close.

"Weird," I agreed, even though I was pretty sure we were talking about two very different things. For me the weirdness was all about Carvin, or rather the space between me and Carvin on the tiled edge of the pool. It was a very small space, so electrically charged that one whole side of my body—the Carvin side—was buzzing. The side next to Celine wasn't buzzing at all.

Celine kicked her long, skinny, perfectly tanned, perfectly manicured Barbie feet over the surface of the pool and stretched her long, skinny arms overhead. I'd never seen her so relaxed. "I thought I would miss Good Fences, but it's so nice here. I could definitely get used to the de Rothschild way of life."

I took a deep, sighing breath. Carvin smelled good, like Ivory soap and the liniment we used to bathe the horses.

"What time is our morning lesson?" I asked, even though I knew perfectly well when it was. "I want to be there an hour early so I can hand-walk Red," I babbled nervously. "Get his spooks out."

"Children, come eat!" Mr. de Rothschild called.

Carvin jumped to his feet and held out his freckled hand to help me up. "You feeling it yet?"

I grinned sheepishly and took his hand. I hadn't ridden in over a month. Every muscle in my legs protested as he pulled me to a stand. "A little." I winced. "Yes. Ow."

We were just sitting down to eat our pizzas when another guest arrived. She looked like Audrey Hepburn in *Breakfast at Tiffany's*—elegant dark bun, giant sunglasses, red lipstick, little black dress.

"Fashionably late as always." Mr. de Rothschild stood up and held out his hand to the petite woman. "Everyone, this is Helena de Rothschild, my wife."

He pulled out the empty chair next to me and gestured for her to join us. I stared at her as she approached. Her tiny feet in their white patent leather sandals barely seemed to touch the ground.

"Hello," she greeted me, kissing the air near both of my cheeks. She smelled as strongly of perfume as Mr. de Rothschild did of cologne. "You are Merritt, yes?" It was the voice from Beatrice's phone, the one that had left that sad, lonely message. She pronounced my name *Merreet*.

"Yes, that's right," I stammered.

She greeted Carvin the same way, standing on tiptoe to kiss him. Celine was so tall she had to stoop.

"Helena is . . . was . . . Beatrice's mother," Mr. de Rothschild explained, his face clouding over at his own mistake. As if to demonstrate, Helena de Rothschild pulled an e-cigarette out of her little clutch purse and switched it on.

I gasped audibly and Carvin put his hand on my arm to steady me. I sipped my water, attempting to regain control. Helena de Rothschild was like a tiny, fashionable, French version of Beatrice. It was bizarrely unsettling.

She sat down and one of the chefs brought her a pizza and a glass of iced tea. Mr. de Rothschild sighed heavily and took his wife's hand.

"Sometimes it takes a great misfortune to bring people together again. Helena and I have had our differences in the past, and many arguments about Beatrice." He paused, his face so bereft a lump lodged in my throat. "I think I have learned the hard way that I must keep my loved ones close. So, once business is taken care of here, I will return to the chateau in France where I will reside permanently, with Helena." He raised his glass and attempted a smile. "A toast. To new beginnings."

"New beginnings," Candace and Luis repeated loudly.

I was careful to avoid eye contact as everyone clinked glasses. The others continued to chat and eat. I was no longer hungry.

Helena de Rothschild didn't eat anything either. She just smoked her e-cigarette. I tried to smile, but I felt like I was going to throw up. How could everyone be so nonchalant? I couldn't do it. It was wrong. Beatrice should have been there, being loud, scarfing down pizza and waving her e-cigarette around, making fun of her parents and Candace behind their backs.

"You okay?" Celine mouthed to me. I shook my head. She pointed at the condo and whispered, "Go lie down and watch TV or something."

I nodded and stood up. "Excuse me," I said, still avoiding eye contact with everyone except Celine. "It's been a long day." I glanced in Helena de Rothschild's general direction. "It was very nice to meet you."

"Good night Merritt," Mr. de Rothschild said. "Yes, please go relax. You'll need your strength to beat Carvin!" He laughed loudly but it sounded forced, almost hideously so.

"Thank you very much for dinner," I managed and then hurried away.

Back in our room, I changed out of Celine's sundress and into my old T-shirt and cut-off sweats. I studied my face as I brushed my teeth. I'd gotten too much sun and my blue eyes had a sort of startled look that I couldn't shake. I went downstairs to the condo kitchen to grab a bottle of water from the fridge. Carvin opened the back door as I was headed back to the bedroom.

"You're not in bed yet," he said, stating the obvious. "Good. I want to show you something."

I blushed as he brushed past me and led the way upstairs. I wished I'd put on something more attractive and taken the time to brush my hair.

"It's in here." Carvin went into his room and I followed. Clif

Bar wrappers and empty juice boxes littered the floor around the wastebasket. "Sorry about the mess. I keep missing my baskets." He handed me the magazine with the picture of me and him on our horses at Hits. "Have you seen this?"

"Kind of," I said senselessly. What was wrong with me? His room smelled like him. I handed back the magazine. "It's a cute picture." I blushed. "I mean Red looks cute."

Carvin tossed the magazine on the bed. "So." He looked at me expectantly. "Are you tired?"

"I think I'm just really nervous," I babbled. "I wasn't expecting to meet Beatrice's mom. That was crazy. And I haven't ridden in over a month. What if I fall off or go off course something?" I wasn't saying anything I meant to say. I was just talking.

Carvin shook his head. "Not gonna happen."

"You already got him so high in the standings, it almost doesn't matter what I do. We don't have to win."

"No, you don't," Carvin agreed. Then he smiled broadly. "Although it is fun to win." His smile disappeared. "But you're okay?" he asked me again.

I nodded and swallowed, blushing under the searching intensity of his green eyes and all those freckles.

"Come here," he said.

I stopped breathing, but I didn't move.

Instead, he closed up the distance between us, cupped my face in his freckled hands, and kissed me. He pulled away almost immediately, still holding my face. Our heads were very close together. "Remember the Hampton Inn at the Old Salem show, when we were all lying on my bed?"

I nodded, still not breathing.

"I've wanted to kiss you since then. And when you drove Beatrice's car to Saratoga. You were so upset. I wanted to kiss you then. And in the bar at Saratoga I wanted to kiss you." He smiled and pulled me toward him again. His lips brushed my cheek. "I've wanted to kiss you a lot."

"But I thought you were gay!" The words escaped in a breathless giggle.

He kissed me again and shook his head. "Not gay." Then he pulled away and grinned. "I thought *you* might be gay. You and Beatrice—"

I blushed and bit my lip, my mind racing. Beatrice was my friend. It seemed irreverent and sort of mean to say that she'd made more of our relationship than there really was. But it was Carvin I'd liked all along, and now I knew he liked me, too.

"She did try to kiss me once," I admitted. "She was just so confident. She did whatever she wanted. And she kind of took up all of my attention. She thought everyone else was a jerk, including you. I guess I was just confused—" I stopped talking. Again I wasn't saying exactly what I meant to say. I'd loved Beatrice, but I'd never felt like *this* about anyone.

Carvin put his hands on my waist. "Me too," he said huskily. "But not anymore." He kissed me again. And again. And again. We couldn't stop kissing.

Outside his bedroom window the sky suddenly erupted with loud, colorful explosions—a fireworks display. We turned to watch them. Carvin took my hand. I'd been too distracted to notice that it was dark out now.

"What are they for?" I whispered.

"Us." He chuckled and gave my hand a squeeze. "It's actually a tribute to George Morris. He never came out to California, but I used to watch his clinics on YouTube. He's like, legendary. I sort of want to be him when I'm old."

"You will be," I murmured, standing very still. The fireworks continued for what seemed like hours. Carvin dropped my hand and wrapped his arm around my waist for the finale, a crescendo of sparkly blue and white bursts that drifted down to earth leaving shimmering, starry trails.

"I swear I didn't plan that," he said when they finally ended. I leaned into him and he turned me around to face him. I put my hands on his shoulders. I liked how soft his gray T-shirt was. And how his shoulder muscles sloped beneath his T-shirt. I liked the way his sun-kissed hair was just long enough to touch the collar of his T-shirt at the nape of his neck. And how the muscles of his upper arms had stretched out the sleeves of his T-shirt.

"I like your shirt," I breathed, stepping even closer to him.

50 | RED

One night, and everything had changed.

Merritt was there, standing in front of my stall, but she hadn't opened the door. She hadn't even said hello to me yet. A cheesy unplugged duet played on my radio, a new release by Ann Ware—who was supposed to be "the next Taylor Swift"—and some English boy band dude who sang in falsetto, as if he was getting prodded with a pitchfork.

"I know it's corny, but I kind of love this song," Merritt said. Then Carvin lunged out of Tang's stall and grabbed her. They started to slow dance in front of me, holding onto each other like they were both drowning. I was so surprised by this bizarre turn of events there was no choice but to tear my stall apart.

I pawed the door and rammed it with my shoulder, but Merritt didn't let go of Carvin. She just turned her face toward me, her cheek pressed against his chest.

"Be patient," she told me. "I'll be there in a sec."

She turned back to Carvin and stood on tiptoe to kiss him while I watched. That went on for a very long time, longer than the song. I kicked at the walls and dug a deep hole in my bedding. They didn't stop.

"Um, guys?" Celine called from the tack room. "It's a little too quiet out there. Everybody still decent?"

"Okay for us to bring out your tack?" Luis yelled. "It's time to get on and ride. Candace is waiting."

"We're good," Carvin called back. He pushed Merritt away. "Cut it out. I have a job to do here."

I pinned my ears and struck my stall door with an angry hoof. I didn't like how he was shoving her around. Merritt kept on ignoring me. She giggled and pulled down her shirt. Carvin flicked his crop at her boots.

Oh my heart, my aching breaking heart. The stray strands of partially chewed hay on my tongue tasted sour. I didn't like this. I didn't like this at *all*. Finally Merritt unlatched my stall door and came inside to take off my grazing muzzle and lead me out into the aisle to tack up.

"That's a good boy," she said and rubbed the white blaze between my eyes like nothing had changed.

But I knew better.

That day and the next I went through the motions of schooling for the horse show. If anything I was better behaved than usual, because my heart wasn't in it. My heart was broken. I just didn't know what to do about it.

The last time I'd intervened someone had wound up dead.

The night before opening day Mr. de Rothschild showed me off to his wife. I recognized her immediately, jolted by agonizing flashbacks to my first and only race.

"You remember, Helena, the race at Keeneland, when he jumped over the rail and crashed into that poor filly? They almost put them both down," Mr. de Rothschild said.

Instead of coming closer, Helena de Rothschild backed away from my stall door. She sucked on a glowing cigarette just like the one Beatrice used to smoke and regarded me coldly. She was very small and delicate, her tiny bare toes polished red like her lips.

"Yes, I remember Beatrice's horse."

Something about the way she looked at me, so impassive, so removed, made me want to scare her. *Beatrice is dead.* I stared her down with my one good eye like a murderer in a horror movie. No one was going to save her from the beast about to strike.

"I need to listen to this." Mr. de Rothschild turned the dials on my radio, tuning it to a horse race he must have had some money on.

"And they're off!"

I tensed reflexively, every muscle in my body quivering. The skin on my neck broke out in patches of sweat. I paced the boundaries of my stall, the excited voice of the radio announcer cuing me to pace faster and faster.

Helena de Rothschild kept smoking her little cigarette. "We're making him nervous," she observed.

That didn't even begin to describe it. I was losing it. I'd already lost it.

Mr. de Rothschild shook his head. "Everything makes him nervous. This one I am more than happy to sell. But not till after Merritt rides him here. Gunnar Soar promised me two million for both horses, with an extra half million if one of them wins tomorrow."

He turned up the radio, listening intently as I paced and paced. So Tang and I were to be sold. What about Merritt and Carvin? Were they part of the package? Merritt had only just come back and I was already losing her again? My mind raced, song lyrics streaming through it like so much cobbled-together, confused gibberish. I was free fallin' over troubled water.

Mr. de Rothschild stood at attention, listening the radio announcer's loud, frantic voice as the horses came down the stretch. "Wait a minute, I think our horse is making a move."

"*And it's Waiting Game living up to his name and swinging wide on the outside. He's gaining on the leaders. Waiting Game is in second now on the homestretch . . .*"

I paced and paced, my coat now slick with a shivering lather. All the lonely Starbucks lovers tell me the good die young.

A horse's life is all about the people we belong to. But I didn't belong to anyone. Not anymore.

51 | MERRITT

I t was eight-thirty in the morning on opening day. The workers were raking the footing in the main ring one last time as Carvin and I went in to walk the course. We were late getting there, having stayed up half the night "talking." Carvin and Tang were on the roster to go forty-first. Red and I were fifty-sixth. The other one hundred seventy riders competing against us in the International Hunter Derby had already walked the course and were getting ready to warm up their horses.

The course had been designed by renowned rider-trainer Scott Stewart. It looked simple, but the jumps were huge, set at odd angles and surprising distances. What looked like a straightforward eight-stride line down the outside was actually a twelve-stride bending line, with the in jump set askance from the out. Antique tractors, hay wagons, carriages, potted fruit trees, and windmills had been used to decorate the imposing course, giving the horses even more to spook at and the riders more choices for the best approach. I had never seen such a complex and beautiful course. It was more like a sculpture park.

"Easy," I joked nervously after we'd walked it three times. I leaned against the fence and mentally retraced our steps, just to make sure I had it down.

Carvin ducked under the brim of my helmet and brushed his lips against my cheek. "If you say so."

I blushed and pushed him away. "Stop, I need to focus," I protested, although I knew it was impossible. I'd never been good at doing two things at once. It was all or nothing for me. Now that I knew Carvin liked me as much as I liked him, it was very hard to focus on the horse show.

Carvin flicked his crop against the top of my tall leather boot. "Tell me the course one more time," he commanded, as if he knew I was having trouble concentrating.

"Do I need to separate you two?" Celine approached us from the other side of the fence, looking very un-horsey in a pink and white zebra-print playsuit with a pink patent leather belt. She held up a paper bag. "Merritt, I got your bacon, egg, and cheese sandwich and iced coffee."

I'd ordered Beatrice's favorite in her honor. Not that I had time to eat. The show started in ten minutes and I hadn't even had time to check in on Red.

Celine pulled a plastic cup full of brownish green murky stuff out of another bag. "Carvin, here's your gross juice. What are chia seeds anyway?"

"Ancient superfood." Carvin reached for the drink and took a long pull on the plastic straw. He smirked at me. "Now I'll definitely win."

"So if I don't win, it's because I like bacon?" I shot back.

Celine reached over the fence and touched my sleeve. She looked worried.

"No, if you don't win it's because your horse is a lunatic. Have you seen him this morning?"

"When I got here he was all sweaty and he wouldn't stop moving," Luis explained. "Someone—maybe the braider, I'm not sure—put his radio on the races. I think it made him nervous." He finished scraping the excess water from Red's coat and handed me the lead rope. "I didn't want to give him a bath and mess up his braids too much, but it was kind of necessary."

"Thanks, Luis." I led Red out of the wash stall, hoping I could find a quiet place to graze him so he could dry off and calm down. "What's the matter, boy?" I rubbed his poll as we walked. "I'm the one who's supposed to be nervous."

Red's radio was tuned to classical music now, soothing strings. Carvin was in Tang's stall, removing her wraps.

"Need any help?" he asked me.

At the sound of his voice Red threw up his head, pinned his ears, and kicked out at Tang's stall door.

"Hey!" I shouted. "Cut it out!"

"I'm coming out," Carvin said.

"No, stay there." I led Red forward. As soon as we were past Tang's stall, his little episode subsided. "What was that?" I asked him, but of course he couldn't answer.

I took him out to graze in the sunshine near the parking lot. While he cropped the grass, I scratched his withers in the spot he usually liked, but he only shook himself in response, as if I were just another pesky fly.

Carvin came out of the barn to check on us from afar. He gave me the thumbs up sign and I gave him one back, even though I wasn't sure if things were okay at all. Then Carvin pointed to his watch and flashed ten fingers at me.

Schooling with Candace would begin in ten minutes.

Luis and I brushed and tacked up Red in a hurry. He seemed calmer, but still not himself. Just as I was about to lead him outside to mount up, my mother stepped inside the barn.

"Mom?" I'd known she might come, but she'd made no effort to let me in on her plans.

"Surprise," she said with a smile. She looked wiry and tan and was dressed like a normal person for once, not a marathon runner, in a khaki skirt and white blouse. Two puppies—more wolf than dog—sat at her feet. They whined uneasily at Red, their canines dripping with hungry slobber.

"I bumped into the de Rothschilds. They told me where to find you." Even though she was smiling, there was a sort of grim sadness pulling at the corners of her mouth. She gestured at the dogs. "Sorry I can't come any closer. I don't want them to mess up your nice clean riding outfit."

I pulled down my stirrups and led Red to the mounting block just outside the barn. "Where's Dad?" I asked as I stepped into the saddle.

Mom hesitated. "Your father is in Canada. We're taking a break for a while. Your dad just can't seem to get his head around you and the horse thing. He thinks I'm allowing you to turn into his mother. I think that's absurd. You're your own person. You're stronger than she was. Gran-Jo was a drunk. She was mean—to him anyway—when he was a child. And I should never have allowed—"

"Mom, please," I interrupted her from Red's back. My head swam. I couldn't think about Gran-Jo now. "I have to go warm up," I said weakly.

"It won't make much difference to you anyway," Mom added, as if that made any sense.

"I have to go," I said again and turned Red toward the warm-up ring.

The International Hunter Derby was a high-pressure two-day affair. All the top horses and riders were there, and the winner would take home over $100,000. I wasn't in it for the money— none of us were—but of course we all wanted to win.

I took a deep breath and tried to focus on the "small moments," the way Kami had taught me at Good Fences. The expansive blue sky. The blazing hot sun. The coppery sheen of Red's shiny poll. The perfect fit of my custom-made riding boots. The soothingly repetitive voice of the announcer as he called out the names of horses and riders. The smell of popcorn and freshly mowed grass. The perfect feel of my gloved hands on the reins. The flexed muscles in Carvin's outer thigh as he and Tang soared over their last warm-up jump . . .

Carvin picked up a decisive canter right at the gate and steered Sweet Tang diagonally across the ring, the coattails of his black hunt coat flapping rakishly. They continued around the far end by the rail, straight up to the high side of the first jump, a brush decorated with ten small, individually spinning windmills. Sweet Tang picked up her knees around her ears and peeked at the jump between her hooves, her muscular neck arched with impressive athleticism and her ears pricked prettily. Carvin kept his position over the jump and then cantered on to the in-and-out in twelve perfectly timed strides. He turned his head in mid-air and opened his right rein so that Tang landed on the right lead and they rolled back in a perfectly round arch to the high side of the wide and airy water jump. If the horses were going to spook it would be at this jump. Tang soared over it without flinching.

Then it was bending line to the looming green hill with flowers aiken jump and three direct but short strides to the low side of the gate, or four long indirect strides to the high side. Carvin took the hill long and landed close to it, so he wisely chose the lower, more direct option, which gave him a smoother, longer turn in the far corner of the ring to the high side of the haystack line with five nicely balanced strides between the jumps. Then it was all the way around the near turn past the gate to the outside line of wishing well jumps with no height options—vertical, four strides to the oxer, five strides to the even bigger oxer.

Tang jumped beautifully but stumbled just a bit in the turn as she changed leads.

If Carvin was at all flustered, he didn't show it. Only one more jump, the long approach to the imposing brick wall set at an angle just left of center-ring. Tang seemed to spot the distance to takeoff the moment she laid eyes on the jump. All Carvin had to do was maintain the rhythm and pose and they were golden.

I sucked in a huge gulp of air as they landed. I hadn't even realized I was holding my breath.

"Hell yeah!" Candace crowed from the gate. "We either have a new leader, or a very close second. Otherwise I'm going to go over and rip the judge a new asshole."

I giggled nervously. Candace's vocabulary seemed to get more florid as the stakes increased.

"Bravo!" Mr. de Rothschild was on his feet in the first row of crowded bleachers, cheering unusually loudly.

Helena de Rothschild sat beside him with her pale legs crossed elegantly, wearing a wide-brimmed straw hat and fanning herself with the horse show program, e-cigarette lodged between red-painted, unsmiling lips. All of a sudden she stood up, dropped the program on the ground, and wolf-whistled the way Beatrice used to.

I flinched. Beneath my seat I thought I felt Red flinch, too. Just behind them, Celine leapt to her feet, towering over Helena de Rothschild as she applauded furiously. Helena wolf-whistled again and again.

Carvin and Tang's score flashed on the board: 289 out of 300. The audience erupted in another round of cheers. Carvin and Tang were in second place—a horse named Teton was a point ahead.

"Ha! Second place, not bad, not bad!" Candace growled. She patted Sweet Tang's neck as Carvin walked the gray mare out of the ring. Tang's dappled gray coat was so soaked with sweat that she appeared almost blue.

"You were awesome," I gushed. "Really grea—"

"Stop your flirting and get going. Now!" Candace shouted at me. "You can beat him if you try. Better do all the high ones though. You got the course?"

My mind inadvertently flashed back to my first show, when Beatrice had taught me how to memorize a course. I repeated today's course, silently mouthing the words as I eye-balled each jump. I gritted my teeth determinedly. "Got it."

"Okay, canter him over the warm-up vertical a few more times, then go wait at the gate." Candace's wizened blue eyes flashed at me, goading me on. "You can win this."

My heart ricocheted against my ribcage. Candace was under the impression that Red and I were already warmed up, when the truth was I hadn't even attempted to trot.

"Red's acting kind of—" I started to explain but Carvin pulled Tang up alongside us. His freckled face was flushed and dripping with sweat. Red pinned his ears and gnashed his teeth.

Carvin loosened his white tie and unbuttoned the top button of his sweat-soaked shirt. He grinned cockily. "I was going to try to kiss you good luck, but better not."

I nodded, too nervous to talk, and urged Red into a canter. We looped around the schooling ring in a wide circle and I bent him to the outside and then to the inside to keep him elastic and focused. At least he was doing what I asked— for the moment. Maybe I would be the one to get us around safely today and Red could close his eyes. No, that would never work. Maybe he just needed some positive reinforcement.

"Good boy," I murmured and reached down to stroke his coppery neck.

52 | RED

"*Good boy.*"

I'd made up my mind to mess it all up. I was going to refuse the first jump, ditch Merritt in a traitorous heap, then jump out of the ring and gallop away in a blaze of glory. It was going to be dramatic, unforgettable.

But the course was magnificent. I couldn't let Tang beat me. Why not give it one last shot, go out with a bang?

Merritt was a nervous wreck, just like at our first show, but she knew more now, and she trusted me more. I wouldn't have to dump her on the ground to make her listen. Even as we warmed up I could feel her allowing me to take over. She might even have had her eyes closed. Do not worry, about a thing . . .

"Big Red, you're up!"

We cantered smartly into the ring and directly to the first jump. That was the way to get the judge's attention. No polite circles, no messing around.

Left lead straight to the high side of the huge brush jump with windmills all over it. Twelve ground-eating racehorse strides to the in-and-out, rocking back on my haunches like a bronc so as not to plow into the out. Then we turned on a dime to roll back to the freakishly airy water jump. I jumped it like it was twenty feet tall.

"*Good boy,*" Merritt whispered again, or maybe it was just her voice in my head.

Long approach around the big hay bale jump to the weird hill of flowers. I hung in the air for a good ten seconds. I heard the yipping of Merritt's mother's dogs and a Beatles song on someone's car radio.

"*Good boy,*" Merritt whispered as we landed.

Then it was four quick strides to the big gate and sharp left to the hay bales. Five strides to the next big hay bale jump, all the way around past the grandstand. I could smell Mrs. de Rothschild's expensive French perfume and Mr. de Rothschild's woody cologne. Wishing wells outside line, four strides, then six strides.

"*Good boy.*"

Then it was all the way around the far turn, past the cluster of old tractors, long approach to the final brick.

"Careful. Come on, don't fuck it up," Candace growled softly from the gate.

Blam. I tucked my hooves up underneath me, pricked my ears, and rocked it. Oh yeah, baby, thunder road.

"*Good boy!*" Merritt laughed as we cantered straight out of the ring, still all business and no frills. She fell on my neck and hugged me. "Good boy."

And that was the last time I'd ever hear it.

53 | MERRITT

The sounds of Helena de Rothschild's wolf whistles and Mr. de Rothschild's bravos rang in my ears.

I dismounted and handed Red off to Luis so he could walk him and cool him down. Our score wasn't up on the board yet. There seemed to be some sort of hold-up in the announcer's box. Mr. and Mrs. de Rothschild were in there with a dapper-looking man wearing a purple bowtie and sporting shoulder-length red hair. Mr. de Rothschild shook hands with Mr. Bowtie, then they both took turns shaking hands with the announcer.

"Will you still talk to me now that you're famous?" Carvin came up behind me and tugged on the tails of my riding jacket.

I whirled around and grabbed him. We were both overheated and sticky with sweat but I didn't care. "I didn't do anything," I admitted, still breathless from our round. "It was all Red."

"Sure," Carvin joked. "You just sat up there with your eyes closed."

"Actually, that's exactly what I did," I admitted, even though I knew Carvin wouldn't believe it.

The scoreboard flashed an array of numbers but I was still too wound up to read them. "What does it say?"

"Two hundred ninety-four. That's going to be pretty tough to beat." Carvin ducked under the brim of my helmet, his freckled face very close to mine. "You know I hate you now, right?"

I bit my lip. "Can we save this for later?" I asked, blushing. "My mom's here, and Mr. de Rothschild and Candace are coming over to talk to us."

"Brilliant!" Mr. de Rothschild strode up behind Carvin, his broad, tanned face radiant compared to the way he'd looked a few nights before. "Absolutely brilliant!"

"Seriously epic," Carvin agreed. He stepped away to shake Mr. de Rothschild's hand. Then Mr. de Rothschild opened his arms and embraced me, smothering me in his cologne.

"I hit the jackpot with you two," he said happily. "I really did."

Helena de Rothschild stood a few yards away, holding her e-cigarette in her delicate, pale fingers, her eyes obscured by an enormous pair of sunglasses. She nodded at me but didn't smile.

"I don't know what you did," Candace crowed loudly as she approached. "But you did it perfect."

Celine and Mom staggered over, each of them dragging a panting puppy.

"Looks like you inherited your dad's competitive spirit," Mom observed with her new unhappy smile.

"Isn't it over?" Celine demanded. "What's with the old lady?"

We turned back to the ring. The last to go was a dark bay Oldenberg gelding named Strauss and his owner-rider, a rail-thin woman in her sixties with a severe nose and circular horn-rimmed glasses.

"She looks like Harry Potter," Celine hissed. She pretended to point an imaginary wand at the horse in the ring. "Mess up, mess up, mess up."

Strauss's round was competent and very polished, until they got to the combination. Strauss picked up his left front foot a moment later than his right so that he appeared to be scrambling over the jump in the air.

The rest of the round was flawless. He floated out of the ring at an extended trot, flashy and proud.

I stood rooted to the spot, staring at the scoreboard. Carvin's arm was wrapped around my waist.

"Oh my God, oh my God, oh my God," Celine murmured, clutching Mom's wrist with her long pink fingernails. "I don't think I can stand this."

Strauss's score flashed on the board. Two eighty-eight.

"You won this round," Carvin whispered hotly into my ear. "But don't forget round two tomorrow."

"Ladies and gentlemen," the announcer called over the loud-speaker. "I'd like you to join me in congratulating the winners of today's round, Big Red, owned by de Rothschild Farm and ridden by Miss Merritt Wenner."

Luis led Red to the gate and I took the reins from him, ready to jog in first.

"Second place today is Teton, owned and shown by Miss Kennedy Sawyer. Third place goes to Sweet Tang, also of de Rothschild Farm, ridden by Mr. Carvin Oliver."

Strauss was fourth. Two more horses whose rounds I hadn't seen were fifth and sixth. We jogged our horses and the judge gave the okay. These would be the standings going into tomorrow's round. I led Red back toward the gate, looking forward to a long shower and a swim in the condo pool with Carvin and Celine. Luis took the reins from me and I unbuttoned the tight collar of my ratcatcher shirt.

"We have just learned from Mr. Roman de Rothschild that both Big Red and Sweet Tang were sold today to Mr. Gunnar Soar of Soar Farm and Vineyards in Victoria, Australia," the announcer added. "Mr. de Rothschild will donate all of the proceeds from their sale to the expansion of Good Fences, his Equine-Assisted Rehabilitation Center in Hamden, Connecticut, in memory of his late daughter Beatrice."

I froze.

"Australia?" Carvin demanded loudly behind me. "What the hell?"

I spun around, barely breathing.

Carvin's green eyes flashed. "He can't do this," he growled, his gloved fists clenched angrily around Tang's braided leather reins. "I won't let him."

I stared at him for a moment, so completely shaken I could hardly hear what he said. Without a word, I turned away toward the stabling area. I couldn't talk to Carvin. I couldn't talk to anyone.

Roman and Helena de Rothschild were already being interviewed by a journalist from *The Chronicle of the Horse*, along with the dapper red-haired gentleman I'd seen with them in the announcer's box earlier. He looked like a lion tamer or a leprechaun, Mr. de Rothschild's lucky leprechaun.

With leaden feet, I trudged back to the barn. All the glory and elation of winning today's round was gone. Red and Tang had been sold. Mr. de Rothschild had hit the jackpot all right. I remembered what Beatrice had said about her father: *"He always has an agenda."* Then I remembered the papers that had fallen out of the glove compartment the day she'd taught me how to drive. Some of them bore the Soar Farm letterhead with a gull flying across the top of the page. Beatrice had known about this. She probably would have told me about it if I hadn't gotten so angry with her. If she were still alive.

Mom was waiting for me halfway to the barn with her ridiculous sled dogs. And she was grinning, as if I hadn't just gotten the worst news of my entire life.

"Mr. de Rothschild is so thrilled," she gushed. "You pulled it off, honey. You did a wonderful job, too. It doesn't even matter how tomorrow goes. You rode so well. He was just telling me that you're basically a professional now. You can ride for anyone and they'll pay you. You even get a commission from this sale." She giggled indulgently. "You've probably made more this summer than I do in a year. You were always so young for your class, still sixteen going into your senior year. Now look at you. I'm so proud."

I stared at her. "You knew about this? You knew Red was going to get sold?"

She was still smiling. "Of course. This was always the agreement. You would ride Red until he was sold. Mr. de Rothschild is a businessman. He saw how talented you were and he put you to work."

"You mean he used me," I said angrily. How was this okay with her? Did she not see that Red was mine? I thought she wanted me to be happy. How could I be happy without Red?

"There'll be plenty of other horses," she started to say.

"No!" I shouted loudly. "There won't!" I was so angry I was shaking all over.

I stomped across the grass toward the barn with Mom on my heels. Luis was waiting for me with Red at the barn entrance. He'd removed his tack and given him a drink of water.

"I'll take him inside and give him a bath," he said as soon as he saw the wild look on my face. He led Red into the barn. I stood rooted to the spot, my heart pounding.

"Merritt?"

I glanced behind me. It was Celine, looking sunburnt and out of place. Her pink toenails and sandals were dirty. Swollen mosquito bites stood out on her skinny legs.

"You were awesome. I'm so sorry though, this sucks." She

wrapped her long arms around me, pulling me close. "Carvin wants to talk to you," she whispered in my ear. "He's over by Tang's stall. I think he's planning something. Go. I'll deal with your mom. Just go."

I pulled away and strode down the barn aisle.

"Those puppies definitely look like they could use some water, Mrs. Wenner," I heard Celine call out loudly behind me. "Pass me a leash. I'll show you where we can get some."

A storm was coming. There was no lightning yet, just distant, rumbling thunder. A hard, steady rain began to drum on the roof.

Six purple cardboard wine boxes were stacked against the wall beside the row of de Rothschild tack trunks. The boxes were labeled *"Soar Vineyards Fine Australian Wines,"* with clusters of green grapes beneath the words and a single gull flying over them—a gift from Red's new owner. Why did so many wealthy horse people make their own wine? I wondered. Because they could, I guessed. They could do whatever they pleased. I yanked off my helmet and tossed it aside. It skidded across the cement floor, coming to rest beneath the boxes of wine.

"Ladies and gentlemen," the announcer's voice crackled loudly through the din of the driving rain. "The rest of the afternoon's events have been cancelled due to unsettled weather in the area. Thank you. We'll see you tomorrow for Round Two of the Classic, weather permitting. Have a great evening, everybody."

Carvin wasn't in the barn and Tang's stall was empty. Luis was in the wash stall, bathing Red.

"Thanks, Luis," I said. "Do you mind if I finish up?"

Luis gave me a sympathetic look and handed me the lead

rope. "Sure. You want to spend as much time with him as you can. I understand."

Red pawed the cement floor. I picked up the liniment-soaked sponge, squeezed out the water, and ran it over the white blaze between his eyes.

"I'm sorry." The words hiccupped out of me in a gasping sob. Tears streamed down my cheeks. I pressed my forehead against his. "I'm so sorry."

Red stood very still. I pulled away and stared into his amber-colored eyes. They were so soft, but unfathomable. All of a sudden his head shot up and he pinned his ears flat.

I spun around. Carvin stood in the doorway of the wash stall. His white shirt was dirty and untucked and his tall black boots were splattered with mud.

"Hurry, we haven't got much time," he said urgently. "I've got Tang in the van. Luis helped me. Let's get Red in there with her and go."

Without asking for an explanation, I turned Red around in the wash stall and followed Carvin down the barn aisle toward the rear exit of the barn. The light was dim now because of the storm. Red flicked his damp ears back and forth as we hurried past the other horses, their heads over their stall doors, peering at us through the din. The rain beat down on the roof like bullets. Carvin was walking very fast.

"Where are we going?" I shouted after him as we stepped out into the rain. A white horse van was parked in the grass, its taillights glowing in the fog. The loading ramp was down and I could see Tang's gray, rain-soaked hindquarters.

Carvin stopped by the loading ramp and waited for me to catch up.

"Where are we taking them?" I demanded.

He didn't answer right away. His forehead was pale beneath

his soaking wet hair. Water dripped off his freckled nose. His green eyes were bloodshot. He'd been crying, too.

He gripped my upper arms and pressed his forehead against mine. "I don't know. California, I guess? I just can't let this happen. Especially not to you and Red."

"So we're stealing the horses?" I said doubtfully. Red's lead rope hung slack in my hands.

Carvin swept the damp hair out of my eyes and behind my ears. "There's a nice barn near my house. My mom has a new boyfriend now so she's not so needy. My dad's in Tahiti for the Billabong Pro." He put his arms around my waist and pulled me closer. I could feel his heart beating beneath his shirt. "Let's just *go*," he murmured into my hair.

I rested my cheek against his chest and closed my eyes, wishing we could stay like that forever, not making any big, life-altering decisions, just hugging in the rain.

Suddenly Red's big head loomed large over both of us, ears flat to his head, eyes rolling, teeth bared. I'd forgotten all about him.

"Red, cut it out!"

I yanked down hard on the lead rope, but Red was bigger and stronger. He lunged forward, bowling Carvin over with the force of his massive body. The back of Carvin's head smacked against the loading ramp.

"I'm okay," he groaned from where he lay on his back on the muddy grass. "Just give me a sec."

Red stood at the very end of the lead rope, his head high, ears pinned back. A familiar surge of anger flared up inside me. This was exactly how he'd acted around Beatrice.

"What's your problem, Red?" I demanded through gritted teeth. "Why can't you just be nice?"

Thunder rumbled and a flash of lightning x-rayed the

sky. Red's eyes rolled in their sockets. His nostrils flared in defiance.

"*Red!*" I growled, my mind racing. When I got angry people died. First Gran-Jo, then Beatrice. Beatrice was with Red when she died. I tugged on the lead rope. Red backed away from me in long, lunging steps.

Carvin sat up. "Hold on to him!" he called out.

The slick lead rope skidded across the palm of my hand, burning my skin. I let go of it. Red reared up on his hind legs as if to test the extent of his freedom. The lead rope swung loosely from his halter. Then he wheeled around and galloped away.

Carvin staggered to his feet. "Tang's okay in the van," he gasped. "I'll go grab some feed from the barn so we can catch him."

I stood where I was, paralyzed. "I don't want to catch him," I said quietly. "Just let him go."

Carvin stared at me, his forehead creased with worry. "What?"

"Let him go," I repeated. My voice sounded cold and hollow.

Carvin's worried expression changed to one of recognition. This was the Merritt from the hotel bar in Saratoga Springs, possessed by a demon she couldn't control. He didn't have a name for it, but I did. The Beast was back.

"Never mind," he said gently. "I'll get him. Go inside and get your stuff together."

"No," I said half-stubborn, half-pleading. "Don't go."

Carvin pressed his lips against my forehead. "There's a fence over there. He can't get far. Please, just get your stuff and meet me back here. I'll see you in a sec," he promised and dashed off into the rain.

I stood where I was for a moment, dazed and shivering in my wet riding clothes. Rain pelted my face. Inside the van Tang rattled her hay net and let out a resigned snort. I turned away and walked back to the barn.

My riding helmet lolled on the cement floor beneath the neat stack of Soar Vineyards wine boxes. The words VIN DU PICNIC were stamped in small black letters on the purple cardboard. I walked over and picked one up.

54 | RED

When a horse gets loose in a crowded place bystanders react in one of two ways—they either back away, scared to death of being trampled, or they lift their arms out on either side of them and get in the horse's way to try to stop him. It was raining hard and misty. No one seemed to notice me gallop across the fairgrounds, the lead rope swinging from my halter.

"*Red!*" I thought I heard a voice in the wind and spattering raindrops, but I knew it was just my mind playing tricks. Nobody cared what happened to me. I was just some horse that they used to know.

I continued on past the food tents, my nostrils flaring at the unfamiliar smells. A musical performance braved on beneath an outdoor stage haphazardly tented in plastic. I stopped short and swung my head in that direction, listening.

A hand reached out and grabbed my lead rope.

It was Carvin. We stood in the rain for a moment catching our breath and glaring at each other. Then he turned me around and began to lead me back to the barn.

I walked along willingly as I considered my options. The legs of his beige riding pants were spattered with mud and his nice leather boots were sodden and ruined.

"Good boy," he said, but I knew he didn't mean it. I stopped walking.

"Come on, Merritt's waiting," Carvin said impatiently.

She was waiting for him, not me. I pinned my ears and tossed my head. If I hurt him she would never forgive me. I ground my teeth together and pawed the dirt in frustration. If you love someone you have to set them free.

A swarm of golf carts was suddenly upon us, crowded with men in matching green rain slickers. I detected Mr. de Rothschild's woody scent. A groom rushed up and wrapped a chain over my poll and around my nose. He took the lead rope out of Carvin's hand.

"That's enough, Carvin," Mr. de Rothschild boomed from beneath an enormous wooden-handled umbrella. Sharing the umbrella was a younger man with red hair that hung down to his shoulders.

"I'll have my grooms take him and Sweet Tang back to my stabling area for the night, the red-haired man told Mr. de Rothschild. "Tomorrow we're off to Melbourne."

"Tomorrow?" Carvin repeated.

The rain had lessened to a misty drizzle. Mr. de Rothschild folded up his umbrella and stepped down from the golf cart to tower over Carvin.

"Mr. Soar was going to offer you a job riding for him, but I think he may have changed his mind. The horse show officials have been notified. Stealing horses is a serious offense. They've put a five-year ban on you, Carvin. Gather your things and go." He glanced at Mr. Soar. "Unless you still want him. He might be legal to show in Australia."

Carvin didn't wait for Mr. Soar's response. He held up his hand and scowled. "Yeah, thanks. But no thanks. You should hire Merritt, though. She's a way better rider."

Mr. Soar shook his head. "Sorry, but I've heard a bit of her story. She's far too unreliable. I can't take on that kind of responsibility."

Carvin let his hand drop. "Fine. Guess we'll see you around then. Or not."

He turned to go. I knew by "we" he meant him and Merritt. He was the real winner and he was taking it all.

My new handlers led me across the show grounds to my new barn. Tang was already there. They put me in the empty stall beside hers, threw in a few flakes of fresh hay, and filled up my water bucket. Then they removed my halter and fed me my grain. No muzzle, which was fine with me. They turned out the lights. I began to nuzzle the latch on my stall door.

55 | MERRITT

"Merritt?" It was Carvin. "Merritt, are you here?"

"Here," I called from the back corner of the wash stall.

Carvin hovered in the doorway. He was soaked through and streaked with mud.

"I found Red," he panted. "He's fine." He cleared his throat, pretending not to notice the plastic cup of wine in my hand. "But that Soar guy's got both horses. He's taking them away tomorrow." He leaned against the wall and rubbed his eyes with the heels of his hands. "He was going to offer me a job in Australia, but I kind of threw it back in his face." He took a deep breath and let his hands fall to his sides. "You're the one who should go."

I looked up from my corner, watching the muscles in Carvin's freckled forearms flex and un-flex in spasms of nervous fatigue. The skin around his eyes was swollen and pink. Still, a wave of relief washed over me. Red hadn't hurt him. He was all right. And if I could get him out of there and away from me, he'd stay that way.

I set the cup down and stood up. "Let's go," I said, trying to keep my voice neutral.

Carvin wrapped his arm around my shoulders and guided me out of the barn to his car. The rain had stopped but the show grounds were still shrouded in a hazy mist.

"Celine's probably worried," he said as we walked. "She knew I was up to something. And you need to talk to your mom. I want you to come home with me, to California," he continued, his voice becoming more and more animated. "I'll introduce you to some trainers you can ride with on the circuit out there. They always have great horses. And we'll be together."

We stopped outside his car. He pulled me close.

"I love you, you know," he said into my hair.

I wrapped my arms around his waist and hugged him in silent response. I wanted to tell him everything that was troubling me, but I didn't know where to begin. It was too much to process and way too much to articulate. Instead, I tilted my head back and kissed him, allowing him to think that this was the beginning of something, not the end. At least we'd have this one night.

Finally I let go and got in the car.

The horse park was quiet after the storm. Carvin pulled over outside one of the larger barns. A team of workers in matching green rain slickers zoomed past us in a golf cart.

"Want to say goodbye to Red?"

I shook my head.

"You sure?" Carvin waited. Then he put the car back in gear.

"He knows I love him," I said as we rolled forward and the barn disappeared from sight.

56 | RED

By the time I escaped my new stall and returned to my old stabling area, Merritt and Carvin were gone.

A pile of strange purple boxes was stacked against the wall beside a tack trunk. The top one had been opened. I stretched out my neck to sniff the spout. The scent was familiar. It was the same fermented fruit scent that had emanated from Merritt's skin when I first met her at Good Fences.

I chewed on the spout until the sweet red liquid began to gush. I drank the whole box and then knocked another one down and found the spout, gnawing at it until more liquid came.

Then I drank another.

I drank until my insides swelled and my vision swam. Then I staggered away to look for my old stall so I could lie down and sleep.

I couldn't find it.

Inside every stall was some stranger, looking me right between the eyes.

My sides heaved. The party was over, I was out of time. I staggered down the barn aisle and out into the open.

I'd reached the end . . . which is where I began.

• • •

I'm outside the barn now. The storm is over and the earth is a just-baked pie left out to cool. Over in the show ring the jumps loom, huge and beautiful in the moonlight. In the morning Merritt and I are supposed to jump that course. We're supposed to win. But now I know tomorrow won't ever exist. This is the day that I'll die.

I close my eyes and then open them again. I'm spinning. In the most peculiar way. My whole body shudders and I fall to the ground.

Another horse bites the dust.

The stars shine bright. I lie with my good eye to the sky until the pain subsides and I'm comfortably numb. It's better to burn out. Not fade away. Like a rolling stone. My direction is unknown.

This is the end, my sweet friend, my girl, Merritt. I'm pulling out of here. Please don't forget about me.

No more magic carpet rides.

EPILOGUE

December

Dear Carvin,

This is a new exercise we have to do at Good Fences: write a letter to someone, living or dead, telling them what's on our minds. We don't have to send it, we just have to write it.

I thought about writing to Gran-Jo. I thought about writing to Beatrice. I thought about writing to Red. But then I chose you, I guess because you're still alive. And because I do want to send it. My thoughts are pretty disorganized, in case you hadn't noticed. But here I go.

I'm sorry I wasn't there when you woke up and I didn't go to California with you. I didn't want you to feel like you had to take care of me. I need to do that myself.

You probably heard that Red died. Red, Beatrice, Gran-Jo—I feel like maybe I'm jinxed, like what happened to them is because of me. It's probably safer if I stay away from you. I'll stick to writing letters. For now anyway.

I know Tang is winning in Australia because I Googled her. It looks amazing there, even better than Florida. We get The Chronicle *here and I see Todd's name a lot too.*

He's back training, mostly little pony riders from what I can tell. They'll be on their way to Florida soon.

Celine is leaving for college, so I'll have my own room again. There are some new girls here but they're all younger. They're getting more horses and a big indoor arena so we'll actually be allowed to ride, but they're waiting until after winter to start construction.

Dr. Kami, the social worker here, thinks I should go to a college with a riding program. When I'm ready. Maybe you could do that too? Colleges have their own show circuit. You wouldn't be banned from that. It could be fun. Please tell me you're still riding? You can still be legendary.

I miss you. I'm sorry it's taken me so long to write. I'm sorry I'm here and you're there. But I think this is where I need to be right now.

Mom says now that I'm exactly like Gran-Jo. I don't think she means it as a compliment, but I really loved Gran-Jo so it can't be the worst thing. My old friend Ann Ware who my parents always thought was so great is in rehab now. And my parents are getting divorced. Life is strange.

Sorry, I'm getting dark.

On mall day I went to the bookstore and found this picture book Gran-Jo used to read to me when I was little. It's about a donkey who finds a magic pebble and gets turned into a rock when a lion is about to eat him. He can't turn back into a donkey unless he's holding the magic pebble, but he's a rock so he can't really hold anything. I think maybe I'm like that rock. I just need to figure out how to pick up the pebble.

Now you know for sure I'm crazy.

We're supposed to talk to the horses here, tell them

our troubles. I'm assigned to an old draft horse named Arnold, but I still go up to Red's old shed and listen to his radio and talk to him in my head. I guess since I'm writing you this letter I'm talking to you, too.

Don't worry, you don't have to answer.

I want to say something profound, something for you to remember me by in case we never see each other again. Beatrice would have quoted some poet. Red would have quoted a song if he could quote anything. Gran-Jo would have just poured herself another Old-Fashioned. I don't want to sound sad or crazy or make you feel like I'm asking you for something because I'm not. I guess I'll just tell you. I think you already know. I love you, too.

—Merritt

ACKNOWLEDGMENTS

I must first thank my editor, Dan Ehrenhaft, for never doubting me or the book, despite not being a horse guy, and for providing just the right combination of kick-in-the-assness and kindness so I'd rise to the challenge. I would also like to thank Bronwen Hruska, Meredith Barnes, Rachel Kowal, Amara Hoshijo, Janine Agro and all the other impressively efficient, smart, and genuinely nice people at Soho Press. Thank you Eric Brown for your legal expertise, amusing anecdotes, and graciousness. Thank you Neil Rosini for additional legal advice. Thank you Bobbie Ford and everyone on the Penguin Random House Children's sales team for your enthusiasm and hard work. Thank you to the excellent Rights People. So much love and gratitude to Boo Martin, Becky Sanborn, Andi Snow, and all the women and girls, horses and ponies of Pony Farm—you inspire and amaze me (and this is not about any of you). Thank you Agnes for sharing my love of horses and riding and for cleaning your boots and reading this sad story a thousand times. Thank you to my mother for driving me to all those lessons and horse shows and for being brave enough to start jumping as an adult. Finally, this book would not have been written without the constant support, love, and humor of my family and friends, especially my husband and children—thank you, you know I love you.

MUSICAL ACKNOWLEDGMENTS

Thank you to the following artists for allowing Red to butcher their songs. After all, he is only a horse:

Coldplay; The Doors; Kate Bush; Don McLean; Fleetwood Mac; Queen, Steppenwolf; Blue Öyster Cult; Pink Floyd; The Raconteurs; Ashford & Simpson; EMF; Tom Petty; Survivor; Huey Lewis and The News; Steve Miller Band; Roxy Music; LMFAO; Eurythmics; James Taylor; Michael Sembello; David Guetta and Sia; Pharrell Williams; Kenny Rogers and Dolly Parton; Peaches & Herb; The Fabulous Thunderbirds; Lionel Richie; Janis Joplin; Nelly; Joan Jett and the Blackhearts; Kool & the Gang; Deee-Lite; KC and the Sunshine Band; Smokey Robinson; House of Pain; Beastie Boys; The Rolling Stones; Frank Sinatra; Tony Orlando and Curtis Mayfield; The Beatles; Tag Team; Stevie Wonder, Rufus and Chaka Khan; Jefferson Starship; George Thorogood and the Destroyers; Michael Jackson; Bill Withers; James Brown; Cheap Trick; The Lumineers; Montell Jordan; Bob Dylan; Crosby, Stills, Nash & Young; DJ Casper; LL Cool J; Otis Redding; Foreigner; Iggy Azalea; Elvis Costello; Carly Simon; Ann Wilson & Mike Reno; Bryan Adams; Taylor Swift and Ed Sheeran; Billy Ray Cyrus; Simon & Garfunkel; Billy Joel; Bob Marley; Bruce Springsteen; Gotye; Sting; ABBA; Prince; David Bowie; Neil Young; Buddy Holly; Simple Minds.